The Traitor's Smile

Patricia Elliott

Holiday House / New York

Holiday House thanks Amanda Cardinale for writing
the historical note and time line in the backmatter of this book.

Library of Congress Cataloging-in-Publication Data
Elliott, Patricia, 1946-
The traitor's smile / Patricia Elliott. — 1st American ed.
p. cm.
Sequel to: The Pale Assassin.
Summary: In 1793, Eugénie de Boncoeur arrives at the home of her English uncle and
cousin, but the French Revolution has pursued her in the form of Guy Deschamps,
who is determined to bring her back to Paris to marry the Pale Assassin.
ISBN 978-0-8234-2361-3 (hardcover)
1. France—History—Revolution, 1789–1799—Juvenile fiction. [1. France—
History—Revolution, 1789–1799—Fiction. 2. Uncles—Fiction. 3. Cousins—
Fiction. 4. Spies—Fiction. 5. Adventure and adventurers—Fiction. 6. Great
Britain—History—George III, 1760–1820—Fiction.] I. Title.
PZ7.E4578Tr 2011
[Fic]—dc23
2011018988

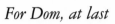

For Dom, at last

Patricia Elliott writes:

Who can you truly trust in a changed world, darkened and bloodied by revolution and the terror of the guillotine? Old loyalties and friendships count for nothing, neighbors betray each other to survive, and ruthless men use the Revolution to further their own ambitions.

    Eugénie de Boncoeur has escaped the dangers in France. She is no longer the spoiled, childish aristocrat of the days of the Ancien Régime. But in England she feels increasingly alone. As the two countries go to war, she cannot place her trust in her strong-willed English cousin Hetta, whose views are so different from her own; and her relationship with the young Frenchman, Julien de Fortin, is falling apart. When her old admirer, the charismatic Guy Deschamps, appears, it seems natural to turn to him for comfort and help....

CAST OF CHARACTERS

Principal imaginary characters:

EUGÉNIE DE BONCOEUR, a young aristocrat who has escaped the French Revolution

HENRIETTA (HETTA) COVENEY, Eugénie's cousin and a staunch supporter of democracy

JULIEN DE FORTIN, former law student and Armand's friend

GUY DESCHAMPS, nicknamed Le Scalpel, a dashing but dangerous spy working for Raoul Goullet

ARMAND DE BONCOEUR, Eugénie's brother, a liberal aristocrat and leader of a failed attempt to save the royal family

RAOUL GOULLET, nicknamed Le Fantôme, or the Pale Assassin, a founding member of the Brotherhood of the Watching Eye

JEM CUTTLE, Deal boatman, spy, and smuggler

THOMAS COVENEY, Eugénie's uncle, a surgeon at the Naval Hospital in Deal

MOLLIE, the Coveney family's maid

LADY FREDERICA and SIR HENRY COVENEY, Eugénie and Hetta's aunt and uncle

VICTOIRE D'ABREVILLE, a well-known hostess before the Revolution

ISOBELLE (BELLE) FLEURIE, a milliner and Eugénie and Armand's former landlady

FABRICE LE BRUN, a balloonist

BART JENKIN, a boatman

FRENELLE, a farmer's daughter

REYNARD GRAUNIER, a bargeman

MICHEL and PIERRE, bargemen working for Reynard Graunier

XAVIER SAINT-ETIENNE, a former aristocrat, now a member of
the Chouan rebels

GASTON, Raoul Goullet's coachman

GEORGES, Eugénie's former groom

MANON, Eugénie's former maid

Among the real people mentioned in the story:
GEORGE III (1738–1820), British monarch whose reign included
the American War of Independence and a number of wars
against Revolutionary and Napoleonic France, culminating
in the defeat of Napoléon in 1815

WILLIAM PITT THE YOUNGER (1759–1806), English prime
minister from 1783–1801 and 1804–1806 who, at age
twenty-four, became the youngest prime minister in British
history and whose years in office, which occurred during the
reign of George III, were dominated by the French
Revolution and the Napoleonic Wars

MAXIMILIEN ROBESPIERRE, lawyer and key figure in the
Jacobian party who clashed with the Girondins and became
the feared "moral" leader of the Revolution

CHOUANS, or "the silent ones," anti-Republican rebels opposed to
conscription, mostly operating in Brittany and the Vendee

GEORGES DANTON, deputy to the National Convention and
leader of the Committee for Public Safety

"Always in the eye of the storm, always in the shadow of the guillotine, we walk in the glint of lightning."

Manon Roland, French Republican and feminist rebel,

1754–1793

PARIS

22 January 1793

A carriage was swaying over the packed earth of La Place de la Révolution, where only the day before the people of Paris had executed their king and celebrated the birth of their new republic. All the way along the rue Saint-Honoré, it had been stuck behind a tumbril taking the latest victims to their execution beneath the blade of the guillotine.

Under an overcast winter sky, a raucous crowd greeted the tumbril's arrival. The first to step down was a young man in his early twenties, an aristocrat. He was white-faced and trembling, his hands bound, and his hair, which had been cropped for the blade, exposed the delicate, youthful neck.

He needed support up the steps to the platform, where the executioner was waiting for him. Firm but merciless hands took hold of him. He murmured something—a prayer?—but his voice shook so much the crowd could not catch his words.

Then he was thrust face downward onto the tilting plank, his head secured in the brace. Gasping, he tried to free himself but could not. The crowd jeered.

It was over very quickly. The executioner pulled on the rope. The blade rushed down between the upright posts. The people nearest the guillotine were soaked with blood, and the head rolled into the waiting basket.

The man inside the carriage had been watching as he went by, his pale, cadaverous face at the window, his light eyes expressionless. He had seen it happen before. It did not disturb, or even excite him. He was an assassin, well acquainted with violent death.

As the carriage jolted away over the cobbled streets, leaving the dark silhouette of the guillotine against the lowering sky, he heard his passenger groan.

Like the victim, he was a young man, scarcely more than a boy. His name was Armand de Boncoeur, and for the last twenty years the Pale Assassin had vowed vengeance on his family.

The Pale Assassin flexed the damaged fingers inside his black leather gloves and glanced over at de Boncoeur with satisfaction. The youth was slumped in the far corner of the carriage, semiconscious. But he would soon know where he was: in the prison of La Force, one of the most notorious of the Revolution, with only one end to his incarceration: death beneath the guillotine.

He, Raoul Goullet, would not bring about that end too quickly. He wanted de Boncoeur to suffer as once he had.

Yes, the first part of his revenge was going according to plan.

The other part was de Boncoeur's sister, Eugénie. She was already contracted to him in marriage. She had escaped Paris the previous day, but he only had to hunt her down, with the help of his most successful spy. Guy Deschamps would find her. After all, they knew where she was going.

England.

Deal, to be precise: a little port on the Kent coast.

PART ONE

A Game of Cat and Mouse

DEAL AND PARIS

31 January—mid-August 1793

ONE

The girl, struggling through the noisy crowds of Middle Street in Deal on the last day of January, had pulled the hood of her cloak up to hide her face. Henrietta Coveney had lived in the small port on the Kent coast all her life, and knew from bitter experience that there was always some busybody ready to tell tales to her father.

And Hetta did not want her father to know where she was going now.

To her relief she could see no one of her acquaintance. It was after three o'clock on a raw afternoon, and dusk was already falling. As for her father, he would not be returning from the Naval Hospital in West Street for a while yet. Besides, the street was so thronged with sailors intent on seeking out the nearest inn that Hetta was able to slip unnoticed through the crowds.

Then someone trod on the hem of her cloak.

Hetta looked around, tugging the hem away, and saw in the light of the street lantern that it was a young gentleman. At least she assumed he was a gentleman by his clothes, which were of a fine cut, and by his demeanor, which was upstanding and manly.

As soon as he realized what had happened, he stepped back swiftly, freeing her, and bowed.

"My sincere apologies, mademoiselle. I hope the cloth is not torn?"

Though he spoke perfect English, his faint accent struck Hetta. It reminded her of the French governess she had had, and of the émigrés fleeing the Revolution in France who disembarked at Deal before they left for London.

"No apology is necessary, sir," she said. "There is no harm done."

She made to walk on, but at that moment three sailors jostled past, blocking her way.

"You walk alone here?" said the young man, frowning after them.

"I live here, sir, and know it well." Hetta pulled her cloak hood further around her face. They were at the entrance to one of the many side lanes that led to the beach, and a chill mist was coming straight off the sea, drifting between the masts of the anchored warships and the huddle of warehouses on the pebbles. "You have come over from France?"

The stranger nodded. She noticed a bandage around his head that had been hidden by his hat; locks of auburn hair gleamed beneath the linen in the lantern light. Hetta had never yet found any of the young men her aunt determinedly produced for her in the least attractive or interesting, but now as she looked at the stranger she felt an unfamiliar curiosity.

"And you are wounded?"

"A little bump." He put his hand to his bandaged head and smiled at her. "I am French, yes, though perhaps that is not a thing to admit just as our two countries go to war! I arrived today, seeking refuge from the turmoil in Paris."

Hetta was disappointed. Not a Revolutionary who had nobly tried to abolish the corruption of old France, but another rich, spoiled émigré, escaping punishment.

"You will not be staying in Deal long then, I think," she said pointedly.

He shrugged in a decidedly French way. "I have some business to complete here, mademoiselle. It may take a while."

"Then we may meet again, sir," said Hetta coolly. "Deal is a small town and my father and I come across many émigrés."

As he bowed, she walked on quickly. She was going to a secret meeting in Bowles Alley and did not want to miss the first speech.

The young man looked after her for a moment, a curious expression on his face. Then before her figure was entirely hidden by the sea mist, he began to follow her.

The storehouse had once been used for confiscated smuggled goods. For the meeting, benches were arranged in rows around a make-shift platform. It was dank and cold. A few candles flickered on the platform, illuminating three men in travel-stained clothes. One, weary-eyed but intent, was already holding forth passionately in a strong northern accent.

Hetta slipped onto a bench at the back. Looking around surreptitiously, she saw in the flickering light that the audience was small: mainly men in stained work clothes—boatbuilders or rope makers from the naval yard.

"Citizens, friends," the speaker on the platform continued, "we want to follow the examples of America and France and bring about a better future. Equality and liberty can be within our grasp. Education for all, we say! The vote for all! Why shouldn't men and women be equal, whether they are workers or aristocrats?"

Hetta listened closely, her excitement rising. She longed to go to university herself, and would certainly like the chance to vote. It wasn't fair that boys could do such things but not girls. Why should women of her class be forced to marry for their keep, when they might accomplish so much, given the opportunity?

The speaker was striding about the front edge of the platform, the planks shuddering under his muddy top boots.

"Social evils are the result of government oppression," he declared. "What use to us are monarchs and governments? Life, liberty, and property, my friends! That is the sole duty of government—to protect those ends."

Someone in the front row shouted, "Fine talk, sir, but does it put more money in our pockets?"

"It's the king what's got the money, and the lords, ain't it?" cried another. "Let's do what they've done in France—get rid of the lot of 'em! We'll have a revolution and be done with the lords and the monarchy, too. Then there'll be more for us!"

A man turned on him. "Silence, sirrah, or you'll have the constables on us for treason!"

Hetta knew that King George III and his government were terrified of the Revolution in France affecting England, as if revolution were a contagious disease. For the last year, radicals who dared to speak out against the monarchy and the government were imprisoned without trial. Secret meetings were broken up by the constabulary, the participants arrested. Hetta was risking arrest herself by coming here this evening. But at the moment she did not care. She sat forward, entranced.

The speaker continued. "If each man and woman has a vote, then everyone will have a say in the running of the country."

Behind Hetta, the man who had followed her stood silently, observing the audience and listening to the speakers on the platform while he kept one eye on the girl sitting a little way from him. Why was she there? She interested him, jaundiced as he was with Paris society. Her face was arresting, with striking dark gray eyes and a direct gaze that he had not encountered in the aristocratic women of Paris.

And soon he would have to come to her rescue. He had seen a

bunch of constables with truncheons hanging about the head of the alley, waiting for reinforcements.

With a bang the door burst open. Uniformed constables stood on the threshold, their faces grim in the light of their leader's lantern. One shouted, "This meeting is officially closed down, by order of the Deal Constabulary and Council!"

A man on the platform called out in protest. "For what reason?"

"Disturbance of the peace! You are under arrest, sir!" Abruptly, several constables moved toward the platform.

Hetta, on her bench, was hemmed in as people began to move, pushing and shoving, anxious not to show their faces. There was darkness on the platform as the candles blew out in the commotion; a cracking sound as some of the supporting crates began to break up. A man stumbled over her foot and swore horribly.

Her heart thumped. She felt a touch on her shoulder and recoiled.

"Come with me, mademoiselle," said a calm voice in her ear.

She was pulled from her seat and propelled firmly through the crowd, away from the main door. Before she could protest, she was hurried around the edge of the platform. A door opened in front of her and cold salty night air touched her face. Other figures were pushing out behind her, but her rescuer held her to prevent her falling.

They had come out into Beach Street. Hetta could hear the sea, a dull sighing over the stones, and see the dark untidy shapes of upturned hulls edging the misty shore. In the yellow light of the street lamp, she recognized her rescuer as the Frenchman she had met earlier.

"That was most kind of you, sir," she said with dignity, "and I am much obliged to you, but you may free my arm now."

"You are not feeling faint, mademoiselle?"

"Not in the slightest," retorted Hetta, though her heart still beat hard in a mixture of shock and relief.

"Forgive me, mademoiselle, but I have been wondering why a young lady should attend such a meeting and risk arrest."

Hetta said nothing.

"Perhaps I overreacted, but I have seen the horror of crowds protesting *en masse*, people crushed underfoot. The Paris mob afire with blood lust is the most terrifying sight, I do assure you. They would pull a living person to pieces and toss the limbs away without a care." He stopped. "I apologize, mademoiselle. I am frightening you, I am sure."

"No, please continue," said Hetta, agog. "I'd be exceedingly interested to hear about the Revolution in Paris!" She knew that women had influenced many Revolutionary events. If only *she* had been there herself! But hearing about it at secondhand was better than nothing.

But he would not be drawn further. "Another time, mademoiselle. For now I should walk you home. May I have the pleasure of knowing your name?"

"Henrietta Coveney." Beach Street was poorly lit and she did not see his expression in the darkness. "And yours, monsieur?"

"Guy Deschamps. I am staying here at the Three Kings." They were walking past the hostelry, a well-known landmark, built on the beach itself.

Hetta stopped. She was in a quandary: She would have liked to have learned more about Monsieur Deschamps, but if he walked her home, she would have to offer him refreshment, and then her father would arrive back and want to know the whole story.

"It is most kind of you to offer, monsieur, but there is no need to accompany me further. Our house is only a little way down Middle Street."

"You wish to walk alone?" said Guy Deschamps doubtfully. "In such a place—full of cutthroat smugglers?"

"Oh, but they would never harm me," said Hetta airily. "I was born here, grew up with them."

"Very well, mademoiselle, as you wish."

Then Hetta was walking away from him, down Oak Street into the brighter lights of Middle Street, her boots tapping over the cobbles.

Two

A short while before, Eugénie de Boncoeur and Julien de Fortin had disembarked at Deal as the last of the daylight filtered through the thick white mist. The sea was heaving beneath the lugger and Eugénie had clutched the side nearest her as she stared at the approaching shore.

It did not fill her with cheer. Causeways of wooden planks ran down to the sea over a flat, stony beach, with coarse sea grass and weeds sprouting from the stones. Along the beach straggled buildings of all shapes and sizes: brick warehouses, boatmen's dwellings of black-tarred wood, ramshackle boat sheds that leaned away from the wind.

Behind the beach was a long road of sorts, with horses tethered dejectedly by the waiting hire carriages—waiting for customers that would never appear, she thought, especially in this weather. The town was blurred by mist, but she glimpsed squat little houses with narrow alleyways leading away from the beach.

There could surely be no *gentleman's* house among them.

She glanced back at Julien for support and he smiled at her encouragingly, his dark eyes lighting for a moment. He was looking exhausted again, the wounded arm hidden beneath his greatcoat, the sleeve dangling loose.

"Does your arm pain you dreadfully?" she asked tenderly, in French.

"It is of no consequence." He gripped the bulwark with his good hand, and spoke with uncharacteristic ferocity. "But I swear to you, Eugénie, if I ever set eyes on that traitor, Guy Deschamps, again, I shall do my utmost to kill him!"

"You were mistaken, Julien," she said, frightened by his vehemence. Her heart sank, for he still must believe it was Guy who had tried to murder him in Calais. "Your assailant was never Guy. How could it have been? Guy is our friend!"

"I fear you are wrong, Eugénie," said Julien shortly. "But I do not wish to argue over it. Let us not speak of it ever again. We are on English shores now and safe from him." As if to make amends for his abruptness, he covered her hand with his. "You are certain your uncle will welcome us?"

"Oh yes," said Eugénie, but now doubt clutched her. "At least, that is what he has said in his letters."

But what would he think when she arrived on his doorstep with salt-sticky hair and a filthy, sand-encrusted cloak? And no luggage—indeed, no possessions of any sort? Would he believe such a wretched-looking creature was a relative?

A mutter came from behind her. It was Jem Cuttle—Deal boatman, spy, and onetime smuggler, who had reluctantly rescued them in their hour of need. He had been listening to their conversation; after numerous adventures of a somewhat dubious nature along the French coast, he was fluent in the language and had developed eavesdropping to a fine art.

"If he don't welcome you, missy, you can both stay with me," he remarked. " 'T'ain't nothing special, but it's home."

"That is most kind, Mr. Cuttle," Eugénie said uncertainly. No doubt he lived in one of the shacks on the shore. "But I do not think it would be quite proper, if you understand me."

Jem grunted. "Suppose not. In any case, I daresay the prime minister will have some new ventures for me across the Channel now we're almost at war with France." He sounded hopeful.

The boatman who had come out to the clipper to ferry them was an old friend of his, and now it seemed Jem knew all the boatmen coming down the beach to pull the lugger ashore, for much joshing ensued between them. Willing arms lifted Eugénie out and set her down on the stones as tenderly as if she were a piece of china.

I am on English soil, she thought. *I have escaped the Revolution!*

Yet she did not feel safe.

The beach swayed alarmingly beneath her and she almost fell against Julien.

"Careful," he said, laughing as he steadied her, "else I'll end up with two bad arms!" He looked over at the carriages. "We should hire one to take us to your uncle's house."

"Goosefield House? 'Tis but five minutes' walk away," declared Jem Cuttle. "I'll take you there myself!"

Eugénie wondered how he knew the whereabouts of the house, but it seemed indelicate to ask; perhaps in England it was acceptable for a surgeon to be acquainted with a smuggler. She walked unsteadily between Jem and Julien, the cobbles tilting beneath her.

Despite the raw afternoon there seemed to be a large number of people about in the misty dusk. Sailors in uniform, men with weather-beaten faces and rope wound around their waists to secure their baggy breeches, a couple of soldiers with painted women on their arms. A stray dog ran along with a fish tail sticking from its mouth; another barked madly at a lamplighter.

They went down one of the dark, crooked little alleyways into a slightly wider street that ran parallel with the beach. Most of the houses here, too, were no more than two stories high, though some had fine pediments over their doors and others were gabled in the new Dutch style. Between them were ancient dwellings of wood and wattle, oozing damp.

Then Jem Cuttle stopped by a small front garden with a gate and an old apple tree. At the end of a path stood a modest brick house, with gabled windows in the roof and pillars on either side of the front door. The glow of candles showed through the fanlight.

There can be no more than three bedrooms at the most! thought Eugénie. Surely a surgeon working at the hospital would command a better establishment than this?

The front door was opened by a maid, a young girl in a crisp white apron. She took one look at Jem and scowled. "I knew t'were you, Jem Cuttle, by the knocking! Miss Hetta ain't at home, so begone!"

"It's you I want, Mollie," said Jem placidly. "I have two guests for you. The mamzelle is Miss Hetta's froggy cousin, all the way from Paris!"

There was no salon that Eugénie could make out, and they waited in a small front room for her uncle to return—a parlor, Mollie called it. She was a little comforted to see a pianoforte in the corner, a Broadwood no less, with a copy of Monsieur Haydn's "Scotch Songs" open on the stand. Perhaps her cousin played, too, and they might sit at duets together.

The fire Mollie had lit was beginning to take the chill from the air, but Eugénie was glad of her borrowed clothes, which were thicker and plainer than any dresses she had ever possessed herself, and of the woolen shawl that lay heavy on her shoulders.

I have exchanged one set of borrowed clothes for another.

She had taken off her damp clothes in her cousin's bedchamber, where Mollie drew the curtains and lit a fire for her. She had washed her face and hands in a bowl with the hot water Mollie brought her in the thick china jug. But she felt tired, so tired, and now she would have to make an effort to converse with a stranger—two strangers—for no doubt soon her cousin Henrietta would appear.

Upstairs, she had looked around the chamber to see what it would tell her about her cousin.

It had remarkably little in it, though the furniture was of good quality. The dressing table was disappointingly bare of toiletries, for she would have liked to dab herself with eau de toilette. She used the pair of silver-backed hairbrushes, however, then investigated the wardrobe; but a rummage through the dresses hanging within merely showed her that they were as plain and serviceable as the one she had been given.

There was a bookcase crammed with novels—Fielding, Defoe, Richardson—English writers, whose names meant nothing to her, but there was a much-thumbed copy in French of Rousseau's novel *La Nouvelle Héloïse*. She remembered reading it with Hortense, her late governess, and a lump came to her throat. This was the household that had dismissed Hortense so arbitrarily! And now she was in the difficult position of having to beg refuge with them, when secretly she could never forgive them for driving Hortense out.

Behind the books, almost hidden, were two volumes that appeared new: *The Rights of Man*. The author's name—Thomas Paine—meant nothing to her. Beneath these was a slim booklet—*Aims of the London Corresponding Society*—in densely written English that looked boring in the extreme.

Her discarded clothes lay on the floor in a damp, filthy heap. "Take them away and burn them, *s'il vous plaît*," she told Mollie. "I never want to see them again!"

"I'll give them to one of the boatmen's wives," said Mollie, shocked at such waste. "There's good wear in that cloak and jacket once they're cleaned up."

She glanced at Eugénie as she left the room. Miss Henrietta was taller, and the French girl had to lift the skirts of the borrowed dress as she walked. She had no look of "Miss" about her at all, though she was pretty as a picture now she'd had a wash and brushup. And, my word, she didn't half give herself airs!

Mollie foresaw trouble.

Thomas Coveney, when he returned to his house a short while later, looked at Eugénie's big sky-blue eyes and saw his late sister's. He clasped Eugénie's small, cold hands in his large, warm ones.

"My dear Eugénie! At last you're here! I wrote to your brother, Armand, many times, begging him to flee Paris with you before it was too late. I am delighted to welcome you and"—he turned to Julien, standing stiff and uncomprehending beside her, and bowed— "Mr. de Fortin." His glance went to the bandaged arm. "I must look at that later." He turned back to Eugénie. "But where is Armand?"

It took time to explain why he had not come with her. Eugénie found herself so fatigued she could scarcely find the right words, though she had always fancied her English fluent.

"So he gave up his place to Monsieur de Fortin? A brave young man, indeed! Let us pray he follows close behind you. Meanwhile, I want you to stay here until the Revolution is over." Her uncle's face grew grave. "I fear we are going to have to fight a war with France. England will not stand for the execution of a king. But I believe your government is all too eager to declare war on us."

Thomas Coveney was a big man, but his movements were neat and deft. He poured them each a glass of wine and sat down, folding his long legs beneath him. Then he remained very still, his intelligent gaze concentrated on Eugénie.

She began to talk, shyly and hesitantly at first, all the while running her eyes over him for she still could not quite believe she had at last found her English uncle. She noticed the deep shadows beneath his eyes, the lines of strain around his mouth, the hair so streaked with gray that it was difficult to make out what color it once had been. It was difficult to imagine someone with so kind and gentle a face dismissing Hortense in such a callous way.

Gradually the wine loosened her tongue. She glanced over at Julien once or twice for confirmation, but, of course, he could understand nothing of what she said—she always forgot that he spoke so little English—and was sitting looking most horribly awkward, his mouth compressed, wearing a morose expression that she knew meant he was embarrassed. She worried that her uncle might think Julien was sulking, and might not realize what a brave, true, and entirely admirable person he was.

In the midst of her story, there were voices in the hall. Moments later the parlor door opened and a girl of about Eugénie's age walked in, looking like a thundercloud.

It was too provoking! The French girl—Hetta supposed she *was* a cousin and not an imposter—had been through her clothes and books! And now, as Hetta saw her next to her father in *her* usual chair, she realized she was wearing one of her dresses.

Though undoubtedly pretty, her cousin was an insipid-looking creature, with her pale gold hair and white face. The hand she held out to Hetta trembled a little, the other clutched her shawl—*her* shawl—around her shoulders.

"Hetta, my love, this is your cousin, Eugénie," said her father; there was, she noted, a trace of anxiety in his smile.

"Father, why is she wearing my clothes?" muttered Hetta, dropping Eugénie's cold hand with alacrity and turning to her father accusingly.

"My love, your cousin has good knowledge of English," said her father with slight reproof. "She has no clothes of her own, that is why. She even had to borrow those that she wore when she arrived on these shores!"

Hetta raised a dark eyebrow in surprise; she did not look at Eugénie.

"She is with us at last," her father was saying, "after what sounds a highly dangerous experience, escaping through France with Mr. de Fortin."

A slim, dark-eyed young man, with hair as black as soot, bowed gravely from the fireside, his arm in a bandage.

"You are the second wounded Frenchman I have met today, monsieur!" Hetta said. He did not smile; he looked puzzled.

"Monsieur de Fortin does not understand a great deal of English," said Eugénie protectively.

She looked at her cousin, Henrietta, with misgiving. Her face was unwelcoming in the extreme. She was undeniably striking, she supposed, probably in an English sort of way, though too tall and her face sadly browned by the inclement weather of Deal. Her *toilette* left much to be desired. That hair, scarcely dressed at all! All long dark curls hanging about her shoulders, though the drab gray dress brought out the color of her eyes.

"I suppose you must come across many French émigrés in Deal, Cousin Henrietta?"

Hetta's expression did not warm; if anything, it grew colder. "There is a feeling that we may have half the population of France here before long. I don't believe the English realized there were so many aristocrats in France!"

"Oh yes, indeed," said Thomas Coveney heartily, trying to cover his daughter's rudeness. "You will find many of your fellow countrymen here, my dear Eugénie. Mr. de Fortin will be able to speak at last! It is too long since I did the Grand Tour. I'm afraid I have little facility with the language."

"Nonsense, Father! You can speak French perfectly well when you have a mind to it."

He looked a little abashed; it was true he feared sounding a fool. "Well, later perhaps..."

"I speak French, monsieur," said Hetta, in French, to Julien. "I had a French governess, who taught me well."

She noticed an odd expression cross the young Frenchman's face at the mention of her governess. Her cousin, Eugénie, looked, if anything, paler still.

"Well, we shall have interesting conversation at supper," said Thomas Coveney. "Each of us will be able to understand at least one other!" He took out his watch from his waistcoat and looked at it with relief. "I do believe it is almost time for Mollie to announce it."

Eugénie went over to the fire, pulling the shawl around her shoulders. It was an excuse to stand close to Julien, but Hetta was not to know that. *Thin blood*, she thought. Her cousin would have to get used to the bitter winds of Deal.

As Eugénie murmured something to Julien in French, Hetta took her father aside. "Father, may I speak with you?"

She led him into the hall. "They cannot stay with us! You must tell them so. We are cramped enough as it is."

"I'm sorry, my love. I have asked Mollie to make up the beds." He looked at Hetta's appalled face. "Mr. de Fortin will find an inn tomorrow, but tonight we cannot banish him. He needs food and rest, and though his arm appears most efficiently bandaged, I should like to inspect the wound—a sword cut, apparently, that needed stitches. Tonight he can stay in the little box room where Hortense slept."

"And Eugénie?"

"I thought she would share with you."

"I cannot share with a French aristocrat, even if she is my

cousin!" protested Hetta in a furious whisper. "It would go against all my principles. It was the extravagance of the aristocracy that brought ruin on France!"

"You know that is not entirely true," said Thomas Coveney, with reproach. "Besides, where is your humanity, your compassion? I had always thought you so mature for your age, my dear." He ran his fingers through his hair.

Hetta could not bear to see him look worried. She said in a low voice, knowing she sounded like a petulant child, "Very well. If I must share with my cousin tonight, I must. But tomorrow, when Mr. de Fortin is gone, I will move into the box room and Eugénie can have my bedchamber to herself."

"Julien, I wish you could stay here with me," said Eugénie sadly. "I'd no notion my uncle kept such a modest establishment."

Since they were momentarily alone, he caught her hand and pressed it. *It was indeed remarkable*, she thought, *how his touch could send such a tingle through her.*

"Eugénie, I will visit each day. You will not be alone, remember that. We are in this together."

"And soon Armand will join us, won't he?"

He looked somberly into the fire. "I hope so."

"But how shall we discover what is happening in our country? It is our only way of knowing what Armand endures!"

"There are newspapers, even here," he said, smiling the crooked smile she had grown to love.

"*English* newspapers." She shook her head. "Most surely they are ill informed and biased."

"But the Deal boatmen will know all there is to know about relations with France. Think how close we are to the French shore! A mere twenty-five miles! We shall see it on a clear day."

That was comforting. She was not so very far from Armand, after all.

They sat around the small walnut dining table and ate dressed crab and a roasted duck.

The crab was unexpectedly good, Eugénie thought. She was pleasantly surprised, for she had assumed English food to be far inferior to French; but she was too tired to finish her meat, and the vegetables, though fresh, were boiled and presented plain, without sauce.

She pushed her plate away, and without warning was overwhelmed by grief. To her horror she felt her eyes fill with tears.

Thomas noted with interest Julien's expression of tender concern. "Tomorrow, Eugénie, we must see about your clothes," he said cheerfully, as the conversation died to a heavy silence. "You cannot borrow my daughter's dresses forever. You must have your own."

"Thank you," she managed to say. At any other time the prospect of new clothes would have filled her with excitement. "I have the money, sir, I do assure you." Upstairs was the pocket belt stuffed with French *assignats*; Julien, too, had his own.

"You are with your family now, my dear," said her uncle gently. "You need not pay for your own wardrobe! Hetta, you must take Eugénie to one of the auctions at the Customs House. I am sure you will pick up suitable material there."

Hetta nodded, without enthusiasm.

The conversation edged around the Revolution.

"Our prime minister saw fit to mobilize the militia last month in case of trouble," said Thomas. "He is clearly worried that France's revolutionary ideals may spread here and cause insurrection."

"Would that happen?" said Eugénie, wide-eyed. *Have I escaped one revolution only to find myself at the start of another?*

Her uncle smiled. "It is most unlikely, my dear. No, our own revolution was more than two hundred years ago. Though there are one or two movements to bring about change. I hear the London Corresponding Society has even come to Deal! The constables interrupted a meeting earlier this evening, apparently, and made several arrests."

The name was familiar. Eugénie glanced at Hetta, opened her mouth and shut it again.

Her cousin stopped eating. "But the Society is pacifist, Father! They believe change can be achieved without the use of violence."

"It only takes one radical among them to inflame the others," said her father mildly. "I believe that is what happens with the Paris mobs."

"Have you seen a mob on the march, cousin?" said Hetta. "It must be a thrilling sight, is it not? To witness the power of the people demanding reform!"

Eugénie swallowed and could not speak. She remembered running in terror; the shouts and screams behind her; the convent where she had lived so peacefully, in flames.

"I heard from my French governess how the women of Paris marched to Versailles demanding bread for their starving families," said Hetta dreamily. "I would have supported them myself had I been there! And King Louis was forced to give it to them, was he not? No wonder he lost his head. He seems to have mismanaged the affairs of his country most abominably! What do you think, cousin?"

It was a deliberate challenge. Eugénie was disturbed by the passion she saw in her cousin's face. Surely Henrietta did not think it right to execute a king? She found herself stammering in answer.

"My brother and I were royalist. We supported the king, but we wanted a new constitution that would give the people fairer laws and control his powers—indeed, Armand fought for reform during the early years of the Revolution. We did not believe that destroying the monarchy and putting a republic in its place was the answer to our country's ills."

The eager light in her cousin's eyes died.

After supper, while Thomas checked Julien's arm in the library, Eugénie fell asleep in her chair. It was only when the men came back that she woke again. Her uncle looked down at her kindly. "Bed for you, my dear, and sleep as long as you wish."

"Is Monsieur de Fortin's arm mending?" Eugénie said anxiously.

"I dare say he will live," said Thomas.

Eugénie could hear Hetta thumping away on the pianoforte downstairs; she did not play well.

Later Hetta came upstairs and found her in bed, sitting up in a borrowed nightgown and yawning over *La Nouvelle Héloïse*. She looked at her curiously. "You read Rousseau?"

Eugénie hesitated. "This novel was a favorite of my governess," she said painfully.

"Mine also. I suppose it is not such a coincidence, since my governess was French."

Hetta's voice was noncommittal, unemotional. It made Eugénie so angry she found herself exclaiming, "I know! I know also that Hortense Tati was dismissed from this household and cast out without money or references!"

Hetta was taken aback. "How can you know such a thing?"

"She was governess to us both in turn, that is why! My guardian gave her your father's address in England when I went to convent school and she was no longer required. So she took up employment here, poor unfortunate creature."

Hetta had not thought Eugénie possessed such spirit. Perhaps she had underestimated her. She sat down on the end of the bed and looked at her with her candid gaze.

"I loved Hortense, as I see you did, too. She was like a mother to me—no, perhaps a big sister—for I had neither mother nor sister. It was not my father who dismissed her, but my aunt Frederica.

She thought she filled my head with radical political views, and indeed she did! I was distraught when she left."

They regarded each other in silence.

"When you meet Aunt Frederica you will understand that she would disapprove of Hortense." Hetta sighed. "She disapproves of most people, myself in particular. But I would so like news of Hortense!" She looked at Eugénie's white face against the pillows and felt a sudden compunction. "Not tonight, though."

Eugénie's anger died. She could not bring herself yet to tell Hetta what had happened to Hortense—that she had been murdered by an assailant in Calais.

Hetta brightened. "And we can compare our views on the significance of the Revolution in France. It will be delightful—almost as good as having Hortense herself here—to discuss politics again!"

Eugénie lay down and turned her head away. She reflected that she was going to be a grave disappointment to her cousin.

When Hetta came to bed a little while later, Eugénie was tossing and turning in her sleep. She did not wake as Hetta climbed in, but seemed caught fast in slumber. Hetta lay awake next to her, wondering what nightmares haunted her cousin that she should cry out in such terror.

THREE

When Eugénie awoke, the room was filled with a bleached light and the sound of seagulls. Mollie had already crept in to light the fire. Eugénie felt a great deal refreshed, especially after she had eaten the English breakfast that Mollie brought her on a tray. Instead of rolls, there were thin slices of bread and butter, and "toast": hot bread burned ingeniously, not black, but a soft golden brown on both sides.

"Would you like my help in dressing, Miss?" Mollie said, when she returned to collect the tray. "I sometimes help Miss Hetta, when she allows me, and I am sure you must be used to having a lady's maid." She added kindly, "I know our two countries are at war now, but I do not blame you for that."

"That is most generous of you, Mollie!" Eugénie said, smiling at the girl, who was not so very much older than she was herself. "And indeed I should like some help in choosing something appropriate to wear." She shuddered inwardly at having to wear another of Hetta's mud-colored dresses. "But I did not know that war had been officially announced?"

"Yes, Miss. It's all the buzz along Beach Street. Jem Cuttle came into the kitchen to tell us."

"I must see him." She swung her legs out of bed. "Is Monsieur de Fortin awake?"

"The Monsewer?" Mollie nodded. "Jem is to find him an inn."

Eugénie remembered now that Julien would not be staying at Goosefield. Her heart sank immediately.

Jem had worked his way around the Coveney household with his news, and he was with her uncle in the library by the time Eugénie was dressed and her hair arranged to her satisfaction.

"Best to knock, Miss," said Mollie. "The Master don't like to be disturbed when Jem's with him."

"Does Jem visit often?" said Eugénie in some surprise.

"Oh yes, Miss. Long chats they have. He gives the Master all the news before the papers print a word."

They did indeed appear on excellent and familiar terms: both of them smoking pipes and sitting opposite each other in wing chairs in the book-lined room. They rose, looking somewhat sheepish, as Eugénie knocked and entered through pungent drifts of smoke.

"I must get to the hospital, my dear," said her uncle reluctantly, pulling out his fob watch. "I did not realize how late it was. Jem has been regaling me with your adventures in the Channel. You were too tired to get so far last night." He examined her with a medical eye. "I am glad to see that you have some color this morning. The fresh air of Deal will soon bring roses to your cheeks."

"Where is Julien—Monsieur de Fortin?"

"Why, he is with Hetta in the parlor, I believe."

Poor Julien, struggling to make conversation in English with her serious-minded cousin! She would rescue him as soon as possible, but first she must talk to Jem.

As soon as her uncle had left, she turned to him. "Mr. Cuttle, do you believe you'll return to France soon?"

He eyed her thoughtfully, sucking on his noxious pipe. "I don't rightly know. Now we're at war with your country things may get a little complicated regarding my future activities."

She lowered her voice. "But surely Mr. Pitt will send you off on another mission? You are one of his most valuable spies, you've said so yourself."

"Did I now?" He stepped closer, breathing out tobacco fumes. "Why do you want to know? Want to go home, do you? Tired of being with the good doctor already?" He gave a chirpy black-toothed grin.

"No, of course not," said Eugénie stiffly. "My uncle is courtesy itself. It is my brother, Armand, I'm worried about, Mr. Cuttle. You remember Julien and I left him behind in Paris?" She fiddled with the grayish lace on Hetta's cuffs. "I thought you might hear news of him, you with your great network of"—she hesitated— "colleagues. I believe Armand will try to reach Calais. It could not be a more dangerous time." She blinked away tears. Outside the library window a herring gull laughed mockingly.

"I'll do my best, little lady. I'll be popping over shortly, no doubt." He winked at her. "Don't like to say this to a Frenchie, but they ain't got a cat's chance in this war."

She was not sure how to take that, for it was difficult to know whose side she should be on—being half and half, so to speak. "Perhaps you should not be so sure, Mr. Cuttle!"

He grunted something. She thought it was good-bye, but he strode over to a corner and opened a waist-high cupboard; inside was a shelf, with the shine of glass decanters holding brandy and whisky.

He turned to her. "If you're ever in trouble, there's a panel on the right-hand side slides back. There's an indent behind the molding of the doorway. Press it, and you'll find steps down and a tunnel leading to Beach Street. It's a smuggler's route. Deal is full of 'em."

"Goodness! Does my cousin know of it?"

"Oh, aye. Miss Hetta uses it often."

"Indeed?"

"And she keeps her clothes in there. Boys' clothes, of course. She couldn't do what she does, dressed like a lady."

Eugénie's eyes grew larger still. "You mean—my cousin is a smuggler?" she said faintly.

"More like she warns us when the excise men are about. Then she'll hide us—get 'em off our backs, see? If you're a boatman in Deal you're a smuggler or wrecker, or both."

Eugénie was speechless. Jem shifted uncomfortably, aware he had said too much.

"Best not to tell Miss Hetta I've let you in on it. She'd be furious, and Miss Hetta in a rage—why, she'd make an army of Frenchies turn tail and run away."

Since Hetta had not yet appeared, Eugénie went to the parlor. The door was a little ajar. From inside, she could hear the murmur of voices and low laughter. That gentle, amused laugh was Julien's; she knew it so well now.

Strangely disturbed, she pushed the door open further.

The two heads were bent over a book on the table, very close. Hetta was saying something, but she stopped as soon as she heard Eugénie enter the room. They both sat back, glancing at each other in what looked to Eugénie to be a conspiratorial way before smiling at her politely.

Almost as if I were a stranger.

"What is so amusing?" said Eugénie coldly, as Julien rose to his feet and bowed. An odd little feeling pierced her heart for a moment.

"Good morning, cousin," said Hetta. "I trust you slept well?"

"Your bed is very comfortable. Thank you." She remained where she was, looking from one to the other awkwardly.

Julien was still smiling at her, but his smile had altered. It was now, she noticed with relief, as warming and loving as always.

"Your cousin has been kind enough to give me an English lesson," he said, in French. "Soon you'll keep no secrets from me, for I shall understand everything you say!"

"I thought I would help Monsieur de Fortin with his English," said Hetta, also in French.

"Mademoiselle Henrietta is teaching me from a child's alphabet book!" Julien grinned ruefully. "I fear that is about my level!"

"Nonsense!" said Hetta. "It was only your first lesson. It won't take long—perhaps an hour a day if you can spare it."

"Mademoiselle, I would be deeply obliged. And perhaps we can have a little exchange, so I help you with your pronunciation?"

A faint flush rose in Hetta's clear skin. "Are you criticizing my accent, monsieur?"

"Oh no, mademoiselle, it is merely a little uncertain here and there," said Julien gravely.

Hetta burst into a peal of laughter. "Very well! I am somewhat out of practice, I admit."

Eugénie was torn between uneasiness at the prospect of Hetta and Julien cloistered together for a whole hour, and the thought that at least it would mean she would see Julien each day. She went over to him, wishing that Hetta were not there, able to understand every word she said.

"Oh, Julien, you know that France has declared war on England?" She wrung her hands. "Why have we done such a thing? We are already at war with Prussia and Austria. We cannot take on the whole of Europe!"

He looked at her strained face and knew she worried about Armand. War would make it even more difficult for him to join them. How would he cross a channel full of warships to reach the English coast?

"Now King Louis has been guillotined, the government feels under threat from hostile monarchs. That includes George III of England. They feel their only course is invasion before they are invaded themselves."

"You mean"—Eugénie put a hand to her mouth—"the French would come *here*?"

"They cannot do it," interrupted Hetta. "Our navy will mow them down!"

"There are other ways of defeating a country," said Julien thoughtfully. "There are other seas and other lands to fight over that both France and England desire for themselves."

He rose and went to the door. "Now I must find that rascal, Jem Cuttle! He's promised to introduce me to one of his innkeeper friends."

In fact, Jem had told Julien he'd be safest in his company—and keeping his French mouth shut, too—but Julien did not want to worry Eugénie. The people of Deal had grudgingly accepted the influx of French émigrés over the last few years since they did not stay long before going on to London, but who knew what they would feel now that the two countries were at war?

"Might I write a letter?" Eugénie asked Hetta after Julien had gone. "My old landlady in Paris, Belle Fleurie, will be wondering if I've arrived safely."

"Of course," Hetta said. "It's best that it's dispatched before we engage in action. Jack, the boot boy, can take it for you. He knows which boats will be crossing."

After the letter was written, Eugénie wondered forlornly when Julien would return; she had hoped that they might explore Deal together their first morning. She sat down at the Broadwood pianoforte and tinkled a dismal little tune.

"Come," said Hetta. "I saw in the *Kentish Gazette* that the Customs House has an auction today. We may be able to pick up some good cloth cheap." She smiled. "I shall need my dresses back some-time, though I vow you look a good deal prettier in them than I!"

"I am sure that is not true," said Eugénie politely, for she could see that her cousin was anxious to be friendly and make amends for her coldness the previous evening.

Or was it for something else? She could not dispel a vague disquiet that was nothing to do with the war.

They wore Hetta's warmest outdoor clothes, since, according to Mollie, there was a bitter wind blowing for all the day's deceiving brightness. Despite the cold, the whole of Deal was agog with the news.

They were hardly out of the garden gate before they were accosted by the Coveneys' neighbor; and after that no less than four other acquaintances stopped to inform Hetta that they were now at war with France. Eugénie thought she detected a note of relish in their voices, almost as if they were looking forward to the impending engagement. She felt their sly, appraising gazes when she was introduced.

How could war be entertainment? It was not a game. How very strange the English were!

The stiff salt breeze made her eyes water; she feared it would tear the curls from her hair. Even the seagulls were forced to fly at an angle, or shelter squawking beneath the chimney stacks. But the light was so clear and bright after yesterday's mist that she could see every detail of the plasterwork over the doors and windows of the houses they passed, each brick clearly defined, each slate as if drawn on the rooftops. She reflected that though they were modest houses compared with those she had known in Paris, there was an appealing quaintness about them.

Then, as they emerged onto Beach Street, she gasped in surprise and admiration.

The entire sea was filled to the horizon with ships.

The previous evening, mist and growing darkness had hidden them from her sight, but today she could see the British fleet in all its majesty rocking gently on the sheltering sea: sails furled but masts piercing the sky, as the rushing clouds lit and shadowed each ship in turn. Other, smaller boats pulled briskly toward them to unload their cargoes, the tiny dark gesticulating figures of the Deal boatmen on their luggers dwarfed by the vast city of wood. Other luggers emerged and pulled back to shore to reload, the boatmen's shouts carried away by the wind.

However can we win against such might? Eugénie thought. But if the French invaded, the thought of revolutionary soldiers charging up the beach, their eyes alight with blood lust, was too dreadful to dwell upon.

An inn stood on the beach, its sign creaking in the wind—the Three Kings. "Perhaps Julien will stay there," she said hopefully. It was not so very far from Goosefield House.

"If he does, he will meet a kind young Frenchman I encountered yesterday evening," said Hetta.

For a moment her mind lingered on Guy Deschamps. He was, without doubt, attractive—so very different from the clods her aunt lumbered her with at dances. "But I think Jem Cuttle will avoid that particular hostelry. It is very popular with naval officers, and Jem does not believe in encountering such exalted people at too close quarters! He had clashes with many an officer during his days of running goods between the Forelands either side of Deal."

"Yet he spies for Mr. Pitt."

"Hush." Hetta looked around quickly, though she knew most of the boatmen were aware of Jem's special activities; indeed, many of them were his accomplices. "That is different."

"Because it is sanctioned by a prime minister, and not illegal and dishonest—like smuggling, or wrecking?" Eugénie watched Hetta's face carefully.

The blood had risen in Hetta's cheeks, though perhaps caused by the buffeting of the wind. She stared back at Eugénie, her gray eyes darkening to the color of a stormy sea.

"Do not condemn smuggling and wrecking when you know nothing about them!"

"I know enough. Both are stealing!"

"Do you realize that years ago our boatmen were allowed to bring in whatever goods they wanted?" said Hetta fiercely. "Now they have that right no longer, yet they still provide the sole defense of our coastline when we're not at war. They still go out in mountainous seas to save the lives of shipwrecked men! They see smuggling as a just reward."

"But the wrecks?" protested Eugénie. "Don't they lure them into dangerous waters deliberately so they can plunder them?"

Hetta shook her head so vigorously that her hat blew off. Strands of dark hair whipped about her face as she jammed it back on. "The Goodwin Sands are perilous for any boat. We call them 'the Ship Swallower.'"

Eugénie was not certain now whether she still thought smuggling and wrecking as wrong as she had some minutes ago. Perhaps as an ignorant foreigner it might be as well to stay on her cousin's good side until she had worked out for herself how things were.

"I understand," she said meekly. "Thank you for explaining it to me, cousin."

Hetta cast her a suspicious look, but was met by Eugénie's wide, innocent gaze.

"Well, then," she said grudgingly, "we had better be getting on to the Customs House or it will be time for luncheon." She put her hand to her mouth. "And Aunt Frederica is coming! I had quite forgot!"

* * *

Eugénie was astonished to discover that the Customs House was auctioning confiscated smuggled goods; even more so that ladies of quality attended the auction, apparently undismayed by this fact. Indeed, they proved to be most competitive and *un*ladylike in their bargaining.

However, she arrived back with Hetta at Goosefield well pleased with her own purchases, though Mollie shook her head over them. "You'll have no chance to wear such finery in Deal, Miss. You need warmth above everything here!"

"I shall go to the draper's tomorrow for some wool cloth," Eugénie promised absently, stroking a length of apple green figured satin, which she had laid out over the end of the bed in order to admire it better. She could not help wondering, though, whether the dressmakers of Deal might not ruin such beautiful material: no doubt their cutting was abominable.

Downstairs in the hall Hetta noticed a calling card on the silver tray where the letters were always placed. A visitor must have come while they were out. She picked it up idly.

It bore a name only—*Guy Deschamps*—printed in black on the stiff white card.

She ran up the stairs to her old bedchamber and burst in, trying not to sound too eager. "What did my visitor say, Mollie?"

"He seemed disappointed you weren't here, Miss. Such a nice-mannered young man for all he was French—begging your pardon, Miss Eugénie." Mollie blushed and patted her cap. "He said he would visit again."

"A Frenchman?" said Eugénie.

"It's the young man I mentioned to you," said Hetta, feigning indifference as she passed over the card. Mollie was already hurrying away to check that clean napkins were laid out in the dining room, ready for luncheon.

There was a pause, then Hetta noticed that her cousin was

looking strangely shocked; indeed, she had gone quite white, as if she were struggling with some great emotion as she stared down at the card.

"Does the name mean something to you?"

"I know Monsieur Deschamps well," breathed Eugénie. "He is a dear friend of both Armand and myself. I had no idea he was in England!"

It was her ill fortune, Hetta reflected, to meet the only attractive man in Deal and then find he had been discovered already by her pretty little cousin. She felt ridiculously put out.

"Then why are you so perturbed?" she said tartly. "Would it not be agreeable to see him?"

"Oh yes, I would like it above all things! He cannot know I am here and it will be such a surprise to him." Eugénie sank down on the bed and the card dropped from her fingers as she put her hand to her cheek. "But what am I to do?"

"No doubt he will return." Under the circumstances Hetta could feel little sympathy for her cousin's surprising agitation.

"But that is the trouble! Julien must not see him! I cannot tell him that Monsieur Deschamps is in Deal!"

"Why ever not?"

"Julien hates Guy! He persists in thinking that Guy tried to kill him before we left France. At first I thought Julien was merely feverish with his wounded arm, but I have not been able to persuade him otherwise."

Hetta's interest was pricked despite herself. "But why does he think Monsieur Deschamps should want to kill him?"

"The idea is too nonsensical! They have known each other for some time; both were members of Armand's circle in Paris; both struggled for reform and a constitutional monarchy. There was no quarrel between them, for Armand would have told me." Eugénie hesitated, biting her lip. "I feel in a way that Julien's delusions are my fault."

"Oh?" Hetta gave in to her curiosity and perched on the bed next to Eugénie, careful not to squash the satin—though her cousin appeared to have lost all interest in it now.

"Julien has misjudged Guy in the past—for various reasons that I confess were a little to do with my behavior." Eugénie looked down and fiddled with the flowered counterpane. "I was flattered by Guy's attentions. I was young and immature then, you understand. Also, Julien has seen Guy in the company of the most odious man called Raoul Goullet, to whom I was betrothed against my will."

"*What?* You are engaged to be married?"

"I have escaped him by coming to England. But Julien believes that Guy knew of this marriage contract and was somehow colluding in it. Mistakenly, I do assure you. Guy knows nothing of it. Why Guy himself"—a blush suffused Eugénie's cheeks—"has made overtures to me, which he would not do, I am certain, if he thought I were already betrothed."

Hetta drooped back against the bed hangings. So Deschamps had courted Eugénie in Paris—was still interested in her, perhaps. Then she rallied briskly.

"Deal is fit to burst with soldiers and sailors preparing for war. The town has never been so crowded. It is most unlikely that they will ever meet. Besides, they are staying in different inns."

"But they might meet here!"

Hetta shook her head. "If Monsieur Deschamps calls while Monsieur de Fortin is here, Mollie will tell him to come back later. It is not etiquette, anyway, to remain when there is another visitor already."

"You will not tell Julien that Guy is in Deal, will you? He must not know!"

Hetta could not imagine that Monsieur Deschamps would be in any danger from the reserved young man to whom she had taught English earlier that morning, but she nodded to humor her cousin.

Eugénie evidently thought she should explain a little more. "Julien has tried to fight a duel with him already—over me. Julien is most honorable, you understand, and will certainly call him out again if they meet. But Guy is so much the better swordsman—and excellent with a pistol, too, I am sure—that if he accepted Julien's challenge, he might kill him." Her blue eyes grew larger. "At the very least they might both be wounded. You do understand, don't you, cousin?"

"Of course," said Hetta shortly. "I shall keep silent." She stood up and went to the door. "Now I must prepare for Aunt Frederica's visit. At least I do not have to entertain her on my own today!"

Left alone, Eugénie pressed her palms to her hot cheeks. Her feelings were so jumbled together—pleasure, trepidation, excitement—at the thought that she might see Guy Deschamps, she wondered if she was going to be sick.

But I love Julien, she told herself. *Why do I feel like this?*

Gradually she calmed herself, sitting at the dressing table and teasing the hair around her face back into its curls. The most important thing was to keep each unaware of the other's presence.

She met her own eyes in the looking glass thoughtfully.

FOUR

Lady Coveney sighed as she finished her last mouthful of ham and mutton pie.

"Of course, in the old days before the present unpleasantness, I often used to visit Paris for a little shopping."

She had eaten luncheon that day with more than her usual enjoyment. She had always found Henrietta on her own somewhat trying—the girl was so argumentative!—but her new niece was altogether delightful company. While she ate, she had inspected Eugénie closely and rapped out questions about her upbringing in France.

Due to her fondness for food, Lady Coveney was a large woman with an impressive bosom, and society from Deal to Dover found her a powerful and daunting presence. Eugénie, however, had been undaunted. She looked her new aunt straight in the eye and answered the flurry of questions patiently and politely.

By the end of luncheon, Lady Coveney decided she was well pleased: a pretty child, with aristocratic bearing and exquisite manners. A marquis for a father, no less, and the French aristocracy so much purer than the English! Raised on a grand estate and convent educated in Paris. Used to mixing in the very best Parisian social circles.

Yes, little Eugénie would be no disgrace to the family. In fact, she was a positive attribute, and Lady Coveney looked forward to showing her off. She sat back in the protesting chair and smiled her approval at Eugénie.

"Henrietta must bring you to Sandicote, my dear. We shall visit the local gentry. They will be enchanted. And so will your uncle Harry, when he comes down from London. I believe I might give a ball in the summer when Parliament stops sitting." She began to compile a list in her head of those she would most like to impress with Eugénie: the prospect was altogether agreeable.

"That is most kind of you, Aunt," Eugénie began, a little overwhelmed. "But I do not want to put you to any trouble."

"It is no trouble, my dear. We are delighted to welcome you to the family, aren't we, Henrietta?"

Hetta nodded glumly.

As she departed, Lady Coveney graciously presented a plump and remarkably unlined cheek for Eugénie to kiss; she smelled of violets, Eugénie noticed approvingly. She watched as the well-trained coachman escorted Lady Coveney to her carriage as reverently as if she had been royalty. It rattled away over the cobbles, scattering passersby in all directions.

Hetta shut the front door smartly as if she longed to slam it instead. "You did well," she remarked to Eugénie. "Now I have to thank you for yet another ball!"

"But it will be most enjoyable, no?" said Eugénie in surprise. "And it was so very kind and generous of your aunt to suggest such a thing." She wondered how she could contrive a meeting between Lady Coveney and Julien, so that Julien received an invitation, too. Perhaps she would have the apple green satin made up into a ball dress. She did not think that Julien had ever seen her in green. . . .

Hetta began to stomp up the stairs, calling over her shoulder, "I am going to read! You may do as you wish!"

Eugénie stood alone in the hall and hesitated. From the kitchen below came the subdued clatter of dishes and pans, but otherwise the house seemed very quiet. She felt extraordinarily fatigued suddenly—she would dearly like to lie on her bed and rest until supper. It was most unlike her: She supposed it was the strain of the last weeks. But she must visit the Three Kings while there was light enough to see her way.

The innkeeper of the Three Kings liked to think he kept a high-class hostelry. He was suspicious of any pretty young woman arriving alone, without chaperone or gentleman to accompany her. When Eugénie arrived, he looked her up and down with misgiving.

But she was dressed modestly, he noted, and her clothes were of good quality. When she spoke, trying to make her voice heard above the ringing upper-class voices of the naval and military officers in the adjoining saloon bar, he realized that she must be another French émigré—one who did not understand that ladies should not go into English inns on their own.

"Can you help me, monsieur? Is there a Monsieur Deschamps staying here?"

She appeared distressed, and the innkeeper was a kind man. Besides, he had no personal quarrel with the French: He had had excellent business from the rich émigrés that had flooded into Deal from France and required somewhere to stay. He had even picked up a little French.

"Indeed there is, mamzelle. Would you like me to send a maid to fetch the monsieur down?"

Eugénie clasped her hands together. She was acting, she knew, but part of it was genuine. *"Oui, s'il vous plaît, monsieur. Vous êtes très gentil!"*

The innkeeper was charmed by the large blue eyes filled with gratitude. "Then let me show you into a private parlor, mamzelle."

The room Eugénie was shown into was like the cabin of a ship, lined in wood but comfortably furnished, the curtains drawn against the dying afternoon. A fire burned in the hearth and she warmed herself while she waited, her pulse calming a little.

The tall, familiar figure came through the door.

He was dressed as exquisitely as ever, his long legs clad in beautifully cut buckskin breeches, but there was a bandage around his auburn hair.

Eugénie started toward him, her hands outstretched involuntarily. "Guy! You are hurt!"

He looked taken aback to see her in the little inn parlor and her heart sank. Then the surprise on his face was quickly replaced by pleasure. "Mademoiselle Boncoeur! Eugénie! How delightful! And how completely unexpected!"

"But your head, monsieur! Oh, Guy, what has happened to you?"

He touched the bandage ruefully. "A fight in Calais. So many starving rogues lurking around the quayside, greedy for one's purse. One took me by surprise. It was a poor fight, though, and I dispatched the rascal forthwith."

He stepped closer and looked down at her. "But you, mademoiselle? I never thought to meet you in Deal!" He took both her hands in his and brought them to his lips. "We never managed to say good-bye in Paris, did we? But now fate has brought us together again so that we need not do so!"

She tried to laugh, though her hands were still imprisoned in his and his greenish hazel eyes very bright as they gazed into hers.

"It is singular, is it not?" she said shakily. "I take it you, too, are escaping the Revolution?"

He dropped her hands lightly and shook his head. "I have some work to do that brings me to England occasionally. It is not so difficult to travel back and forth if your business is nothing to do with the war and you have the right papers."

He rang for brandy and ratafia, though she would have preferred a tisane. After the drinks had been brought, they seated themselves either side of the fire.

He was frowning a little. "How did you know I was staying here?"

"I have relations here in Deal. I believe you met my cousin yesterday, by strange coincidence. Her name is Henrietta Coveney. You left a calling card at her house."

"Of course! The young woman last night." He looked amused. "I would not have expected to encounter a young lady of her background at a meeting of the London Corresponding Society!"

Eugénie wanted to steer the conversation away from her cousin.

"Oh, Guy, there is so much to tell you!" She took a sip of the ratafia. It was agreeably sweet, tasting of peaches, and left her with a warm glow. She drank some more. "I saw you at Calais before I left France. I was about to greet you, but"—she thought of Monsieur Goullet's sudden sinister appearance as he walked along the quay with his umbrella, and shuddered—"in the end, I did not."

An odd expression crossed Guy's face. "You were engaged in conversation with an acquaintance at the time," she explained hastily, fearing that he was put out. "It did not seem appropriate to interrupt."

He leaned forward, the firelight flickering over the handsome features beneath the bandage. *It is ridiculous*, she thought, *that even with a bandage he is so exceedingly attractive!* She saw with relief that he was smiling.

"I am delighted to see you at any time, *ma petite* Eugénie," he said softly. "If I had known you were in Calais...I thought you were still in Paris and feared for your safety."

"Armand wanted me to come to England. We were both to travel here and stay with our English relations until the Revolution was over. I left Paris just after the king's execution, but Armand—was unable to accompany me."

Eugénie was not sure how much Guy knew of the secret plan to rescue the king; she thought he had not been involved. It was best not to mention it, perhaps.

"You managed to cross France alone?" he said, raising his eyebrows. "Few aristocrats manage that now. You passed through all the checkpoints? Remarkable."

"But I wasn't alone," she said brightly, eyes wide. "I had a friend of Armand's with me. You know him, of course—Julien de Fortin."

Guy twirled his brandy glass in the firelight, watching through narrowed eyes as the swirling liquid glowed amber and gold. His long mouth smiled. "Monsieur de Fortin! How pleasant it will be to see an old friend in a strange country. We shall have quite a reunion between the three of us!"

She had known Julien was wrong. Guy could not have sounded more pleased. But they must not be allowed to meet. She pressed her hands together. "Oh no, monsieur, we cannot do that!"

His eyes flicked to hers and he set the brandy glass down carefully. "No? Oh, I know Julien and I had a misunderstanding in Paris a while ago, but we are Frenchmen. We always quarrel over women! It means nothing. And you were the woman in question, were you not, Eugénie?"

"But he hates you!" she burst out.

He laughed, showing his excellent teeth. "For finding you as pretty as he does? Jealousy, *ma chérie*, that is all it is, and who could blame him?"

"Hush, Guy, you mustn't talk such flummery! Please be serious." She hesitated. "I believe he would challenge you to a duel again." She gulped down a large mouthful of the ratafia.

Guy spread his hands; they were smooth, white hands, the nails beautifully manicured. He looked at a loss. "For remaining interested in you?"

"It is all nonsense, of course, but he is convinced you are his enemy."

"Then let us go and convince him otherwise!" He finished his brandy and rose in one lithe movement.

Eugénie was dismayed. This was not going to plan at all. She had wanted to stop Guy from coming to Goosefield again. It was quite possible that Julien, invited to supper, would be returning there at any moment.

She struggled to speak calmly. "I fear you cannot do that, Guy. Monsieur de Fortin is still in France. He was wounded by an assailant in Calais and not well enough to sail with me. I doubt whether he will be able to cross the Channel now, what with the war."

"Not with you? He remained in Calais?"

She nodded. A tiny pause, then Guy shrugged and sat down again. "That is not altogether a disappointment. It means I have you all to myself, Mademoiselle Eugénie! What an enchanting prospect. Have some more ratafia and tell me all about your adventures on your journey across France. I confess, I am most intrigued as to how you—and the good Julien, of course—managed to outwit the guards."

As the last daylight faded outside, Eugénie grew confused in her account and began to falter. Another time she would have enjoyed being alone with Guy in their intimate firelit world, but now she was exhausted, fighting the draw of his magnetism with weakening strength.

He leaned across, his eyes intent on hers. "I have rooms that open onto the balcony. The ships are a pretty spectacle at night with lighted lanterns hanging from their fo'c's'les. Why don't we retire there and look at them, while we partake of a little supper?"

Eugénie hesitated, but he helped her up with the utmost courtesy. The room spun around her. She leaned against him for a second, scarcely knowing what she was doing, and felt the strong muscles of his arm through the heavy silk of his coat.

He looked down at her with concern. "You are fatigued, mademoiselle. Some refreshment in my rooms will set you up."

At that moment, when she did not know herself how she would answer, the door to the parlor opened and a maid poked her head around it.

"Sir, Miss—apologies for disturbin' you and that, but there is a boy, says he's from your household, Miss, and you're wanted back immediate." She looked at Eugénie somewhat smugly. "He's a *French* boy, so I put two and two together when he didn't ask for you by name."

"*Merci,*" said Eugénie, puzzled. She let Guy's arm go. "It has been a pleasure to renew our acquaintance, monsieur." He pressed her hand, and a tremor went through her. She looked up into his face. "When you return to Paris, try to find Armand for me, I beg you! You know all his friends and they may have news of him. Tell him to join me as soon as he can."

In the saloon bar, a boy was standing by the counter with a lantern, wearing a shabby greatcoat and hat, and surrounded by uniforms and loud English conversation. There was something familiar about the slight body and erect stance.

The gray eyes met hers. "*On y va,* mademoiselle." The way her language was mangled was all too familiar.

Outside the cold night air blew through the fug in her head. It also blew off the boy's crumpled felt hat. He caught it deftly with one hand and glared at her.

"What on earth were you doing?" hissed Hetta, her hair tumbling down around her shoulders. She gathered it up and crammed the hat over it impatiently. "Do you not know it is unwise to walk the streets of Deal alone at night and enter an inn full of men, when you are a stranger and French at that? How did you propose to return home? On foot, through the drunkards?"

"You do it, I am sure," retorted Eugénie. She felt no gratitude for Hetta's sudden appearance at the Three Kings; she felt humiliated. "And what is worse, you do it wearing breeches!"

"I pass unmolested like this." Hetta put an arm around Eugénie's waist and Eugénie tried to pull away. "If we look like sweethearts, we will be left alone!" Hetta hissed.

A group of men, in pursuit of a frightened boy who looked no more than twelve, thundered past them over the cobbles of the alleyway. Eugénie shrank back against the walls.

"Press gang," said Hetta, in a matter-of-fact way. "They need more sailors for the war."

"I suppose that is the disguise you wear when you help smugglers!" Eugénie said, as they emerged into Middle Street and she saw her cousin properly under a streetlight. She felt profoundly shocked that her cousin should expose her body in such a way. Any man could see where her legs began under the long open coat.

Hetta tossed her head. "One day women will have the freedom to walk the streets at all times unmolested, and wear breeches if they so wish. Even your revolution—in which women have played such a big part—has not rewarded us with that!"

"*My* revolution?" Eugénie wrenched away. "I wanted nothing to do with it! It changed my life forever, and it changed Armand." Tears sprang to her tired eyes and the wind tore them away. "He gave his soul to it, and it will kill him yet."

Guy swore to himself. So de Fortin had stayed behind in Calais, nursing his sword cut. He should have finished him off properly while he had the chance. What was he to do now, with his quarries either side of the Channel?

And yet, was La Boncoeur telling the truth? Goullet had pursued her along the coast from Calais. Goullet would know if de Fortin had been with her then, but he could not ask that question until they met again. He cursed the fact that communication was so difficult. And what a fool he would look, not knowing de Fortin's whereabouts!

In the meantime he must assume that de Fortin was still in France. There was no reason for La Boncoeur to lie. She trusted him.

But perhaps it would be worth checking all the inns in Deal just in case. Failing that, he could return to Goosefield House one more time. But it was all a damnable mess and he was wasting time.

He reached for his brandy glass, downed the contents, and snapped the delicate stem between his fingers.

FIVE

A week passed at Goosefield House, while Eugénie struggled to settle into her new life.

After the narrow streets of Paris where the confined air was always stale beneath the tall, leaning houses, she felt astonished and disoriented by so much air and space. During those February days the sun did not shine again. The wind was always blowing, day and night: turbulent gusts of cold, salty air that made her hair sticky and her skirts fill whenever she took a walk. She avoided Beach Street, where the sea beyond the Downs was dark and rough, and the black outlines of the sheltering warships seemed harbingers of death.

I am a foreigner in my own country, she thought.

Her other uncle, Sir Henry Coveney, MP, made an appearance not long after Lady Coveney. He looked Eugénie over from head to foot in the most approving fashion, pinched her cheek and tried out some inexorable French on her, to which she responded as prettily as she could.

"I believe we shall deal famously together, my dear," he declared, squeezing her arm in parting. In every way he seemed the opposite of his brother—refined, cerebral Thomas—though she thought she caught a sharpness in the baby blue eyes that belied his bluff and genial manner, as he questioned her about the situation in France.

Lady Coveney—Aunt Frederica, as she must learn to call her—took her out on drives to all the local places of interest, nodding her head graciously at yokels in the country lanes as the landau bowled along, and talking to her of Lady so-and-so and Lord this or that, until Eugénie's head ached and her face was stiff from smiling and the cold.

For her part Lady Coveney continued to be greatly taken with Eugénie. However, she did not think so well of the intense young Frenchman who had accompanied her niece to England. No doubt Monsieur de Fortin had protected Eugénie during the dangerous journey from Paris, but he had no class at all and his manner was dour.

During that first week, Eugénie and Hetta edged warily about each other. The duets for which Eugénie had hoped never happened; they would have to sit too close on the stool. But once Eugénie saw her cousin soften, when she told Hetta the sad news about Hortense. Hetta's eyes had filled with tears. It was a moment when they might have drawn together, but they were still too formal with each other. Hetta had turned away speechlessly, keeping her grief to herself.

And Eugénie soon realized that the Revolution as a topic of conversation between them was fraught with potential friction.

"Whatever your feelings about the end of the monarchy, don't you agree that it is quite marvelous that ordinary people rule France now?" Hetta demanded, her eyes shining. "Now they have the chance to rise to high positions in the army, the National Guard and the government. Surely that must be fairer than before, when the aristocrats"—she looked sideways at Eugénie—"had all the privileges?"

"Yes, indeed," said Eugénie cautiously. "But many aristocrats themselves were in favor of reform, you know. They wanted a constitution that would allow equality."

She felt so irritated by Hetta's skeptical expression that she could not resist adding, "We shall see if the lower classes manage things any better!"

"*Lower classes*!" Hetta spat out, as Eugénie knew she would.

Eugénie thought with a shudder of the radical *sans-culottes* who now ruled in the Paris streets, those starving workers in their striped trousers and red caps. They incited mob violence and executed their own summary justice, murdering at will. How could you control people like that? How would the government prevent anarchy? Hetta did not know what it was to run in fear from the mob; she did not understand what horrors revolution could bring in its wake.

Each day Julien came for his French lesson, and each day Eugénie worried that he would encounter Guy somewhere in Deal. She did not know whether Guy had left for France yet and yearned to keep Julien at her side, at Goosefield.

"We see little of each other alone now," she said wistfully one morning when she had seen Julien coming through the garden gate and managed to reach the front door before Mollie.

His dark eyes were soft as he looked at her. "It cannot be otherwise at the moment. At least you are safe, Eugénie."

"I care nothing for my safety!" she burst out. "It makes me feel so very dull! I shall be swallowed by English polite society. I cannot abide 'safe'!" *Especially when you are not.*

He grinned. "Do not, I beg you, get into any scrapes and force me to rescue you!"

"There are no scrapes to get into in Deal! That is not at all what I meant!"

Julien put his hand lightly on her arm. "There are few ways we can change the future from here. In England, I can only do it by persuasion, by talk with the right people."

She looked at him, her eyes wide. "You mean...?"

He nodded. "The queen and dauphin are prisoners in Paris, and a danger to the new Republic while still alive. They must be freed before they are slaughtered, like the king." He looked thoughtful. "I should try to meet the English prime minister, William Pitt. Perhaps some agreement can be reached between our governments: Marie-Antoinette's freedom in return for an end to the war."

"Armand is obsessed with the queen," said Eugénie sadly. "Perhaps she was the real reason he stayed in Paris. Once his plans for the king had failed, he wanted to rescue her in turn."

A shadow crossed Julien's face.

"I am right, am I not?"

He shrugged. "It is true that we had a plan to rescue her from the Temple prison. But there is little Armand can do alone. I don't know how many royalists are left in Paris alive...."

"Do you think that Armand does not intend to join us?" She clutched him in distress. "That he will dream up some ridiculous escape plan and die himself in the attempt?"

He put his arms around her. It was the first time she had had any real physical contact with him since they had arrived in England, and yet she wondered if he was merely soothing her— humoring her. In her anxiety about Armand, she felt nothing, and stood like a pillar, unresponsive, until his arms fell.

Later, she paced the parlor.

An hour had passed, with Julien closeted alone with Hetta. It was true his English was improving, but why did he want these lessons so much? Was it because he needed to be able to talk to important English people about affairs in France—or because he wished to be alone with Hetta, with whom he could talk politics in a much more interesting and intelligent way than with her, Eugénie?

Out of the pretty little bay window she could see a gentleman walking along the street, his cape blowing back in the wind. He cut a tall, elegant figure among the scurrying passersby in their dowdy clothes, and she idly watched him approach for a few seconds before she realized to her horror that it was Guy Deschamps.

The knocker sounded. She hurried into the hall, and hesitated, wondering what to do.

Mollie appeared at the top of the basement stairs. "Say I am out, Mollie," Eugénie whispered, "and that another visitor is with my cousin. Do not on any account say it is Monsieur de Fortin!"

Mollie looked affronted. "Of course not, Miss. I never give names."

Eugénie ran back into the parlor, leaving the door open a crack. There was the murmur of voices, then Mollie came into the room, blushing and flustered, with Guy close behind her.

"I could not persuade him to leave, Miss," she said apologetically, as Guy executed an elaborate and somewhat mocking bow.

"I saw you lurking at the window, Mademoiselle Eugénie."

She curtsied to give herself time to think, but her voice trembled. "Monsieur Deschamps! I'm glad you have been able to dispense with the bandage. I scarcely recognized you! Indeed, I thought you'd left Deal."

"It has been harder than I expected to find passage." He came closer, lowered his voice. "Did I say something to offend you when we last met that you make an excuse not to see me?" He looked amused. "I insist upon knowing!"

"You may leave us, Mollie," said Eugénie. Her heart was beating hard; the library was the other side of the parlor wall, but fortunately there was no sound to be heard from it.

She turned to Guy. "It is only that I have been feeling quite wretched all morning thinking about Armand. I have no spirits for conversation with a visitor."

"Surely I am not any visitor, am I? But I understand your feelings, Eugénie. I am leaving tonight, and wanted to assure you once more that I will do everything in my power to find Armand, if he is still in Paris."

She was filled with compunction. "Oh, Guy, that is so good of you! Of course, I know you understand—you, one of his closest friends!"

He clasped the hand she held out. "Eugénie, why don't you come with me to France? You will be in no danger if you travel with me. We can look for Armand together. You know I have contacts—influential people in the new Republic."

She stared at him, withdrawing her hand. "You mean antimonarchists? Jacobins, like that vile Robespierre?"

"Robespierre did not call for the king's execution," Guy said gently. "He was outvoted in the Assembly. But he has great influence now, and contacts all over the country."

"Republican spies!"

"I thought you wished for a new regime?"

"Not one that guillotines its king! Armand and I wanted to limit the king's powers by a people's constitution, not destroy the monarchy altogether."

Guy came closer still. "It suits you to look angry," he said softly. She was trembling; she was not sure whether it was his closeness, or the fear that Julien might come in. "We have a Republic now, Eugénie, and must move with the times. What's done is done. But together, you and I, Eugénie, can do much in the young Republic." His gaze became intense. "I beg you—return with me!"

"I cannot," she stammered, taken aback. "Why, I have only just arrived in England! My uncle would not permit it, I am sure." She recovered and curtsied quickly. "Farewell, Guy. Do what you can regarding Armand. I shall be eternally grateful."

She rang for Mollie to show him out. At the front door he turned to her as she stood in the open doorway of the parlor.

"Before I go, I would like to pay my respects to your cousin. Is she at home?"

As Eugénie was about to shake her head, Mollie said, "Oh yes, sir. But there is another visitor with her."

"No matter," said Guy cheerfully. "I shall be brief. A greeting and a farewell, that is all. I shall not interrupt the visitor's flow!" He gave Mollie the full benefit of his most disarming smile.

Eugénie put her hands to her face. She was behind Guy as Mollie opened the library door. There was nothing she could do now.

Hetta was sitting at her father's desk, which was covered in books; she looked as if she had been reading for at least an hour. She rose to her feet as Guy came in, and curtsied coolly. Her direct gaze met his.

"Bonjour, Monsieur Deschamps! Comment allez-vous?"

As Guy bowed, Eugénie could see that Hetta was alone in the room.

From the first day Hetta had been intrigued by Julien.

At first she thought the young Frenchman's stiff, formal manner was arrogance; now she knew it was only a shield to hide his shyness. This gradually wore off as he struggled to get his tongue around some of the more difficult English words. Their lessons often erupted in laughter, and his dark eyes would dance as he looked at her after his latest mispronunciation. She wondered sometimes if he was doing it on purpose to tease her.

But he was intelligent and hardworking; indeed, he seemed almost driven to learn. "How long will it be before I can converse easily in English?" he asked that morning.

Unusually, he seemed a little out of sorts, Hetta thought. *Heavens! Why should I care?* And yet she feared she was beginning to care about him; she scarcely dared examine her feelings.

"Not long, monsieur," she said, "especially as you cannot escape speaking English in Deal!"

An odd expression flickered across his face. "That is," she said carefully, "if you mean to stay? I trust the Hoop and Griffin is comfortable?"

"Oh, absolutely, I assure you. No, I have no plans to travel at the moment." He lapsed into a strained silence.

To divert him Hetta told him the history of Deal. She began in English, but when he frowned pathetically she took pity on him and changed to French. Besides, it was flattering to have all his attention on her for once, instead of on Eugénie.

He seemed particularly interested in the smugglers, so she jumped up to show him the secret panel. The astonishment on his face was delightfully entertaining. Then he bent down to investigate something on the top of the steps.

"A coat and breeches!" he exclaimed, holding them up gingerly between finger and thumb and wrinkling his nose. "Ancient and somewhat pungent!"

"Probably left by smugglers years ago," said Hetta airily.

"Quite so," said Julien, dropping her disguise with alacrity. He peered down into the darkness.

"There is a passage all the way to a warehouse yard near Beach Street," Hetta informed him.

He glanced at her. *I have said too much!* she thought. But his face was alight with excitement, like a small boy's. "May I investigate?"

"You mean, go down there?" This was an aspect of Julien that Hetta had not expected: the secret adventurer.

"Why not? I shall pop out and say boo at the other end to my old friend, Jem Cuttle, who no doubt knows of its existence?"

"Oh yes, indeed!" *And has used it as an escape route from the excise men many a time.*

She lit a candle for Julien from the candelabra on the overmantel, and he took it from her, his eyes sparkling. "No more French today!" he said gaily. *"Merci, mademoiselle! Au revoir* until this evening." And with a flick of his coattails he was gone.

Then outside in the hall someone rapped smartly on the front door.

A little later in the library, Hetta had a short but interesting conversation with Monsieur Deschamps. She learned that, like herself, he was in favor of the French Republic, and that they held many views in common. It was so very agreeable and Monsieur Deschamps so very charming, she wondered why it was that, on further acquaintance, she found she did not like him.

Eugénie, after trying to hide her astonishment at Julien's disappearance, remained in the library with them. Hetta could see that something still bound Eugénie to Guy, and this puzzled her, for she had already perceived—how could she not?—that Eugénie and Julien had feelings for each other. Was Eugénie setting her cap at Guy as well?

During the afternoon, while Eugénie was playing listlessly on the Broadwood in the parlor, Hetta quietly donned her boys' clothes, let herself into the secret passage, and went in search of Jem Cuttle to catch up with the gossip of Beach Street.

They squatted on crates in his shed, where he was whipping a rope end between his knees, the thick coils piled on the sandy floor. It was bitterly cold and the stale air reeked of Jem's pipe, but at least they were out of the wind.

Hetta reached for the box of cards, kept on a shelf; it had become their habit to play on these occasions. Jem had taught her all the games he had picked up on his various expeditions, passing on the tricks learned in the gaming houses of the French ports. Hetta, with her competitive spirit and quick brain, had been a willing pupil.

"You're too good for me these days, young lady," said Jem ruefully, passing over the heap of pebbles that were Hetta's winnings after their latest game. "You won't want to play with an old codger like me much longer."

"Oh, stuff, Jem! Who else would I play with?"

Jem sucked on his pipe. "Got me new boat now," he remarked complacently. "Knew it wouldn't take Mr. Pitt long afore some money came my way. I hear tell he wants me for a new expedition." One bright eye closed in his swarthy face. "The boat's a flat-bottomed lugger, with fine, strong oars, better than a sail for slipping about unnoticed beneath enemy hulls."

"Will you be off soon, then?" asked Hetta wistfully. She knew it was no good begging him to take her, too; he would never countenance it.

He pursed his lips. "Got to wait for my orders, haven't I? Besides, I'd rather wait for mist and a flat sea. I'll take some of the boys with me as crew, of course."

"Jem, what do you know about Monsieur de Fortin?" asked Hetta after a pause.

"Nothin' much. Spotted him and the little mamzelle in Calais and followed 'em. You know the rest, no doubt."

Hetta did; she had heard it from Eugénie. "Was Julien— Monsieur de Fortin—already wounded when you first met him?"

"Oh, aye. Nasty sword cut. Said he'd been set on by an assailant in Calais." He looked at her through narrowed eyes. "Why all this interest in him?"

Hetta blushed. "No particular reason."

"He knows all the tricks, I'll say that for him. Gave a false name at the Hoop and Griffin and bought silence with a big wad of notes. Couldn't have done better meself. What's he up to, d'you know?"

Hetta shook her head, wide-eyed.

Jem grunted. "Reckon he's in the same business. Soon find out."

Behind them there was a rap on the wooden half doors, then a man swung the top open and looked through. Jem leaped to his feet, his hand automatically going to the pocket of his dilapidated coat, where, Hetta knew, he kept a knife. Hetta squinted up at the light; she could see nothing against the glare of the white winter sky.

"*Pardon*, monsieur, may I have a word with you?" said a voice she knew.

Jem came back in shortly afterward, grinning broadly.

"That Frenchie—he's been having 'words' with us boatmen all week. He wants a passage across to Calais, vows he's got the right papers, we'll not be harmed. There's some rivalry as to who's to take him. He's paying well. Wants to go tonight, under cover of darkness."

"He's Eugénie's friend, Monsieur Deschamps," said Hetta.

"And yours, too?" The fierce black brows drew together.

She shook her head, inwardly amused. Jem had always tried to protect her, ever since she'd been a child running bare-legged around the boat sheds. Now it seemed he thought it his duty to approve any young man she encountered. "I was obliged to him, but I do not care for him."

"Good. I smell wickedness there."

She left Jem soon afterward, for the February afternoon was drawing in, and made her way in the early dusk toward the warehouse yard and the secret passage back to Goosefield. She was a little way along the alley when she was gripped from behind. She gave a gasp, struggled wildly to free herself, and her hat fell off.

The strong arms did not loosen as her hair tumbled down around her shoulders.

"Ah, I thought so," the voice whispered into her ear, in perfect English, "I thought it was you, Mademoiselle Coveney! Nothing can disguise so delightful a face and figure. Now, tell me—for I am most interested to learn—what you were doing in a boatman's hut in boys' clothes?"

SIX

After a numbingly cold voyage to France, Guy's search for Julien de Fortin in Calais proved fruitless.

Guy had excellent contacts there, but each one denied any sighting of a dark young man with a bandaged arm. He sent messengers to the staging posts between Calais, the major ports, and Paris, while he lodged uncomfortably and with growing frustration in one of the less-known inns in Calais.

He traveled to Paris. The journey was delayed endlessly as snow blanketed the countryside, but eventually with his papers he passed through each checkpoint without a problem. He went straight to Goullet's house in the Faubourg Saint-Germain, only to discover he was away in the Vendée region south of the Loire, where there had been a huge uprising provoked by forced conscription for the wars with England and Europe.

Exasperated by now, he determined to find the answer to de Fortin's whereabouts himself. Then, when Goullet returned, he would be prepared.

He discovered that all Armand's friends who might have known had either gone to ground without a trace or been guillotined as traitors after their failed rescue of the king. Finally, he went to Victoire d'Abreville's mansion in the Marais. It was a last hope. She had been a well-known hostess in Paris society, acquainted with all Armand's circle.

In the thin, falling snow, the Marais was like an untended graveyard, weeds sprouting between the deserted buildings and growing up through the closed wrought-iron gates; the white stone houses, once so majestic and imposing, already had a look of decay and desolation. Some had been attacked and looted by the mob, their fine cornices and porticoes hacked away. Exquisite furniture that had proved too heavy to carry away rotted in the streets.

Guy had not come by carriage, for they were impossible to find nowadays; he walked along the deserted streets, his boots crunching through broken plates and ornaments. Empty picture frames leaned crookedly against the walls; filthy bed linen—bloodstained, as if the occupant of the bed had been slaughtered while sleeping—lay strewn over the *pavé*. He stumbled over bones chewed by feral dogs: whether they were human or animal, he did not know.

Victoire's courtyard, deserted and deathly quiet, was full of windblown rubbish. Dung and broken furniture were piled high against the walls of the mansion.

He went up the steps to the double doors and raised the knocker. The door opened a crack and the old manservant he remembered, now looking older still, his clothes grubby and frayed, peered through it. He was shaking from head to foot.

"Monsieur Deschamps!" Even his voice trembled. "I will tell my lady."

Victoire was hiding beneath a console table in the vast hall; she crawled out when she heard who it was, and clutched Guy around the knees. She was wearing the tricolor costume she had worn for her last supper party months before. It hung loosely from her skeletal frame and stank overpoweringly of sweat, even in the dank chill of the hall. Her wrists and hands were purple and swollen, her face still rouged, but her lips were covered with sores.

"Guy!" she mouthed, her smile a grimace.

Guy helped her up, averting his face from her breath. "For God's sake, light a fire," he said to the manservant. "It is as cold as death in here! I do not want a chill."

"There is no firewood, monsieur."

"Then fetch some!" He fished a handful of *assignats* from his pocket and thrust them at the man, who stuttered his thanks.

He and Victoire sat down at either side of the yawning fireplace. Clouds of dust rose from the chair seats. Victoire appeared unaware; she gazed at Guy hungrily, her eyes huge in her gaunt face.

He came straight to the point. "Is de Fortin here? Julien de Fortin?"

"Julien?" Her gaze drifted from his. "He came to my party. The last party." She nodded her head up and down. "The world is over now, isn't it, monsieur? Poor Armand de Boncoeur in prison, the others all fled. There is no one left, save you and me."

He felt his anger begin to rise. She had gone mad; he would get no information from her. "Julien de Fortin?" he repeated. "Are you sure you don't know where he is?"

Her eyes focused suddenly. "In England," she whispered.

"He had been intending to go to England, that is true," he said carefully, trying to control his impatience. "But he remained in France."

Her eyes widened. "Oh no, that is not what my milliner tells me."

"Your milliner?" he said, frowning.

She patted her filthy bonnet; beneath it her undressed hair, sparse and gray, trailed over her shoulders. "Of course I cannot afford Belle now," she said, with a grotesque simper. "Who can afford new hats these days? But she is kind to an old customer. She brings me a little food sometimes. She has been trying to visit Armand in prison. So sweet, so kind..."

"You are talking of Belle Fleurie?" demanded Guy. Eugénie

63

had lodged with Belle. Belle had known both Armand and Julien. It was possible...

Victoire made her terrible grimace again and nodded eagerly. "Yesterday she read me a letter she had just received from little Mademoiselle de Boncoeur. You remember Eugénie, monsieur? She emigrated, as I should have done."

Guy needed all his restraint not to leap off his chair and rattle her bones. "What did the letter say about de Fortin?" he said through clenched teeth.

Victoire held her swollen hands out to the ashes in the dead grate as if to warm them. "Eugénie wrote that they are both well—she and Julien—and safely arrived in Deal."

"*Deal!* Are you sure she said Deal?"

"Yes, it is a port on the English coast." She smiled dreamily. "Perhaps I shall join them. I must ask Tomas to pack my clothes when he returns."

"What else was in the letter?"

She shook her head. The vagueness was back. He would get nothing more from her.

He rose to his feet abruptly and went to the door. But she was behind him, clutching his clothes in her frail but surprisingly strong grip. She began to wail, a thin, desperate sound that pierced through his head.

"Do not leave me, monsieur, I beg you! They will come for me! I'm so afraid!"

"Get away from me!" He wrenched her hands from his greatcoat and she fell to the floor, where she crouched at his feet, weeping and nursing her bruised fingers.

Fury and revulsion overcame him as the sobs echoed around the empty spaces of the great hall. He put a hand to his pocket and pulled out a dagger. In a sudden, vicious movement he bent and stabbed it deep into the shaking back.

The meager shanks splayed out as she collapsed; there was a drowning gasp, then silence.

"One less for Madame Guillotine," said Guy, and he kicked the body out of his way.

When her servant returned with firewood a little while later, Victoire's blood had spread like a thin carpet over the marble floor.

Raoul Goullet returned from the Vendée a few days later, and Guy Deschamps had a late supper with him in his magnificent dining room: various pâtés, followed by pork, chicken, duck, each with a rich, velvety sauce; an array of ripely melting cheeses; superb wines with every course. Goullet, or Le Fantôme, as he was known to his network of spies, always dined well.

They had said little to each other as they ate from a dinner service heavily decorated with gold and drank from crystal glasses, for Le Fantôme did not like the discussion of business to sully the appreciation of excellent wine and food.

He was a perfectionist in all things.

If the mob were on the march tonight, it would not be heard up here behind the tightly sealed windows. The roaring fire was the only sound. The soft candlelight bloomed on priceless oil paintings, rich wall hangings, the glowing mahogany furniture set beneath them, corner cabinets filled with ornaments. His collection of Sèvres porcelain was Le Fantôme's particular pleasure; he took none in human relationships.

It was ironic that on the dessert table beside them, a superb example of *biscuit de porcelaine*—his treasured figure of Aphrodite, goddess of love—rose above the fruit and sweet wafers, her naked limbs milky against the glowing colors beneath her, for Le Fantôme had a heart that held no love at all.

As he ate, Le Fantôme watched the younger man carefully and

noted the suppressed fury in his eyes, the clenched hands holding the silver cutlery.

He had seen Guy Deschamps's potential from the day he joined the Brotherhood of the Watching Eye—outwardly a Free-masons' society, but secretly a web of spies spun across France, with Goullet himself the spider at its center. Goullet had appreciated Deschamps's sharp brain; he had recognized his ruthlessness and ambition, for they were attributes that he himself possessed. As a rising young lawyer, Deschamps had contact with some of the most influential people in Paris. So from being Le Fantôme's protégé, Deschamps had become his closest colleague, his "Petit Scalpel," his most successful spy. He was his eyes and ears in places where Le Fantôme himself might be too well known; when necessary, he was a most useful and unscrupulous killing machine.

Le Fantôme wiped his mouth delicately on a linen napkin and leaned back in his chair. Putting his gloved hands together, he regarded Le Scalpel over the top of them; the thin black leather caught the candlelight and gleamed eerily. Le Scalpel thought it was possible to glimpse the naked, damaged hands beneath the skin of the gloves and shuddered inwardly: Once, he had had to touch them.

"You bring me no news," said Le Fantôme flatly, "neither of my fiancée nor of de Fortin. I am disappointed in you, Scalpel."

Le Scalpel did not intend to admit to his wild goose chase after de Fortin. But somehow and disconcertingly, Le Fantôme already knew that he had nothing to report. It was not the first time that Le Fantôme had uncannily read his mind. Working together, they had become closer and closer, in thought as well as deed. But when Le Fantôme raised his heavy lids and the strange, light blue eyes glared at him, he let his own gaze drop in discomfort.

"Let us take them one at a time, Scalpel. My fiancée first."

"I tried to persuade Mademoiselle de Boncoeur to return here with me to find Armand. I almost succeeded. Next time I will be successful."

"And if you are not?" Le Fantôme picked up his discarded napkin and began to play with it idly. "You cannot kidnap her. It must be seen to be legal, otherwise I shall never be able to retain my place in the National Convention, nor remain in Robespierre's favor. And soon he will be the most powerful man in France...." He spread his gloved fingers, still regarding Le Scalpel with cold, half-hidden eyes. "She must return with you of her own free will to keep the marriage contract."

"Give me more time, monsieur." Though outside it was freezing, it was suffocatingly hot in the room; surreptitiously, Le Scalpel wiped the sweat from his upper lip.

"Time! Soon she will turn sixteen. She will be legally mine! Yet I do not see any prospect of having her in my possession." Le Fantôme crumpled the square of fine linen into a ball and flung it on the polished floorboards. "If she should go to London, we shall lose trace of her!"

"The society in London is small," said Le Scalpel quickly. For the sake of his future, he needed to succeed in the tasks Le Fantôme set him. The man was his ladder to power. And as for La Boncoeur, she had outwitted him once too often; after his previous trip to Calais he had had a sore head for some while. Now she had tricked him over Julien de Fortin's whereabouts. He had wasted a great deal of time.

Revenge would be sweet.

He leaned forward over the table. "I will bring her back to you wherever she goes—I vow it to you, monsieur! She suspects nothing. I am still her trusted friend."

That trust would not last long after he had dealt with her as he intended. There were many ways to persuade.

"She suspected nothing after the fight in Calais?"

"The mask was down over my face, and when I came around, I would swear it had not been disturbed. She cannot know."

"And her new English family—what of them?"

Le Scalpel shrugged. "The uncle is seldom there during the day. He works at the hospital. I have not met him. He is of no consequence."

"And the cousin?"

Le Scalpel hesitated. Le Fantôme raised pale eyebrows that seemed to melt away into the unlined forehead beneath the old-fashioned powdered wig. He was oddly ageless, though Le Scalpel knew him to be in his late middle years.

"She is interesting," said Le Scalpel cautiously. "She could be dangerous. She disguises herself as a boy, associates with the smugglers and riffraff along the shore. If she were French, she would be a radical revolutionary and would have marched to Versailles with the fishwives."

"She suspects nothing either?"

He shook his head. He thought of the direct gray eyes, the tumbling hair. Even when he had exposed her boy's disguise, she had looked neither abashed nor frightened, but had given him a cool, dismissive little bow and walked on. He had wanted to drag her head back by those dark, curling locks and press his mouth on hers until she submitted to him.

She would do so in the end—as all women did.

But yet...she disturbed him with her honesty, her naive passion. Why should an English girl be so interested in the Revolution in France? She seemed to feel that it would bring about greater freedom for women on both sides of the Channel. God help the man who loved her!

He became aware that Le Fantôme was watching him with a cold smile. "If you wish to bed her, wait a little while, *mon petit*

Scalpel. You have more pressing business." His eyes grew colder still.

Reptile's eyes, thought Le Scalpel. *No lustful feelings have ever stirred those loins.*

Except for Le Fantôme's obsession with Eugénie. But was that lust? What did he want of her? To shut her away and gloat over her perfection, like one of his pieces of Sèvres porcelain? What was his motive exactly?

"So you vow you will bring Mademoiselle de Boncoeur to me?"

"It will give me as much pleasure as you, monsieur." Le Scalpel traced the gold rim of his plate and smiled to himself. "I have only to tell her that her brother is in prison here in Paris and she will return with me at once, I am certain of it. She does not know of his imprisonment yet. And then she will be yours."

"How can you make certain of that?"

"I shall think of a way. Leave it to me." He added casually, so as to make it look like an afterthought, "I take it that you've no more information from Armand de Boncoeur regarding Julien de Fortin?"

"De Boncoeur has closed like a clam. The informers at La Force say they have learned nothing, but that he weeps and cries out for a lawyer. I do not believe there is anything more to be prized from him."

"So what will you do with him?"

"Let him suffer and dream of La Guillotine. In due course he will be sent to La Conciergerie and brought before the new Revolutionary Tribunal on a charge of treason against the Republic." Le Fantôme smiled. "Then I'm afraid his worst dreams will come true."

He pulled at one of his gloves as if to take it off and expose the distorted hand beneath; the soft, slipping sound of the leather was sinister. "So that brings us back to de Fortin. You have not tracked him down?"

Le Scalpel shook his head ruefully. "He is still at large in Deal."

"After all this time? *Deal!*" A fist thumped down on the table, glasses sprang and rang on the cloth. "A tiny port!"

"Full of secret passages and smugglers' hideaways."

Le Fantôme leaned over the table. "If he remains in England much longer, he will go to London and stir up English political support for Marie Antoinette. I am certain he was behind de Boncoeur's plan to rescue her from the Temple. He must be assassinated. He is too dangerous left alive." He gave Le Scalpel a measuring look. "If you rid the Republic of him, Robespierre will be well pleased with you—and me. But since the uprising, your return passage to England will not be so easy to arrange this time."

Le Scalpel looked at him in some surprise. "You refer to the Chouans? A few antigovernment guerrillas in the west should not affect my journey, surely?"

"The Chouans are attracting other rebels to their cause. The people there don't like the new Republic and its wars coming on top of the changes in the Catholic Church and the new land taxes. Robespierre is anxious to keep his spies—particularly the Brotherhood of the Watching Eye—in the provinces. He fears France will move toward civil war." Le Fantôme shrugged. "I must try a different tactic to ensure you return to England."

The pale eyes turned icy. "But I warn you, Scalpel, this time you must not fail."

SEVEN

Madame Isobelle Fleurie was on her way to the prison of La Force, where Eugénie's brother, Armand, was an inmate.

Belle, who had, in happier, wealthier times, been milliner and *modiste* to the ladies of the Paris *haut monde* and, during the early days of the Revolution, Eugénie and Armand's landlady, picked her way, slipping and sliding over the uneven paving stones, down the sordid little alleyway that was her usual route from the rue Saint-Antoine to the rue Pavée, where the men's prison La Grande-Force stood.

No matter how carefully she trod, her hem was always soaked from the filthy puddles and the sewage and waste leaking out from the murky little hovels on either side. Yet Belle carried herself proudly, her emerald green costume bravely defiant in a world that was as dark as the lowering sky overhead. Her face bore the marks of hunger, anguish, and lost love, but it was meticulously powdered and rouged in the old style, and her eyes, however sad, were always beautiful.

Whenever she could, ever since she had first heard the terrible news of Armand's imprisonment from one of his friends, now in hiding, she had loyally struggled here. She had never been allowed to visit him. Few visitors were permitted at La Force: lawyers, perhaps, out to make money from their hapless clients, but never friends.

But still Belle came to charm a guard into checking Armand's name in the records office. While Armand was imprisoned here, he might still have a chance to escape the guillotine. If he were taken to the dreaded La Conciergerie, it would all be over: Prisoners were only transferred there to be tried before the Revolutionary Tribunal.

Belle had written to Eugénie to tell her of Armand's capture and imprisonment. She had agonized over the letter, wondering if it was right to worry Eugénie when she was safely out of the country, but then she thought: *He is her brother. She should know, and who else is to tell her?*

She had known it was most unlikely that her letter would get through; some mail crossed the Channel, but there were delays because of the war with England. Nothing was certain. And in due course, as she feared, the letter was returned to her by the authorities.

Belle made for the entrance gates beneath the forbidding stone facade. No matter how often she came, its grim appearance still struck fear into her heart. Once one of the palaces of the Marais, it had been a debtors' prison for the last ten years. Now it was split into two: La Grande-Force for men; La Petite-Force for women. The inmates were all suspected traitors to the Republic.

There was already a group of people huddled there, waiting desperately for news; she knew their anxious faces by sight now. Today would be the same as all the others; none of them would be allowed in.

But unexpectedly and shockingly, a guard approached the gates and addressed her. "Madame Fleurie?"

Flustered, frightened, she pulled herself together. She had given shelter to two aristocrats—Armand and Eugénie de Boncoeur.

"*Oui, citoyen*," she said, her voice shaking. "*C'est moi.*"

"I have a visitor's pass for you, *citoyenne*."

In a daze of astonishment and fear, she was taken brusquely across stone flags and through two further gates. She looked up in horror at the tiny windows high above her. *I would lose my soul here.*

There were dark stains around the base of the walls. She knew with a shudder of certainty that they had been made during the September Massacres the previous autumn, when thousands of prisoners had been dragged into the courtyards and slaughtered.

She was waved past the records office, down an endless passage.

At last, at yet another closed door, the guard stopped. From within came the mutter of many voices. She heard weeping and her heart chilled: There was something terrible about the sound of a man crying.

"Twenty minutes," the guard said roughly, as he unlocked the door. "I will signal to you when the time is up."

He banged the door shut behind them, locked it again, and squatted before it on the stone flags, resting his musket on his knees. He made no effort to help Belle find Armand, but glowered suspiciously at the prisoners, while he chewed tobacco and occasionally spat out a stream of dark saliva. Belle hesitated by the door and gazed helplessly around.

The large stone room was filled with men.

Some lay curled on straw pallets, their eyes open and staring, or weeping, as if they had already given in to their fates; others stood smoking and talking to companions in a nervous, desultory way; some sat playing Vingt-et-un and backgammon, or paced about like caged animals. Many prisoners wore fine clothes, silk and lace, the mark of a once-prosperous aristocrat, and their linen shirts looked clean; but there were also beggars in rags.

The room, lit only by a couple of small barred windows high in the stone walls, was dark and bitterly cold. There was, of course, no fire in the vast fireplace. The room had never dried out after the guards flooded it during the September Massacres to drive out the prisoners, who had barricaded themselves inside in a desperate attempt to escape slaughter. It stank of damp, despair, and death.

As Belle stared around looking for Armand, she noticed how polite and considerate the prisoners were to one another, bowing to acquaintances, speaking in low voices. A gentleman came up to her and in the most courteous manner inquired about her business.

Armand was pointed out to her. He was sitting on a chair in a far corner, his head bowed over his hands. Her shocked glance took in his bandaged wrists and hands. The bandages must be old: They were gray with the endless prison days.

He raised his head as she came closer and she saw how the bloom had gone from his cheeks. He was clean shaven and his linen shirt had been laundered recently, but his face was thinner under the too-long fair hair, and the blue eyes, once so eager and full of fire, were haunted now.

But they blazed again when they saw her. He raised himself— with difficulty, she noticed—and came stiffly toward her, his wounded hands outstretched.

"Belle!" He took her hand clumsily in his bandaged ones and kissed it, and stepped back. "You look wonderful as always." His voice was hoarse, out of practice. "I never thought to see you again!"

"Monsieur." She dipped a curtsy out of long habit and struggled to keep her voice steady. "Nor I you."

A man at the nearest table offered her his chair and she took it, whispering her thanks, and brought it close to Armand's.

"Oh, Armand," she said in a low, fervent voice, "my dear Armand, *mon petit marquis!*"

He gazed at her anxiously, as if to drink in her face. "How are you, Belle? How are you surviving in the world outside?"

She pulled herself together. "It is not easy. There have been food riots in Paris, as you probably know, monsieur. The value of the *assignat* has fallen by half. It is hard for people to afford food. These foolish wars are costing too dear if it means that France cannot feed her own people!"

"But you? Do you make enough money to eat? How is your millinery business?"

"The days of glorious hats are over, monsieur, but I would not have the heart to make one now. There is no demand for them in any case. It is all drabness and gloom and counting the cost. I have even stopped producing silk cockades. I make them from wool now. *Wool!* At least the government disapproves of women wearing the *bonnet rouge*, for I'd have to force myself to make those dreadful things!"

She sighed and lifted her chin. "But you know your Belle Fleurie. I adapt to these terrible times. I supply the *bourgeoisie* now, I, who once was *modiste* to the nobility." She tried to smile. "My clients are Republican ladies and anxious to appear so. They must not seem extravagant, you understand."

"I wish you had gone to Coblence while you could." Armand hesitated. "And Fabrice le Brun? Have you heard anything of him?"

A shadow crossed her face at the mention of her former lover, making her look old and worn. "Fabrice? I have heard nothing. He is either dead, as he deserves—that foolish, flying daredevil—or in some other woman's warm bed!"

"Never that. No other woman could compare with you, Belle!"

She touched her hair, overcome. "How do you fare—in here—Marquis?" she whispered, casting a glance over her shoulder.

"Well enough. The company, as you see, is excellent. Indeed, I find I know many of the prisoners. We have here the cream of Paris society, Belle, though you might not believe it!" Armand laughed shakily. "This is what we are come to! And tomorrow, who knows? I am trying to live each day for itself, and not dwell on the future, though it is damnably hard. I know what my future is, of course."

He gave a rueful smile, and made a chopping movement with his hand. "No, do not look so appalled, Belle. I must be realistic. I am a traitor to the Republic and an aristocrat. Soon, no doubt, I will be transferred to La Conciergerie and face trial. They have put together a trumped-up Revolutionary Tribunal especially to try suspects like me. There is only one judgment and sentence it can make when I come before it. A visit to Madame Guillotine!"

He sighed and looked around the room, his smile fading. "Unlike the guards, we behave in a civilized way to remain sane. We know we are all facing death."

"There are some who are not so civilized, you are right!" Belle whispered fiercely. "Why are your fingers bandaged, monsieur, tell me that?"

"It is nothing, I do assure you. I have healed well—at least on the outside. Take the bandages off for me, Belle. I can't do it myself."

It was an order, not a request, and she had done the aristocracy's bidding all her life. Very gently, she unwound the bandages, and saw the shining purple of recently healed skin. He flexed his hands gingerly. "You see, Belle? As good as new!"

Her voice trembled, as the dirty coils fell to the flagstones. *"Ces bêtes!* What did they do to you, monsieur?"

Armand hesitated, while she stared at him in outrage.

"They tortured me," he said in a low voice at last—his mouth twisting—"with a burning brand. The pain, Belle—unimaginable. There were men all around me in the darkness, drinking in my screams, and on the wall an eye looking at me."

"What do you mean, monsieur?"

He shrugged. "A huge eye, watching me. I didn't know where I was. Perhaps I was delirious. I'd fought when they took me and they had to knock me on the head to drag me away. When I came to, I saw him in the shadows."

"Who?"

"The man who discovered me." His lips curled in self-disgust. "I was hiding like a dog in the cellar of the house in the rue des Trois Chats. It was freezing, dark, foul smelling. I knew I couldn't stay there long. I thought—just until the commotion over the king's failed rescue dies down. But suddenly there was light above me—soldiers of the National Guard. I saw one man clearly, not in uniform. It was Raoul Goullet!"

"I know the name, Goullet," she said slowly. "We call him Le Fantôme in the streets. He walks them like a ghost. Children run from him, afraid."

Armand nodded. "He is one of the richest, most powerful men in Paris. He has the ear of Robespierre. Some say he encourages the mob in its violence. He is a master spy and assassin for the government. He reports directly to the Revolutionary Tribunal. Those pale eyes"—he shuddered—"see guilt in every man's face, and he saw it in mine as I crouched below him in that cellar."

"What guilt? You are innocent, *mon petit*! You worked for a people's constitution! Let me tell them that, *les imbéciles*!"

He smiled at that, a genuine, amused smile. "And you would, Belle, I know it! But it would do no good." He leaned closer.

"There was another man standing behind Goullet when they found me. He was holding a lantern before him as if to hide his face, but I knew him." There was a tremor in his voice. "I believe it was none other than Guy Deschamps! I'd always considered him a loyal friend."

Belle remembered the charming young man who had brought several of his mistresses to her for new hats, and always paid his bills on time. He was older than Armand, already a successful barrister, and had been something of a mentor to the young law student. "Are you quite sure, monsieur?"

"I don't know!" He looked at her wildly. "I'm not sure now whom I can truly trust. All I know is that with me out of the way

Goullet will lay his hands on my estate, and pursue my sister until he finds her!"

"Eugénie?" said Belle in horror.

"He has always desired Eugénie for himself."

"But she is safe in England now."

He shook his head in despair. "I've no idea whether she and Julien ever reached the coast."

"I've had a letter from her in England," she said quietly.

Armand gasped, and color flooded his cheeks. She fumbled in her pocket for the crumpled paper. "Read it, monsieur, and reassure yourself."

He scanned it urgently, screwing up his eyes in the poor light. He tried to smile. "Her writing was always appalling." A tear trickled down his face and he rubbed at it impatiently. "Thank God! She has reached our uncle in Deal, and Julien is with her." He looked at the date. "She says she arrived the day before writing this. But that's over two months ago now!"

"I have been trying to see you ever since I received it, monsieur, but they would not let me in until today. I tried to write to her to tell her you were here in La Force, but the letter was returned. Nothing is getting through to England."

He looked at her for a moment and leaned closer. "Would you write to her again for me, Belle?"

"But, monsieur, there is no point..."

"Listen carefully." He lowered his voice further. "I have a friend at the Sorbonne. He has been corresponding with an English professor at Oxford University over mesmerism. Academic papers are allowed to cross the Channel."

Belle drew in her breath. "*Je comprends.*"

"I will give you his name and department, and you must deliver the letter into his hands and no one else's. He will understand immediately what he is to do."

He said a few words to her under his breath. "Can you remember that, Belle?"

She nodded.

"Write today," he said urgently. "Tell her to remain in England with Julien. On no account must they try to return to France. Émigrés are to be executed without appeal if they set foot in our country. I can never see them again—neither my sister, nor my greatest friend!" The purple fingers brushed his eyes. "And, Belle, trust no one, remember that. If you are questioned today about what we have said to each other, say nothing. You must not visit me again here. No, do not protest. It is too dangerous."

He looked around at the prison walls. "Will the world ever return to sanity?" His face was white against the dark stone. "We gave France a new constitution, but have lost everything else. How can anything good survive?"

She had to shake her head, then, and felt her own eyes fill with tears.

The guard showed her out in the same truculent, condescending manner with which he had taken her into the prison. She did not relax until the gates had shut behind her and she was scurrying away down the rue Pavée.

There were people about, hurrying like Belle herself, heads bent. No one met anyone's eyes these days unless they had to: It was safest that way. Only the Guards in their red caps, the *bonnets rouges*, stationed on street corners, watched with suspicious eyes anyone who passed.

When she heard her name spoken softly behind her, Belle thought her heart would stop.

"Citoyenne Fleurie? Isobelle Fleurie?"

Her mouth dried with panic. They had come after her. She would be taken to La Petite-Force. It was all over.

She turned and looked up at the man wildly. "Monsieur Deschamps!"

He was smiling at her. "You remember me, *citoyenne?* I saw you come through the gates of La Force. I take it you have been visiting our mutual friend, Armand de Boncoeur?"

She nodded dumbly: It was useless to deny it.

They had stopped in the middle of the street. It had started to spit with rain. He put his hand on her arm courteously and guided her to a doorway where the porch gave them shelter; she was too afraid to resist.

"You were fortunate, madame. Few manage to visit those in La Force. Tell me, how is Armand?"

A surge of anger rose in her but she forced it down and made herself answer calmly. "As well as can be expected, *citoyen.*"

"I hope to be allowed to see him myself." He shook his head. "Such a terrible thing! I have been in England. I returned when I heard the news—I'll see what I can do for him."

She stared at him, noticing the shining raindrops on his unpowdered auburn hair. Such a handsome young man she had once thought him—why, she had even been foolish enough to flirt with him on occasion. She blushed with shame to think of it now. *If I had the strength and courage I would gladly kill him for betraying Armand!*

He was staring down into her eyes with his slanting greenish hazel ones. "If, by any chance, Armand wanted you to write a letter for him, *citoyenne,*" he said softly, "let me take it for you. I am due to return to England shortly." He flicked the rain from his hair with a careless hand. "It would be natural for a brother to wish to write to his sister."

Belle shook her head. "I have written no letter for him, monsieur, and he cannot write himself. He was wounded. His hands are only recently healed." She wanted to sound accusing, but dared not. A gulp rose in her throat.

"But perhaps he asked you to write a letter for him when you returned home?" There was little room beneath the porch and he seemed to press closer still, so that she thought she could feel the heat from his body. It was so long since she had been close to a man—too long—and she was disturbed to feel a sudden treacherous attraction.

"It would be much safer to entrust it to me than to the mail coach," he said, looking down at her and smiling, as if he could read her mind. "Letters are taking an age to reach England—that is, if they get through at all."

His voice was so persuasive, his smile so beguiling. Could Armand have been mistaken? Armand, his eyes half closed, fainting with pain?

Guy Deschamps was watching her carefully, his eyes glints of green light in the dark doorway. "As I am sure you understand, madame, any other way of sending a letter is decidedly—risky."

At the trace of threat, Belle broke away, as if from a trance. "*Merci*, monsieur, but there is no letter. He could scarce speak... He is much altered." She bowed her head. "*Bon voyage, citoyen*," she managed, though the words choked her.

Guy looked after Belle as she hastened away in the rain, almost tripping over her skirts in her rush.

He could go after her. But then it was hardly worth the bother. As soon as he saw Eugénie again himself, her reaction would tell him how much she knew. Besides, it was most unlikely that any letter from Belle would ever reach her.

EIGHT

Danton, deputy to the National Convention and now the recognized leader of the new Committee for Public Safety, was sitting at a large oval table in the mirrored chamber that the Committee used for meetings. Beyond it lay a maze of smaller chambers leading off the queen's staircase in the Tuileries Palace. Once the royal family had lived here, forced by the mob to Paris from their great golden palace in Versailles. Now the little dark rooms were crowded with government officials going about the business of revolution, while outside the walls of the palace, lines of soldiers of the National Guard paced up and down in the wan April sun.

Raoul Goullet, Le Fantôme, sat facing Danton. The room was filled with thin, green spring light from the gardens. It moved across the green wallpaper, intensifying it, and for a moment, as it touched Danton's face, he looked like some great amphibious beast rising from a deep woodland pool, massive and bloated with water, the pockmarks on his face standing out like the scars of an underwater attack.

They could not have been more different. Raoul Goullet's clothes were impeccably cut, a silk tricolor rosette in his buttonhole the only relief in his elegant black suiting. His eyes were cold and clear beneath the old-fashioned powdered wig, his thin lips pursed. Danton, younger by some twenty years, was unshaven, the starched linen undone around his bull neck, his eyes bloodshot, his full, sensual lips drooping.

It was ironic, especially in the light of the conversation they were about to have, that the only things that united them were the rumors of corrupt financial speculation that circled about them both.

"A safe conduct pass, Goullet?" Danton said. "Robespierre won't approve. He believes there are more enemies within France than without. Your Brotherhood are his eyes and ears in the provinces."

"But he is aware that false *assignats* are being smuggled in to inflate the economy and damage the Republic." Goullet leaned across the table, avoiding the ray of sunlight from the window; he disliked light on his face and gloved hands. "We know the forged notes are coming from Britain, smuggled across in flat-bottomed boats from the Cinque Ports—in particular, the port of Deal."

It was a delicate subject. Goullet suspected that Danton himself might be taking personal advantage of the amount of *assignats* in circulation.

"If Le Scalpel has safe passage to Deal he can track down the ringleaders."

Danton's lip curled. "Le Scalpel? These ridiculous names, *citoyen*. Of course you are well known to Paris society as Le Fantôme, but must you hide the identity of one of your underlings?"

"The Brotherhood of the Watching Eye is a secret society," said Goullet coldly. "None of the Brothers' names is generally known. Le Scalpel is my most successful spy. It is particularly important that his identity remains hidden."

"He reports to you?"

Goullet nodded. "And as you know, I report to the Convention."

Danton pursed his lips. "To our mutual friend Robespierre!"

"To Robespierre and to you, *citoyen*. It was Le Scalpel who discovered de Boncoeur's part in the plot to rescue the king."

"So?" Danton raised his eyebrows. "You want your most successful spy to leave France, where surely he is most useful?"

"I believe Julien de Fortin may well be one of the counterrevolutionaries behind the passage of false notes to Paris. De Fortin was among other conspirators in the failed rescue of Louis Capet. No doubt he is already raising support for the queen from the English government."

Danton frowned and hesitated. "He'll report back to the government, this Le Scalpel of yours?"

Goullet nodded. "Through me, as always."

"We can do nothing official about a counterrevolutionary while he is on enemy soil. De Fortin will be out of our reach."

"But you don't want him to continue scheming freely with the enemy against us?"

"What I want, Goullet, is a full report from your spy on the situation." Danton sounded belligerent. He narrowed his eyes, already almost lost in the thick folds of flesh.

Why was it, Le Fantôme wondered, that Danton was so attractive to women? That powerful animal presence? He thought of Eugénie: golden hair and white skin, pure as porcelain. He would shut her away forever, away from the temptations of men like Danton. She would be his alone to gloat over.

"And if Le Scalpel should discover that de Fortin is involved in the smuggling of *assignats* . . . ?" he said.

"He must bring de Fortin back with him to face the Tribunal's justice."

"That may not be possible. He has no powers of arrest."

Danton leaned back and half closed his eyes. "Then he must deal with him in England. Just don't tell Robespierre. He abhors murder."

That is why I came to you, Citoyen Danton, thought the Pale Assassin.

NINE

In Deal, the old apple tree below Eugénie's window had put out curled green foliage and fragile white blossoms that sprinkled their petals every time the wind blew from the sea. But there was a new mildness on the April wind, and Eugénie would open her window to feel it on her face and imagine that this same wind was bringing Armand to them.

But he did not come, and neither did any word from him. Guy was still away, and Jem Cuttle, busy with his own secrets, had no news of Armand when he returned from a trip to the French coast.

To distract herself from worrying, Eugénie threw herself into the social life of Deal. But after the theater, the salons, and balls she had once attended in Paris, it all seemed very parochial and the young men decidedly gauche, even the naval officers at Dover Castle. It was Julien whom she wanted to admire her—Julien whom she wanted to be with. She would remember their escape across France and long for those days and nights again, fraught with danger as they had been. In all that time together he had never laid a finger on her, never attempted to kiss her. Now she wondered if perhaps he did not wish to do so.

His mind is elsewhere, she thought, and a pang went through her.

On Hetta! It is most improper that they are shut up for hours together in the library!

She did not think anyone would know it was her birthday when it came. Who would care? Not Julien.

But Julien came early that morning and surprised her, as she was coming down the stairs after breakfast in her bedchamber. She did not care for the heaviness of the English breakfast and usually left her uncle and cousin to have theirs together downstairs, while Mollie brought her coffee and toast on a tray. *It is hard to break old habits*, she thought guiltily, *but in other ways I am trying so very hard to stop behaving like a French aristocrat!*

Her heart gave a sudden painful leap as Mollie opened the front door and she saw who it was. "Why, Julien," she faltered. "You are early this morning, monsieur!"

He came toward her as Mollie melted discreetly away. "That is because it is a very special morning, *n'est ce pas, ma belle?*"

She looked up at him and he looked down at her tenderly, his eyes so soft and dark that she would willingly drown in them.

He still loved her, then—or did he?

"*Bonne anniversaire, ma chérie,*" he whispered. "Happy birthday, my darling."

He did love her, he did!

"Oh, Julien, I am so very happy that you have remembered!" She added hesitantly, "That is, if it is not too frivolous to think of birthdays at such a time? I read in *The Times* that our war is not going well. We are fighting almost all Europe!"

"Birthdays are much more important than wars," he reassured her, "especially yours, Eugénie!" He brought a thin oblong package wrapped in tissue from behind his back and presented it to her somewhat sheepishly. "I had to ask for it *en anglais*!" he said with his dear crooked smile. "Imagine the humiliation, for I hadn't the correct word and was forced to mime!"

Inside the tissue was a gauzy silver fan, as delicate as a moonbeam when she unfurled it, with a mother-of-pearl handle.

"I saw it in a window and it spoke to me," Julien said solemnly. "It said, 'You must buy me for Eugénie.' And so I did."

Forgetting the war, Eugénie giggled, and reached up so that it shimmered like a butterfly's wing as it caught the gleam from the fanlight over the front door. Then she turned and looked at him over the curve of the fan, her eyes crinkling in delight. He took her free hand; his arm had long healed. The tissue paper rustled to the floor. "Does it please you?"

She longed to kiss him there and then, but knew propriety dictated she should not. "It is beautiful, Julien." She pressed his fingers. "What pleasure to own a fan that's not painted with scenes from the storming of the Bastille!"

"So long as it does not hide too much of your face from me, Eugénie," he said softly.

Eugénie lowered the fan. His face was very close to hers. They looked at each other for a long moment.

Then the door of the dining room opened and Hetta came out. An odd expression flickered across her face as she saw them. Julien released his pressure on Eugénie's hand at once, but Eugénie kept her fingers on his a few seconds longer than she needed before she let go, to make sure that Hetta had seen.

"It is Eugénie's sixteenth birthday today, Mademoiselle Hetta," said Julien a trifle awkwardly, as if to explain.

"I know, monsieur," said Hetta stiffly, "and indeed I have a present for you, Eugénie."

She presented Eugénie with a slim volume. Julien looked at it inquiringly.

"*A Vindication of the Rights of Woman*," Hetta said.

He looked amused. "A most interesting choice, *n'est ce pas*, Eugénie?"

Eugénie was touched. It was Hetta's own copy she knew, from the small ink stain in the corner that Hetta must have tried to remove with milk, for it was now smudged.

"The author, Mary Wollstonecraft, lived in Paris for a while," said Hetta eagerly. "She is something of a heroine to me. Did you know her, monsieur?"

Julien shook his head solemnly. "Paris is a city of more than six hundred thousand souls, mademoiselle. Larger than London, I believe."

"Happy birthday, my dear," said Thomas, appearing behind Hetta. He pulled a long velvet box from his coat pocket. Inside was a string of gleaming freshwater pearls.

"Thank you, Uncle," breathed Eugénie. "Nothing sets off the complexion so well as pearls, you know."

"Indeed?" said Thomas.

Later, before dinner, they drank champagne, which Thomas told them Jem had brought him in return for a good deed. Eugénie and Julien, accustomed now to how things were done in Deal, were too tactful to inquire further.

Eugénie held her glass to the candlelight and watched the glittering bubbles stream upward. She shivered suddenly. "If I were in Paris now, I would have to marry that odious Raoul Goullet! Why, I had almost forgotten about the contract until today. Thank God I am saved such a fate!"

Thomas patted her arm affectionately. He had been appalled when told about the marriage contract. "Don't spoil your birthday with such a thought, my dear. You are safe with us. He cannot touch you here in England."

It was an altogether pleasant evening. Indeed, it would have been quite perfect if only Armand had been there.

But her happiness did not last.

TEN

Two weeks later, Eugénie was parading with Hetta down Beach Street in the sunshine, aware of the admiring glances thrown at the two of them from the young naval officers strolling along the front on shore leave. There were a few ships in the harbor revictualling, but most of the fleet had sailed: Deal looked out over a vast expanse of glittering water.

Hetta's mind was not on the young officers. "I don't understand why there is civil war in southern France," she said to Eugénie. "Surely now the people have their Revolution and their Republic they should be content?"

"They do not like the ways of the revolutionary government in Paris. The Jacobins are becoming as tyrannical as the Ancien Régime."

"Surely not! Nothing could be as bad as when the aristocrats held sway!"

Eugénie turned away, not wishing to argue. "If the civil war spreads, Armand will never reach us."

"You believe he will still come? But what can have prevented him coming already?"

Something in Hetta's tone made Eugénie defensive. "It is not easy for an aristocrat to travel through France."

"You managed to do so."

Eugénie frowned. "You know nothing! Even if Armand has managed to escape Paris, the countryside is full of danger. National Guards demand to see your papers at every stop. He will have to travel under a false name, as I did."

Hetta stared at her for a moment, and they both walked on in silence.

Julien's English progressed so fast he went to see Mr. Pitt, when the prime minister visited Ramsgate. When he came back he seemed restless and out of sorts, and refused to discuss the meeting.

His lessons with Hetta continued. Sometimes Eugénie would catch Hetta watching her with an odd expression in her dark gray eyes. And how beautiful her cousin looked these days! Eugénie had not noticed it when she first arrived, but now Hetta seemed to glow, her cheeks pink beneath a light tan from the spring sun, her dark glossy hair, loosened as always by the sea wind, curling about her shoulders as she strode along Beach Street between Eugénie and Julien, or argued animatedly at the dinner table.

I am not clever enough for Julien, Eugénie thought sadly.

One morning she woke late, with dried tears stiff on her face from a night of bad dreams. When she went downstairs at last she found the house oddly quiet, the only sounds coming from the kitchen below. The library was empty, save for Mollie dusting the bookshelves.

"Where are Monsieur de Fortin and my cousin?"

"Why, Miss, they went out for a walk some while since. The monsewer's lesson was over. They thought it best not to disturb you."

So they had gone out together without her, without a chaperone! They had seized the chance to be alone together! For a moment she felt so hurt tears started in her eyes. But then she heard the front door open, pulled herself together, and went out into the hall.

"Good morning," she said coldly as they burst in, bringing in a wash of May sunlight across the oak floorboards and a billow of spring air.

Hetta had been laughing at something Julien said. Her eyes sparkled; she looked happy. But something in Eugénie's face made her expression change.

"Why, Eugénie! We thought you were still asleep, didn't we, Julien?"

So it was "we" now.

"It is a trifle late for anyone to be asleep," Eugénie said, with chilling dignity. "If you'd knocked and entered my chamber, you would have seen that I was thinking. A person can lie in bed and think, and not be asleep."

"Indeed they can," said Julien solemnly. "I often do it myself."

She could see that he was laughing at her.

"I am sorry," Hetta said. "You and I could take a turn around the shops now, if you like."

"No, thank you, Cousin. The shops here have little to interest me after Paris."

Julien raised his eyebrows. Eugénie ignored him.

Hetta looked surprised: Eugénie had never shown any reluctance before. "As you wish," she said, and then, as if sensing the atmosphere, disappeared with some alacrity into the library, where they could hear her telling Mollie to purchase a chicken from the market for dinner.

Eugénie stared accusingly at Julien, but he was turning over the visiting cards on the tray and did not see. There were three there from yesterday afternoon that she had not bothered to pick up.

"I see you have many admirers." His tone was neutral. "Is that why you are so often out, Eugénie?"

If she had not still been feeling upset, she would have assured him that the salons in Deal and the dinners at Dover Castle were initiated by her aunt and boring in the extreme, and that she attended to divert herself from missing Armand. But she did not.

"I find myself much sought after, it is true," she said, pretending coyness.

Julien frowned. He read out the name from the top card, "Sir Rupert Standish."

Eugénie patted her hair. "A most delightful young Englishman. I hope he will call again."

Julien's frown deepened. "And where did you meet him?"

"At a supper party here in Deal, given by Madame de Montebas, another émigrée. It was a most amusing evening." She smiled as his expression darkened, and her sore heart lifted a little. "Why, I do believe you are jealous!"

"Not at all," he said shortly, and lowered his voice. "Be careful of what you say at these dinners."

So he was not jealous. She bit her lip. "What can you mean?"

"Those who profess to be émigrés may well be spies. No one— French or English—can truly be trusted in these times. Guard your tongue."

She flared up, not caring what she said. "You don't believe I can be discreet, is that it? You have always thought me a foolish chatterbox, haven't you?"

He looked bewildered. "Don't put words into my mouth, Eugénie."

"But you think I've no clever opinions. It is useless to deny it!"

"What is the matter with you this morning?" He sounded exasperated. "Perhaps you had better go back to bed."

Now he was humiliating her, treating her like a child. She felt suddenly overwhelmed with feelings that she did not know how to deal with. She looked at his pinched, reproving face under the dark hair and thought she hated him more than she loved him.

"I believe I will do so, monsieur, if only to have the excuse of leaving you! It is clear we have little to say to each other these days, or feelings to share."

"Eugénie!"

But she had already mounted the stairs and did not turn. All the same she heard his gritted words clearly, "Very well, mademoiselle, if that is how you feel about me, I will leave immediately. I believed differently in the past, but perhaps I was always mistaken!"

The front door shut behind him.

Hetta came out of the library. She looked up at Eugénie in surprise. "Has Julien gone? He did not say good-bye."

"Then go after him!" Eugénie shouted down. "You will have him all to yourself, just as you like!"

She sat at her bedroom window for the remainder of the morning, staring out, watching the people walking by the garden gate, waiting for the click of the latch that would tell her Julien had come back, that he forgave her for her foolish words.

But he did not return. Perhaps he would never come back to Goosefield House, he was so insufferably proud and cold.

But the next morning, as rain from the sea spattered against her window, he returned at his usual time. She ran downstairs as soon as she heard his voice, but he had already gone into the library. For hours, it seemed, she hung about in the front parlor, waiting for the lesson to end. Then the library door opened.

She went out into the hall, and hesitated. Julien and her cousin were at the front door. How could she say anything with Hetta present?

"Julien, I . . ." she began in a faltering voice.

He turned, and with a sinking heart she saw his face stiffen. *"Bonjour, mademoiselle."* He made her a curt bow.

After making some mundane remark about how changeable the spring weather was, he nodded to them both and disappeared into the drizzle.

"Julien seems unlike himself today," Hetta remarked.

"Is he low in spirits?" Immediately Eugénie felt contrite.

Hetta shook her head. "It is more that he appears impatient— for what, I don't know." She added awkwardly, "Eugénie, what you said to me—about Julien…"

"Think nothing of it, cousin," said Eugénie airily. She looked away from Hetta's candid gaze in case her own eyes should reveal too much. "I was feeling out of sorts myself yesterday."

Life somehow went on as usual. Eugénie went to a country dance in the Assembly Rooms, smiled and talked and flirted charmingly, and it all meant nothing to her. She had no desire to play on the Broadwood anymore.

She and Julien made stilted, polite conversation whenever they saw each other, and they never saw each other alone. During that dismal time Eugénie began to doubt that Armand was still alive. Her spirit felt weighed down by doubts and sadness, her old certainties gone. *I am losing Julien*, she thought, *have I lost my brother, also?*

Julien had been invited to supper. Though the evenings were light, they were still chill, and afterward they sat before the fire in the front parlor as dusk fell. Eugénie was acutely, uncomfortably, aware of Julien's presence and said little.

Even Hetta was silent, busying herself with sewing a tear in a shirt belonging to her father; her stitches looked large and grubby against the bleached linen. She did not meet Eugénie's eyes, but Eugénie noticed her looking at Julien. She thought he looked back at Hetta with significance in his gaze; he avoided glancing in her direction altogether. The atmosphere quivered with unspoken emotions as Thomas struggled manfully to keep a semblance of conversation going.

"The book you thought would interest me—perhaps I might see it now, monsieur?" said Julien.

"Of course, de Fortin," Thomas said in his courteous way, putting another log on the fire. "Come into the library and I'll find it for you."

They were gone some time. Eugénie and Hetta sat in awkward silence, Hetta bent over her sewing in the candlelight. Eugénie could just make out the urgent mutter of Julien's voice in the next room, interrupted occasionally by her uncle's; she wondered what they were saying. Why were they taking so long?

It grew dark outside.

Hetta sucked a pricked finger. "I believe I shall go to bed. I confess I am a trifle tired tonight. Will you bid Julien good night from me when he returns?"

Eugénie nodded. At last, *at last*, she might have a chance to see Julien on her own. Seconds after Hetta had left she heard the men come out of the library, but her uncle entered the parlor alone.

She tried to hide her dismay. "Has Julien left already?"

"He is just taking his leave of Henrietta."

She rose at once. "Uncle, forgive me..." She mumbled something about bidding Julien good night, and rushed to the door. But to her astonishment her uncle shut it behind him.

"Eugénie," he said gently. "Stay with me awhile."

"Uncle, I..." she began, flustered, at a loss to know why he was barring her way. "I cannot at present. I'm sorry." She reached past him frantically for the door handle.

She heard him say, "My dear, it is not a good idea to interrupt..." She thought he looked at her with compassion, pity. He stepped aside reluctantly, and she was outside in the hall.

And there they were, Julien and her cousin close together. Julien was talking in a low voice, his head bent to Hetta's. He was holding her hand.

ELEVEN

Eugénie did not sleep that night. In the darkness her tired mind pictured again and again the scene in the hall, and what had happened afterward.

They had stepped apart immediately, but she had seen the guilt on their faces. Then Julien had left, bowing formally to them both, not meeting Eugénie's eyes.

Somehow she had mounted the stairs, undressed, let Mollie brush out her hair. She felt like a stiff, wooden doll, no feeling where her heart should have been. She made conversation with Mollie in a high, artificial voice that was not hers.

When she was alone at last, she sat in bed in the candlelight, staring into space, unmoving. When there was a knock on the door, she did not answer. She knew it would be Hetta, and she could not bear to speak to her. When Hetta knocked again, a little later, she lay down swiftly, so that if Hetta entered, she might think she was asleep.

The night passed somehow. At some dreadful empty hour her tears came, until she was bled dry and there were none left.

Her heart was beating fast as she went downstairs the next morning. It was now about the hour that Hetta's lesson with Julien usually finished. She had prepared a defiant little greeting for him, casual, carefree. *I will not show him how much he has hurt me!*

The library door was still shut. She glanced toward the silver tray on the hall table. There was a letter lying on it and, puzzled, she saw it was for her—addressed in unfamiliar writing to Mademoiselle de Boncoeur at Goosefield House, Deal, England. It must have come on last evening's coach and been delivered after she had gone to bed. They had all retired somewhat earlier than usual.

There was an official seal on the fold, waxed but muddied, and when she broke it, she saw lines of elegant looped handwriting. Her heart gave a lurch as she recognized the writing as Belle Fleurie's: All the stock in Belle's shop in the rue des Signes had been labeled in Belle's own hand.

The letter was dated some months before.

> Ma chère Eugénie,
> I am well, but your brother is in La Force. I visited him today and he is in good health. He was arrested in January and is awaiting trial by the Tribunal. Let us pray it will be a fair one.
>
> I know this news will be most upsetting for you, ma chère, but he does not want you to attempt returning to France to see him. It is too dangerous. Aristocrats are executed if they return and people are guillotined daily. They are calling it "the Terror."

She clutched the hall mantel as the floor rocked beneath her feet. She must have made a sound because suddenly her uncle was there, guiding her to a wing chair in the library, pressing her head down between her knees, calling for Hetta to bring a glass of water.

"May I?" said Thomas gently, and he took the letter from her. He read it in silence, his face carefully composed. He passed the letter to

Hetta while Eugénie sipped the water. She heard them make sounds, she could not make out the words. She had quite forgotten: Today was Sunday and they were about to go to church. Of course, Julien would not be coming for his lesson today. She told them to go, not to worry about her: She would sit quietly until they returned.

And she did sit there, unmoving, for an hour or more, until everyday things began to intrude on the stultified blankness of her mind. She heard the slow tick of the brass clock on the mantelpiece, Mollie singing as she laid the table in the dining room, a blackbird's full-throated song beyond the window.

Finally she picked up the letter from the drum table and read it again.

It was shocking, and yet it was not; as if all along part of her had been certain that her worst misgivings would be confirmed one day, and it had merely been a question of waiting for that day to come. And now it had.

"Armand! Armand!" she whispered. "How empty-headed I am, how foolish!" All this time, while she had been leading a merry life of frolic and flirtation, he had been a prisoner in one of the most appalling jails in Paris.

When Thomas and Hetta came back from church, they brought Sir Harry and Lady Coveney with them for luncheon. They entered the library quietly, as if she were a convalescent, and clustered about her, their anxious faces for her, not for Armand.

Aunt Frederica heaved herself onto the chair next to her and clasped her hand. "My dear, such dreadful, dreadful news. How are you feeling? A little *sal volatile* to restore you?"

"Brandy—what do you say, Thomas?" said Sir Harry.

"You still look pale," said Hetta. She looked troubled and somewhat white-faced herself.

"Give the girl air," said Thomas.

They withdrew a little, but continued to regard her carefully.

"You know, my dear niece, it does not mean..." Thomas began, and stopped, evidently not knowing how to go on.

"...that he will be executed," said Hetta.

"Henrietta!" exclaimed Aunt Frederica, her hand to her mouth.

"Someone has to say it," muttered Hetta. "That is what you are thinking about, is it not, Cousin?"

"He will be acquitted," said Sir Harry firmly. "He needs a good defense lawyer. The boy has done nothing. He was not one of those who took active part in the failed rescue of the king."

"He was one of the conspirators, though," said Eugénie in a flat voice. They all looked startled, as if they had not been expecting her to speak.

"They need evidence of that," said Thomas, looking at his brother.

"He has been betrayed," said Eugénie bitterly. "There will be evidence, and if there is not, then someone will find it, will forge it, if necessary. He is known to be a royalist." She looked down at her clenched hands and whispered, "And now there are no royalists left alive in the streets of Paris."

She looked up and saw them watching her with grave, uncertain faces. "I must tell Julien. He is Armand's best friend."

"Julien is away at the moment," said Thomas. "I believe he has gone to Ramsgate." He looked vaguely out of the window, as if he could sight the distant port on the horizon.

"Julien de Fortin? That young Frenchman?" said her aunt, her mouth quivering with disdain.

"I did not know he was going away," said Eugénie. Another pain shot through her heart. "But he is a lawyer. He will know more about the trial process than I."

"The Revolutionary Tribunal will be no ordinary court of law," said Sir Harry in a grim undertone to Thomas. "God knows what form it takes. The jury probably consists of savage *sans-culottes*!"

Eugénie had sharp hearing. "You are right, Uncle. And that is why I do not expect Armand to be acquitted. That is why I must return to France to see him before he dies."

There was a collective intake of breath in the room. She might have found it funny at another time. Four English faces looked at her, aghast.

"Return to that benighted country?" gasped Aunt Frederica. "Oh, my dear, it would be most unwise! And you couldn't possibly travel alone!"

"Far too dangerous," said Sir Harry. "If émigrés return to France now, they face the death penalty."

Thomas came closer and leaned on the wing of her chair. "Eugénie, my child, it would do no good. What can you do for Armand?"

"I can comfort him!" cried Eugénie brokenly. She turned her face away and whispered, "I can say good-bye."

He put a hand on her shoulder, steadying her. "Things must take their course, my dear. We'll all pray for the best outcome." He looked around. "Let us go and take some sustenance. I think we need it."

Eugénie found herself helped to her feet, Thomas's arm through hers. Aunt Frederica led the way. "The important thing is to *distract* her," she said in a loud whisper to Hetta.

Thomas gave Eugénie's arm an encouraging squeeze. "Show us all how courageous you can be, my dear."

"Thank you, Uncle," Eugénie said softly. "I intend to do so."

Since rereading the letter earlier, she had been busy plotting.

TWELVE

Jem's black shed was empty later that afternoon. Eugénie pulled down her cloak hood and peered about in the gloom, wrinkling her nose at the stink of old fish and tarred rope. She waited until the smell became too much. Disappointment filled her. She had missed him: Jem, who was so essential to her plan.

But he would be back.

The next day she went again, and the next. As a young French girl alone, she was wary of approaching the rough-looking boatmen on the beach and questioning them as to Jem's whereabouts. Antagonism to French émigrés was growing. Even the local shopkeepers were not as friendly as they once had been; in the streets she was spat at when she spoke French.

"How long is it until Julien returns?" she asked Thomas. Her pride prevented her from asking Hetta.

"I'm not certain," Thomas said and looked at her with sympathy. "Do not dwell on Julien, my dear."

She flushed. "I do not."

When she entered Jem's shed one afternoon, there was a dark figure sitting on a barrel. A boy, arms folded, legs in breeches thrust out.

"You!" said Eugénie.

"I know you've been coming here," said Hetta. "I know why you want Jem." She jumped up. "You're planning to return to France, are you not?"

"Of course," said Eugénie coldly.

"Wait, Eugénie, don't go. We can talk in here. No one can hear us." Hetta came closer. "You must not even consider going! You will die if you return. What use is that to anyone? Your duty is to go on living." She sighed. "I know the frustration you feel. It is so hard for us women. We can do nothing by ourselves, it seems. We are constrained by society, which is ordered by men. Yet we need them for our protection and so much of our enterprise, and when we use them we must not show it."

She could not let herself soften, Eugénie thought. "Where is Jem?"

Hetta hesitated. "He is away on a mission. For the prime minister, for Mr. Pitt."

"He told you, and not me!" Outrage and hurt filled her.

"It's awkward. You are French, Eugénie."

"I am English, too," said Eugénie, frowning. After all that she and Jem—and Julien—had been through together, he should have trusted her! "What is this mission?"

"I know little." Hetta spread her hands. "I've no notion when he'll be back." Her voice sank. "If he does come back."

"You know Julien's business, too, I suppose?"

It was too dark to see Hetta's expression. "Eugénie, I am so sorry..."

"I am merely asking when he is likely to return."

"He did not tell my father and me. I thought we might have some message from him by now. I fear for him."

"In Ramsgate?" said Eugénie incredulously.

Silence, then Hetta said, "There are assassins. There is so much we do not know." She appeared to gather herself forcibly together. "Only tell me you will not go to France!"

"It seems I have no means of getting there," Eugénie said tartly.

Another week passed, drearily, anxiously, with no sign of either Julien or Jem. She longed to show Julien the letter from Belle; above everything she yearned for his comfort, his wise words. *I must forget Julien*, she told herself. But she could not.

Lady Coveney paid a visit, flourishing theater tickets. *She has come to make sure I'm not languishing too long and will be recovered by the time of her ball!* thought Eugénie. But she felt ashamed when Frederica patted her hand with genuine affection and concern. "I am happy to see you in better spirits, Niece."

When Eugénie and Hetta returned to Goosefield one afternoon after an outing in the carriage along the Dover road to Sandicote, there was a new calling card on the hall tray. "Guy is back!" cried Eugénie.

Hetta took the card from Eugénie and looked at it, frowning. Eugénie, sensing her disapproval, said nothing more, but inside was filled with hope where before there had been none.

Guy had offered to take her with him to France not so long ago. When he heard of Armand's imprisonment, surely he would want to return—and take her with him? It seemed he traveled between France and England with little difficulty. And he was a respected lawyer. If she could persuade him to present Armand's defense when Armand came before the Revolutionary Tribunal . . .

She slipped upstairs to her chamber, quickly wrote a note to Guy, and sealed it with a wafer.

> I am to visit the Old Playhouse tomorrow evening in
> my aunt Coveney's party. Please attend our box. I have
> news of the utmost importance to impart to you.

Then she sent Jack, the boot boy, to deliver it to the Three Kings.

THIRTEEN

The Old Playhouse was performing two plays: *Wild Oats* and a farce called *Sprigs of Lavender*.

Eugénie, expecting a theater much like the Théâtre Français, which she had attended so often in Paris, discovered to her disappointment that it was a plain, square building and the seating shabby and hard. Even the boxes were cramped. There was no uniformed attendant to take their velvet cloaks, only a row of brass hooks stuck into the painted wall.

At least in a theater so small I shall have no difficulty in seeing Guy, she thought, gazing down from the box where she sat next to Aunt Frederica. As in Paris, it seemed perfectly acceptable to talk throughout the performance. The young man whom her aunt had placed on her other side looked a little dejected at her abstraction as he struggled gamely to make conversation. Finally she took pity on him.

"Forgive me, but I believe an old friend is to attend tonight and I must speak with him."

He nodded, crestfallen. This ravishingly pretty creature must have a lover; all French ladies had lovers and thought nothing of it, so he had heard.

But still she could not see Guy. And then, between the plays, there he was suddenly, drawing aside the curtain, bowing to Aunt

Frederica, the candlelight shining on the chiseled features beneath his auburn hair.

"Lady Coveney. *Mes sentiments.* Do I intrude?"

Somehow her aunt knew all the most presentable French émigrés, Eugénie thought. There was always one invited when she entertained: English society thought them romantic.

Aunt Frederica rose in her full finery, her skirts billowing about her. She extended a hand for Guy to kiss and smiled up at him. "Why, my dear Monsieur Deschamps! What a pleasant surprise! I'd no notion you were back in town. I'd concluded you would be absent from my ball."

"Oh no, madame, I would not miss it for the world. I have returned for that alone, I do assure you."

She tapped him roguishly with her fan and turned. "Girls, is that not good news?"

Eugénie realized to her dismay that it would be impossible to speak to Guy alone. She knew she could not mention Armand's imprisonment on a social occasion: It was simply not *de rigueur*— not acceptable in company.

He kissed her hand and looked into her eyes. "Beautiful, as always," he murmured, but it might have been a mere gallantry. She needed to make him want to do anything for her, including, of course, an escorted safe passage to France. Above all things, she needed to be able to trust him: Now he was all she had.

Hetta removed her hand swiftly after his kiss; she appeared in low humor.

Aunt Frederica talked of the ball, of Sandicote. "We have a shell grotto, monsieur. It is much commented on by our visitors on Thursdays, when we open the house and grounds to genteel company. And I have arranged a little secret surprise for our guests between the dancing."

"What is it, Aunt?" demanded Hetta. But her aunt would not say, shaking her head and smiling mysteriously.

The theater boy was doing his rounds, with his little bell; the second play would start in a minute. Guy lingered.

"A shell grotto?" he said to Eugénie in a low voice, as her aunt's party took their seats again. "Now does that not sound the most romantic meeting place?"

He took her hand and kissed it in farewell. She felt the fervent press of his lips. In his eyes was an unmistakable question.

"Indeed it does, monsieur," she whispered, and her heart beat hard.

When he had gone and she turned to take her seat, she was conscious of Hetta's eyes boring into her back.

Aunt Frederica left the theater in her own carriage; Eugénie and Hetta were alone on the return journey to Goosefield. Somehow their relationship seemed to have deteriorated even further, and Eugénie was not sure why. *She thinks I have a* tendresse *for Guy! But then she should be relieved that Julien is all her own....*

Her heart twisted painfully. She tucked her hands further into the comforting warmth of her swansdown muff as they rattled along, for the night had turned chill.

Something was wedged in her muff. Puzzled, she explored with her fingers: paper. She thought she heard it crackle and swiftly took her hands out before Hetta heard it, too. It was surely a secret message from Guy!

It took an age for a yawning Mollie to undress her and brush out her hair. At last when Mollie had unlaced her and she was in her chemise, she dismissed her for the night. "Thank you, Mollie," she said, suddenly filled with gratitude. "You are so kind to me."

Mollie looked startled. "'Tis nothing, Miss. I gets paid, see? Besides, I feel sorry for you, Miss, I don't mind saying."

"Sorry?" Could Mollie know about Armand? But they never discussed family matters in front of servants.

"Sorry for you being French, Miss," and she dipped a curtsy and winked.

As soon as the door closed, Eugénie took her muff from the wardrobe and reached inside to pull the paper out. It was a letter; she felt the hardness of a wax seal.

She took the letter over to the little dressing table where the looking glass reflected the candlelight. *It is a billet-doux!* she thought. A love letter—from Guy!

For a moment the despair she felt at Armand's imprisonment and the constant ache in her heart over the loss of Julien lessened a little. *Guy will do what I want, I know. He will escort me back to France and Armand!*

The letter had her name upon it in unfamiliar handwriting; the pressure on the nib had pierced the paper.

Eugénie hesitated, staring at the seal. The letter was not from Guy at all. The crest imprinted in the wax was disturbingly familiar. She had known it all her life: the stag's head surrounded by a wreath of ivy. It was the proud, ancient crest of her ancestors, the de Boncoeurs of Chauvais. Though her name was not written in Armand's hand, he must have sealed the letter himself with his signet before it left his prison cell.

She broke the seal with shaking fingers, then tried to hold the letter steady under the candlelight and take in what it said.

And that was how Hetta found her, minutes later. Hetta had come in, dressed in her nightgown, a shawl around her shoulders, to bid her cousin a polite good night.

Eugénie was sitting motionless at the dressing table. In the looking glass her eyes were desperate.

"Hetta, what must I do? However can I agree to this?"

FOURTEEN

She held the letter out. "It is from Monsieur Goullet. He proposes a bargain with me." She bent her head. "I don't know what to do. I cannot think."

Hetta read it slowly.

Ma chère Mademoiselle Eugénie,

We have met on several occasions in Paris. You may remember me, and you may also be aware that four years ago, your guardian, at the time the Comte Lefaurie de Haut-bois, signed a contract agreeing that you, Eugénie de Boncoeur, should marry me upon your sixteenth birthday. That date has now passed, and in effect, the contract has been reneged upon. If you were in this country, I would begin legal proceedings. However, you are in England, beyond the reach of French lawyers and myself. You know I am a powerful and wealthy man, with significant contacts in the National Convention and the committees. Meanwhile, your brother, Armand, is in La Force and in due course will face the Revolutionary Tribunal. There is documentary evidence against him. He will be found guilty. The sentence will be death by execution.

But I can help him. In turn I expect compliance from you.

If you agree to marry me as stated in the contract, then through my contacts I will arrange for your brother to be freed. He will escape the guillotine.

As for you, if you agree to this and convey as much to my courier, Guy Deschamps, he will escort you safely back to France. I have made arrangements for this, and neither of you will come to harm. If you decide against my proposal, then without my intervention your brother will die beneath the blade.

Eugénie's eyes, wide and fearful, met Hetta's in the looking glass. "What can I do? If I marry Monsieur Goullet, it will be a living death!"

Hetta was silent a moment, then she spoke flatly.

"If I were in your situation, I'd marry Goullet."

"But God knows what he has in store for me! He hates my family!"

"But he is willing to save Armand if he has you as his bride." Hetta began to pace about the room, her dark hair streaming down her back. "I have always longed for a brother, a brother with whom I could play boys' games, who would teach me how to shoot and fence and drive a pair of horses at a gallop! If I were lucky enough to have a brother, I would treasure him above all things."

"I treasure Armand," Eugénie said heatedly. "He is the most beloved of brothers! But he would not want me to do this for him. I know he dislikes Goullet intensely. Something happened in the past—what, I do not know. Goullet has been trying to steal Chauvais from us for years. Somehow he has come by Armand's signet ring." She turned and faced her cousin. "You have no notion of what my life will be like! Goullet is old and repellent. He wears black gloves. I believe his hands are deformed beneath them."

She pinched the tender flesh of her thighs under the thin chemise, imagining those gloved hands crawling up her white legs, and shuddered. "Must I give my body in return for my brother's life?"

"If Goullet is old, he will die soon."

Was that meant to console her? "But not so very soon, Cousin."

"You can have lovers. That is what the French do, is it not?" Hetta flashed a dark glance at her. "You can take Guy as a lover, for instance!"

"*Guy!* You believe I want Guy as a lover?" said Eugénie, appalled that Hetta should think such a thing.

"Is it not so? The way you behave when you are in his presence... and he to you."

Eugénie put a hand to her hot cheeks. "I have found him attractive, I admit—in the past...."

"Why has Goullet used him as a messenger? Because he thinks Guy will be able to persuade you to accept the bargain? I do not trust Guy Deschamps."

"Oh, you are as bad as Julien!" Eugénie flashed. "Julien's suspicions have influenced you. Monsieur Goullet must have heard that Guy was returning to England, that is all. They move in the same circles in Paris."

"But what must Guy think of such a contract? Will he not consider it most unsavory? Yet he is the one delivering Goullet's bargain into your hands! Do you think he knows what is in the letter?"

"If he does, then like you, he will want me to accept for Armand's sake. Armand is his friend." Eugénie shook her head and turned away. "If only there were some other way! I'd hoped..." But now she could see how futile her original plan to return to France with Jem had been.

This was the only way.

* * *

She could not sleep. As soon as it was light she composed a short letter to Guy, informing him that she had received Monsieur Goullet's letter, and that on the night of her aunt Coveney's ball she would meet him in the shell grotto, when she would give him her answer.

There was a knock at her door later, while she waited for Mollie to dress her hair. Her cousin came in, ready for the morning in her walking dress.

She clasped her hands nervously together. "Eugénie, forgive me. What I said last night..."

"What of it?" Eugénie said coldly.

"I gave you the wrong advice. I have been awake the entire night, dwelling on it. I sometimes speak—too impetuously. Of course you must not accept Goullet's bargain!" Hetta lifted her head and gazed at Eugénie. "One must never give in to villains."

"I understand why you did it, Cousin." *You wanted me out of the way so that you could have Julien to yourself!*

"Then you won't accept?"

"It is too late. I've made up my mind to do so."

"Then I must try to remedy matters. I will tell Father before he leaves for the hospital."

Eugénie stepped toward her, eyes blazing. "No! He will only forbid me to leave the house!"

Hetta gazed at her in distress. "But Eugénie, you must not go! It is because of what I said so foolishly—so thoughtlessly—isn't it?"

Eugénie's lip curled. "You think what you advised me had anything to do with my decision? You are wrong! We Frenchwomen can think for ourselves, incredible as that may seem to an English girl, with all your high-flown political notions and clever words. I knew I had to accept the bargain as soon as I read the letter." This was not altogether true, but she carried on regardless. "It is the only way to save Armand. And save him I will do, Cousin!"

FI7TEEN

A week later they were on their way to Sandicote for the ball, with Mollie in attendance.

On the cliffs to the seaward side there were unpromising views of gorse and fern and hunched dwarf trees; on their right, small farms and cottages, out of which swarms of wide-eyed children and barking dogs appeared as the carriage jolted past over the dusty road. It had been swelteringly hot for the last week, with little breeze and no rain. Even inside the carriage with its opened windows, the wind of their passing made little difference. Eugénie felt sweat trickle between her shoulder blades and hoped it would not stain her new carriage dress.

Hetta's father would not be able to attend because of his duties at the hospital, where daily more wounded were arriving, but the two girls had been invited a day early. Lady Coveney had guests staying, and particularly wished to show off her nieces to the assembled company.

"That means," said Hetta darkly to Eugénie, "she wants some rich booby to fall in love with me, while you impress everyone with your aristocratic airs!"

Hetta's paternal great-great-grandfather, a wily businessman, had made his fortune in the fruit business. He married into minor but moneyed aristocracy, and set about acquiring land as cheaply as he could, building a grand establishment appropriate for his new station in life. The next generations added to the house, until, in due course, Sandicote was inherited by Hetta's uncle, the Right Honorable Sir Henry Coveney, MP, who had made his own modest fortune in the East India Company, enough to buy his way into Parliament.

The house sat back from the Dover road, surrounded by lawns, landscaped gardens, greenhouses, and apple orchards—the work of an endlessly toiling army of gardeners. Its tenanted farmland was set discreetly to one side, hidden by parkland.

There were several wearying changes of dress that first day, and each seemed hotter than the one before. They had been paid for by Lady Coveney, who was determined that her nieces should look their best. Eugénie and her aunt had spent a most agreeable hour in the spring examining the latest fashions in the *Ladies' Magazine*, and choosing which she and Hetta were to have copied and made up by the best dressmaker in Dover. Eugénie thought how excited she had been at the time, how meaningless it seemed now, when Armand was in prison and Julien lost to her. Now she had only a hollow where her heart should be.

Downstairs in the drawing room, she smiled and curtsied automatically and made polite conversation, flirting behind her fan with a group of admiring middle-aged men while her thoughts dwelled anxiously on her forthcoming meeting with Guy. Out of the corner of her eye she could see Hetta, hot, furious, and uncomfortable in her new clothes, stuck with a gangling, blushing young man who drooled with excitement every time she spoke to him.

"Very rich, my dear," whispered Lady Coveney in Eugénie's ear as she swept by, casting an approving glance at the audience Eugénie had gathered around her. "No brains, but very rich! Do persuade your cousin to encourage him!"

*   *   *

Eugénie, dressed for dinner, had gone down the wrong staircase. It was narrow and dark, and turned out to be the servants' staircase. Overcome with horror as she reached the ground floor, she saw a short, stocky man in bright clothes looking about him, evidently as bewildered as she. His back view was familiar.

She rushed toward him, almost tripping over her skirts in amazement and joy. "Monsieur le Brun?"

"*C'est moi*," the man replied, and turned. "Fabrice le Brun, aeronaut at your service," and he swept an extravagant bow. As he straightened, his face lit with recognition. "Mademoiselle Eugénie?" He came closer. "*Quelle surprise extraordinaire!* I never thought to see you again!"

"Nor I you, monsieur!" Tears pricked behind Eugénie's eyes.

He took her hand and kissed it, gazing at her. "*Si belle.* You have grown up, *ma petite*! Whatever do you do here, in this English house?"

"Oh, Fabrice, there is so much to tell you!"

"Then let us sit down and tell it to each other."

"I must not be late for dinner."

He made a face of disgust that made her laugh through her tears. "Ah, the hearty English dinner. Meat at every course and boiled vegetables, and so many toasts between! However can they eat and drink in this heat? And afterward, to banish all the beautiful women! Come, we find somewhere quiet to talk."

As if he owned the house, he led the way jauntily down the passage away from the noise of the kitchens, and pushed open the first door they came to. It turned out to be the billiard room, which at that hour before dinner was empty of the gentlemen of the party.

Eugénie knew nothing of billiards. Vaguely puzzled by the racks of sticks, the enormous tables, and heavy smell of tobacco and male sweat, she settled down eagerly in one of the leather chairs to hear Fabrice's story.

He was little changed, she thought fondly. His eyes sparkled with *joie de vivre* and gaiety as much as ever, and he seemed to have lost no weight at all in pining for Belle. Indeed, he appeared to have lived life rather well since she had last seen him.

"Why did you never write, monsieur?" she demanded reproachfully. "We waited and waited." She thought of Belle hiding her hurt in brave defiance, while fearing that her daredevil lover had finally killed himself.

He had the grace to look ashamed. "I never had time for schooling, mademoiselle. A pen and ink are no use to me." He went on grandly, "I, Fabrice le Brun, have other talents. Earth cannot hold me, or any woman, for long. I am a creature of the air!"

"But you might have sent word, Fabrice!"

"I was engaged in making my fortune," he protested. "It was all for Belle, you understand. I thought I would then return to marry *mon amour*. But now"—he gave a vast shrug—"it is war, and how can I do so?"

"So what are you doing here?"

"I am famous now, *ma chère* Eugénie. The name of Fabrice le Brun and his balloon *l'Audace* is known along the south coast of England! Indeed, I'd thought you one of my admirers when you called my name. Tomorrow at the ball I am to put on a display for the guests." He snapped his fingers in glee. "In my balloon I shall rise like an arrow into the night sky! They will all think I fly to the moon!" He winked. "But, of course, I have the tethering ropes hidden in the darkness."

"So you are Aunt Frederica's secret!"

His brown eyes, as liquid as ever and fringed by dark curling lashes, widened in horror. "You are the niece of that woman *très formidable*? Are you English now, *ma pauvre*? How has this happened?"

Bit by bit, with constant interruptions from Fabrice, Eugénie told her story. "And now I have to agree to Monsieur Goullet's bargain in order to set Armand free."

"He does not sound a good man. Can you trust him?"

"I have to do so, Fabrice."

"But to undertake such a dangerous journey!"

"Armand's old friend, Guy Deschamps, comes here tomorrow. I know he will protect me on my return to France."

"And can you trust *him*?"

"Of course. He has always cared for my safety. Why, he has rescued me from danger at least twice before!"

But something of Fabrice's doubt touched her. She was about to say more, when a footman, hearing voices, put his head around the door and saw the fancy entertainer clasping the hand of his mistress's niece. The footman hurried away in shock to report the scandal to his sweetheart, the third housemaid.

In his haste, he almost bumped into Hetta, who had succeeded in persuading her gangling young man to teach her billiards. With a resigned Mollie in tow as chaperone, they entered the room shortly afterward.

"Oh, Miss Eugénie, it's you!" gasped Mollie, folding her lips primly before she could say more.

An intrigued grin spread across Hetta's face. "Are you going to introduce us, Cousin?"

The next day, on the rolling expanse of neatly cropped front lawn, *l'Audace*'s great gold and blue dome rose steadily above its gondola-shaped basket as it filled with hydrogen.

Guests clustered around the base of the launching platform, marveling at the size of the hydrogen casks and the complex network of pipes that conducted the gas to the balloon. Every time Eugénie went upstairs to change her dress, out of the window she saw the small, bustling figure of Fabrice as he inspected the rigging, or issued orders at intervals to his assistants in an impatient mixture of French and English. She could hear his commentary as he held up choice examples of his equipment to the admiring crowd below.

"My barometer, *très cher*, worth two hundred guineas! Silk cushions for your comfort! The best binoculars, a brass compass, the sharpest knife..."

Aunt Frederica had decreed that Eugénie and Hetta were to wear white to the ball, since they had not yet "come out." Their season as debutantes in London, which she was already assiduously planning, was to come after they had been finished at Miss Birdsall's Seminary for Young Ladies in Harley Street.

Eugénie felt profoundly guilty as Mollie dressed her in the exquisite ivory satin ball gown, its silver lace overskirt adorned with pearls. How let down her aunt would be, having lavished so many hopes on her newfound niece, when she suddenly absconded with a Frenchman in the days to come! And what of Julien? Would he ever forgive her? He wouldn't realize she had done it for Armand's sake.

But she was forgetting: Julien did not care about her any longer.

She looked wan, as white as her dress. "Ask Lady Coveney if I may beg a little rouge, Mollie."

The pot was duly brought. She dabbed delicately: a hint of a glow on her cheekbones, her hairline, her shoulders where they rose naked from the dress, and between her breasts.

"You look beautiful, Miss," Mollie breathed. "You will have every man after you!"

The only one she needed was Guy.

SIXTEEN

After Mollie had dressed her hair so that curls gathered artfully around her face, Eugénie drifted to her chamber window to view the guests arriving in the evening light. As the hubbub of noise gathered below, she felt suddenly shy and not a little nervous of such very English company when their two countries were at war. When Guy Deschamps's curricle rolled up, its horses snorting, and the familiar elegant figure leaped down, she could not help feeling a surge of relief at the arrival of a fellow countryman.

It was Hetta, however, who knocked on her door, as if she understood she might be apprehensive—"Shall we go down together, Cousin?"—and it was Hetta who took her arm, so that they descended the staircase side by side to murmurs of admiration from below.

Hetta, in her ball gown of deep cream silk, with an overskirt of gold spider-gauze, had been transformed from the gauche, hoydenish tomboy that Eugénie knew. The richness of the cream silk brought out the warmth of her complexion and contrasted dramatically with the darkness of her hair, now neatly smoothed and teased into ringlets that fell softly around her cheekbones.

"What a pair of beauties, eh?" one young blade spluttered to his friend, choking on his wine in appreciation.

Lady Coveney, resplendent in violet satin, her skirt hooped in the style still worn in court circles, eight magnificent ostrich feathers rising from the jeweled tiara on her head, overheard and smiled to herself.

In the ballroom the musicians started to play. Dinner would not be served until the fashionable town hour of nine o'clock. Lady Coveney took Eugénie's elbow. "Come, my dear. Let me perform some introductions. That dance card will not be empty for long!"

She was right. There were many young men eager to partner a prodigiously pretty girl, new to the neighborhood, especially when they discovered to their profound relief that although Mademoiselle Eugénie de Boncoeur was French, her English was excellent; it seemed to them, then, that her beguilingly exotic accent merely added to her charms. Before long her card was filled, and her first partner whisked her away in triumph to dance the cotillion.

Before dinner the guests gathered in the long drawing room so the young people could recover from their exertions. Eugénie expressed her urgent desire for a glass of lemonade to her latest partner, and as soon as he had disappeared, sought Guy out.

He was standing with a group of young military men, but somewhat apart, a stormy expression on his handsome face. Eugénie thought he was staring at Hetta, glowing and beautiful in her ball dress, and closely shadowed by her gangling young admirer and several other hopefuls; but she could not be sure.

"Monsieur Deschamps!" she exclaimed, coming upon him as if by accident. She swept a curtsy. "How delightful to see a familiar face!"

He bowed deeply, and as he stood up, his eyes met hers. Her heart began to thud despite herself; she could not breathe. She unlooped Julien's fan from her wrist and fluttered it before her face.

"Mademoiselle Eugénie!" He looked around and whispered

wickedly, "A pleasure to me also in this so-English society!" Smiling, he bent toward her, taking her arm so that they could take a turn around the outskirts of the chattering groups. "Our arrangement later," he said in a low voice. "It still holds?"

She nodded, fanning herself vigorously, and whispered, "But there is much that needs discussion, Guy. There are matters you may not know...." At the same moment she saw that her dancing partner had followed and was pushing a determined path toward her, precariously shielding a glass of lemonade and glowering to see that she had already been usurped in his absence.

"Then let us meet as the guests are distracted by the balloon demonstration." Guy, an eye on the lemonade's rapid approach, disengaged himself gently. "The grotto, as arranged?"

She nodded; he bowed and withdrew. It was almost a relief to have before her again the round, placid person and undemanding conversation of her dancing partner. Thanks to Aunt Frederica's careful planning—for he belonged to the county's most eminent family—he was also to sit next to her at dinner.

Afterward, the men remained at the table to drink port in the English custom. Eugénie made an excuse to her aunt—who was seated in pride of place in the withdrawing room surrounded by an attentive circle of ladies—and ran up the silent staircase to fetch her new satin cloak. Aunt Frederica had insisted that she and Hetta both have cloaks made up for the evening of the ball, pointing out the dangers of night air even in summer.

Dusk was falling. She might need a candle in the shadow of the trees around the shell grotto. She took one from her bedside table, together with a tinderbox, and pushed them both into her stocking bag on top of some money already in it. Then she slipped down the same servants' staircase she had discovered by accident the night before and out through a side door.

She stopped to get her bearings, breathing fast. She should not have worn her cloak: The air was humid and her palms were damp with apprehension.

The light dusk of an evening in high summer was only now starting to fall and she could still see remarkably well, even to making out each individual stone on the path before her, the feathery yew leaves of the Gothic maze on her right and the pale statues of nymphs standing at the entrance, their stone faces inscrutable as she flitted past.

The path ended, as she remembered, with a flight of stone steps down into the sandy hollow with its gorse and little trees. The air was heavy against her face. The shell grotto beneath her was still lit with candles from earlier that day, when she had been taken in a party of guests to admire it. Outside it appeared a romantic ruin, but inside the walls were made of shells and glistened with water that trickled down from spouts hidden in the roof.

Guy was already there, standing in the entrance. He came forward as she crossed the hollow. Behind him a shadow moved across the lighted shells.

Why has he brought a companion? Eugénie thought in dismay, and pulled up her cloak hood so she would not be recognized.

Guy did not observe the formalities of a social occasion, neither bowing nor kissing her hand. He sounded tense and impatient. "Mademoiselle Eugénie! We have little time before we are missed."

She glanced past him. "But I must talk to you alone, monsieur!"

"It's only Bart Jenkin. He'll not heed us."

"Jenkin the boatman? Why is he here?" Once, leaving Jem's hut, she had bumped into Jenkin. As she righted herself, Jenkin had held her arms too long in apology and lechery had gleamed in his eyes.

Suddenly there was an edge of danger in the air; as she stared at the figure lurking in the shadows she wished that she had brought a chaperone.

"Jenkin is to take us across the Channel," said Guy. "His boat is ready, and his crew. The tide is right and there's little wind to hinder the rowing. We can slip away and no one will know. My carriage waits outside the stables." He looked her up and down. "You have nothing with you, no reticule or case?"

"Wait!" She was astonished. "Guy, I cannot come with you *tonight*! I must make my farewells. I cannot simply disappear!"

"You wish to save your brother?" He said it so coldly she was taken aback.

"You know what has befallen Armand?"

He nodded.

She gripped her hands together. "I must save him, Guy!"

"Then you have to accept the bargain you have been offered by Raoul Goullet."

Dismay and bewilderment at the uncaring way he spoke filled Eugénie. "Then you are aware of what was in his letter?"

He nodded again, curtly. "I thought it the only way to save Armand. I offered to escort you back safely if you agreed to the bargain."

"You mean—it was *your* idea?" A feeling of betrayal crept through her.

He sighed. "Eugénie, I gather this marriage contract was signed by your guardian, giving his permission to the marriage. It is legal and binding. It is you who are in the wrong since you've not kept to it."

Now she was indignant. "Julien says it would not hold up in a court of law!"

"Julien de Fortin is not yet qualified. He knows nothing. And we are not in a court of law now." He sounded exasperated. "Do you wish to save Armand, or not?"

"Of course I wish to save him! But I do not want to marry that vile reptile Goullet!" She shook her head violently. "I am sorry if he is a friend of yours, but I cannot like him! He wants to take Chauvais from us, did you know that? It has been in my family for generations! He has even stolen Armand's signet ring with our family crest. Besides that, he is a most odious-looking creature and I believe his heart is as cold as his visage!"

Perhaps she had been too outspoken and offended him by speaking in such a way of a friend. She ventured closer so that she could see his expression more clearly in the gathering dusk. "Is there not some other way to save Armand?"

She made her voice deliberately soft and feminine. Guy had feelings for her, she was sure. She had charmed him in the past; surely she could do so now?

"You are his friend, *mon cher* Guy." She put her hand on his sleeve in a winning manner, looking up so that the rising moon would shine becomingly on her face. "Can you not defend him before the Tribunal? A few words from you in Armand's defense would make all the difference. You are a respected lawyer, known to Fouquier-Tinville, the chief prosecutor."

"Your brother is accused of being a traitor to the Republic, mademoiselle. I cannot defend him."

"But you know that is not true, Guy! Why, he struggled to achieve a fair constitution for the people of France! He worked for a revolution of ideas, and when it came, he rejoiced." She stared at him. "Everything Armand did was for his country. I believed you were of the same mind!"

"Armand is a royalist." He spoke shortly, almost viciously. "Your brother did not believe in the destruction of the monarchy. But the king is dead and so is his divine right to rule. Louis Capet had his head cut off and tossed away into a basket like any man in the street. France is a Republic now, and we must bow our knee to the state and not to royalty." He shifted irritably. "There is little point in this conversation, Eugénie. If you wish to save your brother, you must come with me now."

She was aghast. "I cannot!"

"This is your only chance, mademoiselle."

"So I must sacrifice myself to Goullet, and you will not help me at all?"

Was this what the Revolution had done to friendship—all those years Armand had looked up to the older lawyer? And what of her own relationship with Guy? Did he not care for her at all, that he should suddenly behave in such a coldhearted manner?

Guy looked down at her, his voice hard. "It is too dangerous for me to help an aristocrat who is known to be a royalist. I have to think of my career, my own safety. You have no idea of what the situation is like in Paris now. Soon they will arrest on charges of guilt by association. The numbers taken to the guillotine are increasing—anyone, high or low, suspected of being a traitor to the Republic. You've been offered the way to survive—both you and your brother."

She was silent. At last she said in a small voice, "Then let me come tomorrow. It is too late tonight. How can I tell my aunt when she has done so much for me? I cannot say my farewells in the midst of a ball!"

His hand was heavy on her arm. "No one must know you are leaving. It must be tonight."

"Please understand. Postpone the journey a few days, I beg you!"

She tried to pull away, but to her astonishment he did not loosen his grip. She stared up at him in shock and saw, suddenly, a very different face. The moonlight glittered in his eyes; there was a wolfish curl to his lips. He jerked his head behind him.

"Jenkin!"

The dark figure loped forward. Surely they were not going to take her by force? She reacted involuntarily; fear of the boatman pushed away every thought in her head.

"No," she cried, in disbelief and terror, "*No!*" She jerked her arm up abruptly and twisted away, taking Guy by surprise.

The slippery satin of her cloak slithered free under his fingers before he could grasp it firmly, and then she was running— running clumsily, with her skirts hitched up high, to the steps that would lead her to safety.

SEVENTEEN

Guy Deschamps drew his lips back over his teeth. The little minx had escaped just as he thought he had her! But it would all add to the excitement of the chase. She had no chance of getting away, wearing those ridiculous dancing slippers and with two fit men after her. He only had to snare her before she sought refuge indoors.

Starting to run, he yelled over his shoulder at Jenkin, "Give chase, man! Between us we'll catch her!"

At the top of the steps he paused, the boatman Jenkin grunting behind him. The oaf had been drinking: His breath stank of it. No doubt he could hold it, though; all the boatmen could. But it took the edge off the man's urgency.

"She's there at the end of the path!" he said impatiently over his shoulder. "Go around the shrubbery and cut her off!"

But La Boncoeur, seeing Jenkin's dark bulk lumber behind the bushes toward her, was running into the maze. She would lose herself without doubt, the little fool, but she would not lose him.

He went swiftly in past the statues, and yes, there she was, darting down a path a little way away, her ivory satin cloak clearly visible between the dark lines of yews. He began to follow the most obvious route, the way she had taken. If necessary he could return to the entrance and post Jenkin at the exit. Then they would only have to wait. In due course she would have to come out.

Zut! He had run into a dead end. But then he saw that so had she, for he glimpsed the pale cloak against the far hedge. She was cowering against the yews, her shoulders bowed, her back to him, too frightened to run anymore. He had her trapped!

He strode down the shadowed path and grasped her shoulder. She gave a gasp and turned, and her cloak hood fell back.

"Mademoiselle Coveney!"

He recovered from the shock quickly, bowing, trying to collect his composure while breathing hard. "My apologies, mademoiselle. I must have startled you."

"Monsieur Deschamps!" gasped Hetta. "It is indeed confusing in here! I fancied myself quite lost earlier. Now I must retrace my steps to the entrance before it gets too dark. Will you escort me?" She fluttered her fan; the moonlight shone in her beautiful eyes.

"I regret, mademoiselle, but I must find your cousin first."

"Are you two playing hide-and-seek?" she asked brightly. "You will miss the balloon demonstration! Oh, there is no need to be so bashful, Monsieur Deschamps! I know you have a *tendresse* for Eugénie." She dropped her gaze, smiling confidingly. "I saw her a moment ago through the hedges, you know."

"Where?"

"I fear your little game is but short-lived, monsieur! She was returning to the entrance."

He cursed inwardly. "Then a thousand apologies, mademoiselle, but I must leave you!"

As soon as he was out of her sight, he began to run again.

Where was Jenkin? Damn the man! But it was easy enough to see Eugénie's white cloak glimmering in the dusk. He pursued the pale figure past the formal flower beds and topiary hedges, through a walled rose garden. He was not yet even out of breath—but she would be, he thought gloatingly: Ladies did not run.

"Eugénie!" he called, making his voice wheedling. "Mademoiselle! There is no need to run from me in this way! Please stop!"

The figure ran on.

He had already studied the layout of the Sandicote gardens during one of the public opening days. He was certain his knowledge of the gardens would be better than hers.

"Mademoiselle!" he called again. "This is tedious! Let us talk at least!"

He began to pursue her in earnest, cursing to himself. She would not be able to run much longer.

He lost her somewhere along the row of ornate glasshouses where fruit was ripening. She had been dodging between them, not keeping to the path, probably hoping to confuse him. He was growing increasingly angry and frustrated.

But then he heard footsteps behind him, whirled and caught sight of her pale cloak whisking behind the corner of the glasshouse he had just run past. Grinding his teeth, he was about to double back in pursuit when he saw out of the corner of his eye her cloaked figure already in the open, running for the kitchen garden.

Taken aback by her speed, he raced after her, passing the darkening rows of beans and cabbages. He could see her figure behind the raspberry canes before she disappeared through the open wooden door.

The back of the house loomed against the deep purple sky, lit by lanterns along the terrace. Panting, he ran up the steps.

Two identically cloaked figures were disappearing around the east corner, running hand in hand.

* * *

"Hetta, I can't go on!"

"You must! We can lose ourselves among the guests!"

But few guests had yet come out on the front lawn. The ladies were fetching cloaks and pelisses, the gentlemen lingering over their port. The two girls hesitated, their breath coming in gasps.

"Fabrice! He will protect us!" panted Eugénie.

"I doubt it," said Hetta. She could see that they were most horribly exposed; there was nowhere to hide on the expanse of moonlit lawn. "We must go indoors!"

Too late. Already Deschamps was emerging around the corner of the house. But it would be a pleasure to tell him how despicable he was face-to-face. She felt fearless and furious. She had followed Eugénie secretly, suspecting she was going to meet him, and had witnessed the struggle in the hollow. It had been delightful to confuse him during the chase. But when he had accosted her in the maze, she had felt the hardness of a pistol hidden beneath his coat.

"Go back inside, through the kitchen entrance!" she said to Eugénie. "I will stay here and confront Deschamps!"

"I won't leave you alone, Cousin!" For a second they glared at each other, then Eugénie grabbed Hetta's hand and pulled her toward the balloon, calling out, "Fabrice! Fabrice!"

Fabrice, checking a tethering rope below the platform, straightened and saw them. *"Mes belles!* But how distracted you look!"

"Guy Deschamps!" gasped Eugénie. "He is coming for me!"

"He shall not have you, *ma petite*!" He gestured grandly at the basket. "You must come with me on my ascent!"

"But..." Eugénie began.

Hetta's eyes shone. "Come on!"

The house overlooked the lawn, and as Guy Deschamps approached from the eastern side, he was forced to slow down in case the sight of a man running across the grass caused alarm and suspicion. That fool Jenkin was, of course, nowhere to be seen. He'd be halfway back to Deal by now, on that lean-shanked pony of his. But perhaps that was as well; he would have only drawn attention to them both.

The guests were beginning to emerge, confusing him when he needed to focus on the two girlish figures. For a moment he lost sight of them behind an interested group examining the grappling irons. The lantern light flickered in the breeze that had begun to blow. Against the light it was difficult to distinguish one dark figure from another. He could hear that ridiculous aeronaut announcing his imminent ascent. The crowd hushed and fell back.

Then he saw them! *Mon Dieu*, they were on the launching platform and climbing into the basket! Forgetting that the balloon tethers ran to an ascent of a mere eighty feet, Guy had visions of losing Eugénie altogether, of seeing his quarry disappear forever among the stars. How he hated to be outwitted! What would he say to Le Fantôme—what of his career, his future?

The aunt, Lady Coveney, was sailing up to him with her husband, the so-important Member of Parliament. "This is exciting, is it not, Monsieur Deschamps? And one of your countrymen, too! The French have truly created a road in the sky!"

"Madame, do you not see who is with the aeronaut?" he said levelly, keeping tight control of himself. "It is your nieces!"

"What?" Lady Coveney peered at the three figures in the basket. "Heavens, Sir Harry, he is right!" She dug her husband in the ribs. "Do something! They cannot be in there unchaperoned!" She lifted her skirts and strode forward over the grass. "Henrietta! Eugénie! Climb out this second!"

Sir Harry followed her with a resigned sigh.

In the balloon's basket there was no sign that her instructions were being obeyed, let alone heard. The murmurs of anticipation around the circle of lantern light were growing as the guests waited for the balloon to begin its ascent. Hetta leaned out, searching for Guy Deschamps among the figures gathered on the grass below the platform.

"Guy has a gun," she whispered in Eugénie's ear, as she waved cheerily down.

Below them, Lady Coveney wrung her hands. "The shame of it!"

Sir Harry patted her soothingly. "My dear, since the intention is to entertain our guests by giving them rides in Mr. le Brun's balloon, we could hardly have forbidden Henrietta and Eugénie to do the same. Henrietta certainly has talked of nothing else since she first set eyes on that contraption!"

"But to be the first to go up, with all eyes upon them! It will appear so very forward! At least Henrietta has Eugénie with her."

"Eugénie! I hardly think Eugénie will prevent anything improper happening," said Sir Harry dryly.

They had both forgotten Guy Deschamps. He began to skirt around the outside of the guests, keeping in the shadows to avoid suspicion. He did not want any of the guests to realize that the charming young émigré, to whom many of them had been introduced earlier, was not what he seemed—particularly when France was at war with England.

His mind worked coldly and clearly. His hand touched the pistol beneath his coat.

EIGHTEEN

Fabrice le Brun lifted his arm, the signal for his assistants to loosen the tethering cords from the grappling irons that anchored the balloon to the ground. Slowly they began to feed the cords out.

L'Audace began to lift. The basket beneath the balloon, as if sensing its coming freedom, gave a shiver of expectation, lurched, and rose experimentally, settled back briefly and lifted again more strongly. It was now about four feet above the ground.

The balloon rose higher, the basket the height of a man.

In the darkness away from the crowd, Guy took the pistol from his coat. Raising his right arm, he pointed up into the empty air and fired.

The shot split the air with devastating noise. There was a short, stunned silence broken by cries of terror. The guests drew together instinctively, wild-eyed with shock, then separated as they realized that one of their number must have a gun.

Husbands began swiftly to escort their wives toward the house, throwing dignity away and almost running in their haste. Lanterns toppled and went out, the darkness only adding to the chaos. Young men lingered irresolute, gaping with fear, ashamed of losing face among their peers. Fabrice's bemused assistants stood their ground below the platform, waiting for his signal.

Above them in the basket three white faces stared at one another as the balloon lifted further. Eugénie, crouching inelegantly in her ball dress, clutched the basket's wickerwork side—so frail, so flimsy against a bullet. She imagined it tearing through, ripping the wickerwork in half, killing one of them. They would crash to the ground, smashing bones, cracking skulls, losing their lives' breath from their bodies in one violent shock.

"Give your men the signal to descend, Fabrice," she whispered. "That was Guy's gun and he will shoot us all!"

Her emotions had been in turmoil since the meeting in the grotto: She was still too shocked and confused to think clearly. Guy, whom she had trusted so long, a traitor! He had betrayed her, was behind Goullet's dreadful bargain, was now willing to kill her. . . .

"Deschamps wants you alive, Eugénie," said Hetta. "He won't risk aiming near us."

Fabrice thought wildly of the journeys he had made in his beloved l'Audace. He could not bear to see her destroyed by a madman's bullet. But to descend meant that Mademoiselle Eugénie would be seized by that scoundrel.

"We shall have to descend in a moment in any case," he moaned. "We are reaching the limit of the tethers!"

That was exactly what Guy had planned. From his hiding place in the darkness, he watched the panic among the guests with satisfaction. As soon as l'Audace was brought back to the launching platform he would seize Eugénie, and in the darkness and confusion hurry her away. It would look as if he were protecting her; no one would see the pistol jammed in her back.

But first he would make certain that the panic continued.

He reloaded swiftly, and fired. Guests fell flat on the grass in terror, shielding their heads. He tucked the pistol away, smiling, and waited for the right moment to make his move.

The pungent smell of burning powder had reached the basket. "We are hit!" wailed Fabrice.

But the balloon was steady above them. She strained at her leashes, a live thing.

The remaining guests pressed together. Eugénie saw a figure creep forward, dress sword gripped in his right hand. It was her uncle, Sir Harry, peering about in the shadows. Behind him, her aunt swung her reticule as if at any moment she would join her husband in battle against the unknown gunman.

Guy will have no compunction in killing them both, thought Eugénie in horror. She knew now the lengths to which he would go.

"Fabrice, give the signal!" she cried again.

"Wait!" said Hetta.

She reached behind her in one quick movement and drew something from a locker. Before the other two realized what she was doing, she stretched about her, making slashing movements. A last flash of the knife and all the restraining cords were cut.

The balloon moved upward in a sudden rush of cool air, its shadow falling over the guests, too frightened now to look up and marvel as the great gold and blue dome lifted against the darker blue of the sky.

Far below, a tiny lone figure stared up for a moment as if in disbelief, then edged around the lawn and raced toward the stables.

They were free and rising fast.

"Oh, Hetta, what have you done?" gasped Eugénie.

"*Tiens, mes amis!*" said Fabrice, his dreadful vision of *l'Audace* in tatters diminishing rapidly. "Unexpectedly, we make a little trip, *oui*? And we have escaped that madman! It is thanks to your cousin, mademoiselle." He pulled a map from under his seat and calmly unrolled it on his knee. "The breeze—it takes us toward Dover, where we shall make a landing."

Eugénie dared to look over the edge of the basket. She gasped at the smallness of the farm outbuildings, the dark silhouettes of trees like the wooden cutout toys she had played with as a child. She could see their own vast shadow moving over the grass, the white dots of sheep running in terror from it.

She looked up. Above them was the huge hanging lamp of the moon, almost blinding in its intensity, and the bowl of the sky decorated with bright stars. It seemed to her that soon she might reach out and pick them like flowers.

How paltry are the affairs of men, she thought. Her turmoil at Guy's betrayal seemed as nothing. Even the bloody struggles of the French Revolution were puny, dwindling to insignificance when contrasted with the vastness of space. And now it was about to swallow them.

"Shall we go on rising forever, Fabrice?" she asked fearfully.

"*Non, non, ma petite*, I can control our height. I have my valve, which I let out a little, so, by pulling on this rope. You see? And thus we descend a little. It takes half an hour to release enough *gaz* for us to land, so I start our descent now."

Half an hour! Eugénie shivered. She wondered if she didn't feel a little sick. Certainly she felt cold. The satin summer cloak had no warmth in it. The next moment Fabrice had bent forward to one of the lockers and revealed a collection of fur-lined capes, beaver flying helmets, and chamois leather gloves. Next came a bottle of brandy and a telescope.

"*Voila!* You see, I have everything," he said smugly.

They took it in turns to swallow some brandy, after which Eugénie's nausea miraculously disappeared and she felt positively courageous, wrapped in one of the fur-lined capes. The wind did not jerk or tug at the balloon as she had expected; they might not have been moving at all. It was the earth that slowly revolved beneath the basket while they seemed to hang motionless in the air. Yet she could see the needle on Fabrice's compass steadily turning.

Then the land beneath abruptly rolled away. The balloon instead of descending was rising.

"We are caught in the updraft!" Fabrice exclaimed. "I cannot control the direction of the balloon!"

"Updraft, monsieur?" said Hetta.

He moved his hands. "Where the sea meets the land there is much rising air always."

"But what does that mean?" said Eugénie. "Where will we go?"

Fabrice shook his head. "We have to rise with it until we meet the next airstream." He sounded worried, and they soon knew why.

"I think," Hetta said, in a matter-of-fact way, as she looked over the side of the basket, "we have left the cliffs behind."

"No!" cried Eugénie, aghast.

But she could see for herself that it was true. Far below, tiny waves curled white against the dark expanse of stony beach, and now even they were receding. As the balloon steadied, there was nothing to be seen below but a glossy blackness lit by the moon and scored in all directions by the thin lines of waves, like a scratched slate.

They were over the sea.

Guy Deschamps saw the balloon float away over the Channel out of the back window of his coach, which, rattling with the speed of its galloping horses, had already left the estate of Sandicote to return to Deal. He was shaking with fury and humiliation, but there was some compensation to be had in the way the balloon was so clearly out of control.

The passengers in *l'Audace* would either be killed in due course as the balloon fell into the sea, or they would survive the journey and land in France. Le Fantôme's spy network stretched throughout coast and countryside. It would not take long before someone reported a balloon sighting. Balloon flights were no longer regarded as entertainment, but with the deepest suspicion, for it was one of the ways the enemy might invade.

He would be the sole passenger crossing the Channel on that mutton-head Jenkin's boat tonight. But Le Fantôme need never know of tonight's disaster. He, Guy, would hunt down Eugénie de Boncoeur, as he had already tracked down Julien de Fortin.

He had failed tonight. He would not fail again.

In the basket Fabrice was groaning with despair.

"But can we not go back?" cried Eugénie.

"*Ce n'est pas possible.* One cannot navigate a balloon. We are at the mercy of the wind's direction, mademoiselle. It blows from the northeast. We are forced to continue over the Channel until it changes its mind."

Hetta swigged some brandy in a most unladylike way. "But that is what you wanted, Cousin, was it not? To reach France?"

Fabrice looked at her in horror. "But *non*, Mademoiselle Coveney, this way is an enterprise *trop dangereuse*! Once before I have crossed the sea—*oui*, a famous crossing witnessed by many— but that was before we were at war and *certainement* not in the night! Now is not safe."

To emphasize his point he pulled out three cork life jackets from his seat locker. Eugénie stared at them in dismay. "It is an insurance, *seulement*," he said. "In case we are forced to land in the sea. Let us pray we have no need of them." However, he put his own on without further ado and signaled to them to do the same.

The girls did up each other's tapes. Eugénie fumbled: Her fingers were shaking with fear. Once on, the jacket was uncomfortably stiff and bulky beneath her cape. "How long will it take before we reach the French coast, Fabrice?" she asked tremulously.

"For me before—two hours to fly to Calais from Dover." He

shook his head. "But this time, who knows? With the wind in this direction we will be blown down the French coast." He shook his head tragically. "Madness! To land in *ma pauvre patrie* in the middle of her revolution! Why has fate brought this upon us?"

Hetta's eyes were wide with excitement. She stood up and stared ahead as if she could see already the French coastline approaching in the moonlight. In her flying helmet and cape and with her dark hair flowing over her shoulders, her tall figure looked magnificent and dauntless.

"Why, Monsieur le Brun? To rescue Eugénie's brother from prison—that is why fate has given us this chance and that, *mes amis*, is what we are going to do!"

PART TWO

The Game is Over

FRANCE

Mid-August–September 1793

NINETEEN

The balloon did not fly in a smooth level path, but in a series of looping ascents and descents between wind streams that did not disturb the balance of the basket.

Eugénie and Hetta were only aware that the shimmering darkness below them turned more quickly or more slowly, and that the silvery road across the sea cast by the moon curved away more to their right or to their left. Sometimes it felt as if the sea were the sky, and the balloon and its basket were sailing upside down, while above them the moon and stars were reflections in the sea's waves.

Around them was an awe-inspiring stillness and majesty. The world of earth and sea and air was suddenly immense, sublime, and timeless, without anything familiar in it. They gripped each other's gloved hands without speaking.

They were aware that Fabrice was checking and rechecking his instruments as they flew. They heard the basket creak as he stood up and sat down, but otherwise it was utterly silent, so that they heard him suck in his breath if they sank too low. Then they would clutch each other in terror, imagining the dreadful plunge into the dark, cold depths below. When he sighed and relaxed as the balloon gained height once more, they turned away in relief to gaze around them.

It was high summer, a cloudless night that never became completely dark. Gradually the whole bowl of the sky became luminous, as if lit from behind.

"Morning comes," said Fabrice. "*Merci, mon Dieu!*" He crossed himself elaborately. "And now, *mon Dieu*, one last thing—I beg you to grant us a safe landing! At least we shall see where we are going!"

The sun was not yet up, but the horizon ahead bulged darkly between sea and sky. It was the coast of France.

In that time before dawn the wind dropped. The balloon began to lose height.

The sea rolled closer. They could see the white tips of waves, like the edges of vellum, poking up from the dark water.

"We must get rid of our weight!" exclaimed Fabrice.

Uncomprehending, they stared at him in alarm as he began to empty the lockers in frantic haste. He threw out grappling irons, bags of sand ballast, the leather flotation devices from the rigging, rugs, cushions, technical equipment, even his compass and maps.

There was no sound as they fell rapidly through the air and into the sea, but they saw the splash the ballast made. He seized the half-empty bottle of brandy, reconsidered, and stowed it away again. He tore his cape off and flung it over the side, signaling to the girls to do the same. Their capes spiraled down, looking horribly like falling people. The water was now terrifyingly close.

Then the balloon steadied and began to rise. The sea rolled away beneath them like a spool of crumpled silk. As they caught the onshore wind, their ascent turned into a great arc that took them high over the dark land. The earth whirled away so fast the girls dared not look. Rigid with cold and fear, they shut their eyes, clutching the basket and each other. They did not have the breath to scream.

The balloon was beginning its final descent. When they opened their eyes they saw a wide sandy estuary opening to the sea, the tiny roofs of a port, then fields, cottages, church spires.

"I know that estuary!" Fabrice shouted. "Le Havre, I do believe!" He was using the venting rope to control their descent as best he could, but an airstream was carrying them swiftly down over wooded countryside. They could see the shape of each tree, the pattern of the branches, each leaf.

A yell from Fabrice: "We are falling too fast!" But there was little he could do to stop it. There was no time left to release enough hydrogen for the balloon to become manageable.

In a moment they would crash into the trees.

There was a terrible sound of splintering wood as they hit. They all screamed. The basket jerked so violently they were almost thrown out. But, perhaps because they had jettisoned so much and the basket was lighter, it did not plunge through the wooded canopy but bounced roughly across the tops of the trees.

Fabrice seized passing branches, desperately trying to stop the balloon's progress. They were still wearing their leather gloves, and the girls, gasping and ducking as thin branches whipped across the basket, tried to do the same.

Around them, the wickerwork was breaking up. A whole side was torn away; holes ripped in the floor.

Then at last the balloon stopped. It swayed above the wrecked basket, deflating gently.

"We're jammed between two trees," said Hetta breathlessly. She and Eugénie sat, with thumping hearts, not daring to move in case they unbalanced the basket.

"We must climb down before we break up altogether," said Fabrice urgently. "Mademoiselles, I help you."

It was not easy to climb out of the basket and down the nearest tree while wearing a ball gown. Fabrice did his gallant best to assist, reaching up from the lower branches to guide their feet, still shod in delicate dancing slippers. Then he jumped to the ground with great bravado and offered to lift them down.

"I should be wearing boys' clothes!" Hetta muttered, furious with her trembling legs. She refused to let Fabrice lift her from the lower branches and jumped down by herself, her dress hitched up around her knees, while he averted his eyes discreetly.

At the bottom they staggered about to stretch their stiff limbs, half stunned with shock and shuddering with cold. In the dawn light of the wood, the sun not yet risen, the world was gray and chill: cold dew on the grass and not a bird singing.

Tears fell down Fabrice's plump cheeks as he stared up at *l'Audace*'s bright balloon canopy, hanging in the branches overhead.

"My balloon, destroyed!"

"But, Fabrice, you are alive!" said Eugénie, rubbing her bare shoulders. "And," she added, for he still looked decidedly disconsolate, "you are the very first man to cross the Channel at night!"

He looked thoughtful, then gave a small, pleased smile. *"C'est vrai.* I have indeed beaten Jean-Pierre Blanchard, have I not?"

"And you have saved our lives," added Hetta, her teeth chattering. "You are a hero, Monsieur le Brun! When we return to England I shall ask my uncle to purchase you a new balloon even more magnificent than *l'Audace*!"

For a moment Fabrice swelled with pride. Then he clasped his ankle and groaned.

"What is it?" said Eugénie. "You are hurt?"

"I believe so," he said, puzzled, and sank down against a tree stump. "Yet with all the excitement, I do not feel it until this very moment." He looked white, with grooves about his mouth.

"You must lean on us, monsieur," said Hetta. "We cannot stay here without dying of cold. We shall find a friendly farmer to look after us."

"Cousin," Eugénie said sadly. "I fear you have little idea of the situation in France. Wherever we are now, we shall be regarded with the greatest suspicion."

It was almost a relief to think about nothing save survival. *I have much to teach my cousin. It is my turn at last,* she thought, but with little satisfaction. "There will be *sans-culottes* and soldiers of the National Guard everywhere. We have arrived out of the air, with no papers, nothing. They will think us spies from England!"

"I fear you are right, *ma petite*," whispered Fabrice, and he closed his eyes, as if he had no heroics left. "Look behind you."

The girls turned. In the shadow of the trees not far from where they stood, the barrel of a musket was pointing straight at them.

TWENTY

The person holding the musket was not a soldier but a young peasant girl of about the girls' own age. The weapon trembled dangerously in her hands, and above it her thin, darkly tanned face looked determined and ruthless.

She called out something in a harsh voice, the accent so strong Hetta could not understand what she was saying. But Eugénie, keeping her head, drew herself up and shouted back, "Hold your fire, *s'il vous plaît, citoyenne*, I beseech you! We are friends, not enemies! I am a citizen of France and so is my friend here!" She gestured at Fabrice, who was lying against the tree, one wary eye open. "We have escaped from l'Angleterre to return to our mother country in her hour of need."

The girl's eyes traveled up to the wreckage of *l'Audace*, draped over the tops of the trees. "The others ran from the flying monster." Her lip curled. "But I have seen such a thing before." She lowered the barrel a little.

Eugénie held out a hand. "My name is Eugénie. May I introduce Monsieur le Brun, the famous aeronaut? He has had a bad fall and broken his ankle." Fabrice let out a groan. "And this is my cousin, Hetta, who has the misfortune to be English, yet has the heart of a revolutionary."

Hetta glowered.

"You are not armed?" the girl demanded.

"No, I assure you, *citoyenne*." Eugénie patted her dress to indicate it had no hiding place.

The girl came closer, lips pursed. She stared at the girls' ball dresses, torn but still beautiful, and at Fabrice's colorful flying outfit. Then she stretched out a tentative brown hand and stroked the silk of Hetta's dress. Hetta stood stiffly, eyeing the musket in the girl's other hand.

"*Si jolie*," the girl whispered, sighing. She pinched the material between her fingers. "*Si cher*, so expensive." She whirled on Eugénie. "You are not aristos?"

Eugénie hesitated. "There are no aristocrats in France now. We are all citizens." She shivered. Early sunlight edged the trees, but beneath the leafy canopy the air was cold and the grass wet beneath her feet, soaking her satin shoes and the hem of her dress. "Can you help us? We are in dire trouble. Monsieur le Brun needs to rest his ankle."

Without answering, the girl went over to Fabrice and crouched down beside him, the musket dangerously close to his good leg. He reared away as she felt his ankle with her dirty fingers. "It is not broken," she declared contemptuously, "it is only sprained."

Eugénie looked at her helplessly. The girl had a sulky face and a sour, tight little mouth. She could see no kindness in her expression.

"I will pay you if you give us shelter," she said, then stopped in dismay. "Oh, but I cannot! My purse is in the basket!"

They looked up at the ruined basket, balancing precariously in the treetops. The girl seemed to come to a decision. She put down her musket, her glare challenging them to steal it, then hitched up her skirt and shinned up the tree. Minutes later she was down again, the stocking purse clenched between her teeth. She shoved the purse at Eugénie and seized the musket again.

Eugénie took out one of her two *assignats*. "Is this enough, *citoyenne?*"

The girl's eyes widened. She grabbed it, held it to the light, then pushed it somewhere deep in her ragged skirt. "Come, help him up," she ordered. "We go before you are seen!"

They skirted the wood and crossed a field, Fabrice hopping between the girls and moaning piteously from time to time. The corn had not yet been harvested; in the weedy meadow beyond, a few scrawny cows clustered by the gate bellowing to be milked.

"The men have gone to fight the war," the girl muttered. "We women do what we can."

They discovered that her name was Frenelle. They also found out that they had been blown at least sixty miles inland, not far from the ancient cathedral city of Rouen. Eugénie assumed Frenelle was a farmer's daughter, but instead of a farmhouse, they were taken to a hovel.

On the cobbles outside, a goat stood chewing nettles, watching them malevolently. Three mongrels came running out, snarling, hackles up, but at the girl's command they sat instantly, their eyes on her face. She stroked their heads with surprising gentleness. "In," she said to Eugénie and Hetta, jerking her head at the open door. Hauling Fabrice between them, they staggered through thankfully.

Inside, it was dark and windowless and smelled strongly of animals, hay, and sweat. The dogs curled up in a corner together, eyes gleaming. Their tails thumped the earth floor: The strangers had been accepted. Frenelle put the musket on a high shelf; it seemed she had accepted them, too.

There was a hard wooden settle drawn up to a makeshift table, a couple of three-legged stools, but nowhere to sit comfortably, save a woven mat on the floor before the empty grate. They propped Fabrice against the wall, next to a pile of logs.

Frenelle looked at their ball dresses gleaming in the darkness, envy and wonder in her face. They could see that she had to stop herself from reaching out and touching the silk again.

"Citoyenne Frenelle," said Eugénie, "we are very cold. You may have our dresses if you have anything warmer in exchange."

"My clothes?" said the girl in disbelief. "In return for yours?"

"*Oui*," said Hetta, trying out her French. "And for me, men's clothes would be *très bien*."

Frenelle considered her grudgingly. "You may have my brother, Bernard's, second best."

"Won't he need them?" said Eugénie.

Frenelle looked away, her face pinched. "He will not be back."

Up a ladder there was a screen dividing the space under the roof rafters in half; in each there was a pallet, piled with dirty blankets, and a chest containing pitifully few clothes. They undressed while Frenelle watched every movement suspiciously, as if she could not quite believe they would keep their word. Her face registered awe at their lace-edged chemises.

Once Eugénie had undone the laces, Hetta flung off her stays with relief. Eugénie did not like being watched by Frenelle; she turned her back modestly, fumbling with her clothes. After years of having a lady's maid, she still found it hard to cope with all the fastenings herself.

Another ladder, narrower and more rickety than the first, with several rungs missing, was propped against the far wall. Frenelle pointed at the ragged thatch poking through above their heads.

"In the corner over there is a big gap between the rafters. If anyone comes, climb up and pull the ladder after you."

"Who would come here if all the men have gone?" Hetta whispered to Eugénie.

"Soldiers of the National Guard. They will find *l'Audace* soon and wonder about her passengers. What about Monsieur le Brun?" she asked Frenelle. "He cannot climb ladders!"

Frenelle shrugged; Fabrice was not her problem.

They climbed down into the ground-floor room again in their unfamiliar, pungent-smelling clothes. Eugénie had shuddered as she put the cleaner of the two greasy kerchiefs over her hair and the other around her throat; she could feel the cloth of the waistcoat already prickling through the blouse. The boots they were wearing were ill-fitting and filthy. Fabrice stared at their transformation in horror.

Hetta looked down at herself with satisfaction. The trousers were a little long, but she had tucked them into her boots. Eugénie blushed in shame for her cousin—she hoped that Fabrice would avert his eyes.

"Where is your brother now?" she asked Frenelle.

The girl spat into the empty grate. "Conscription," she said. "The soldiers took every man that passed the crossroads by force. It was our ill fortune to walk that way. Bernard had wanted to join the Chouans—the anti-Republican rebels behind the recent uprising—and avoid conscription. But he left it too late."

"Do you not support the Republic then, *citoyenne?*" said Eugénie. "You need not fear answering. I once hoped for a constitutional monarchy myself."

"I have danced around the Liberty Tree in our village square. I thought myself a revolutionary then. But the Revolution has not brought us freedom. Times are harder than ever." Frenelle kicked away a charred stick. "At least I need not pay the rent. The soldiers took the farmer, too!"

Eugénie went to kneel by Fabrice. "Do you have any wine?" she asked Frenelle, looking at his white face.

"Wine?"

"To restore him." *And us, too*, she thought, as Fabrice opened his eyes hopefully.

"You think I have money for wine? You can drink water." Frenelle nodded at a bucket on the floor. "From the well outside."

Eugénie soaked a rag in well water and bound it around Fabrice's swollen ankle. Then she looked around the dismal room. The battered stockpot contained a few bones; otherwise there was no sign of any food.

She took her stocking purse from beside Fabrice and pulled out the other crumpled *assignat*. "Is there a market near?"

The girl seized the note so eagerly it almost tore. She nodded her head vigorously. "In the village. I'll bring back food. Stay here." She glanced slyly at the stocking purse. "How much longer do you wish to stay?"

Eugénie looked at Fabrice. He had said little so far, only groaned now and then, but at this he opened his eyes and mouthed, "Do not leave me with this terrifying woman!"

"Until our friend is better," said Eugénie firmly.

Frenelle's expression became almost pleasant.

The heat mounted all day; it became sweltering in the hovel. In the afternoon Frenelle came back with a loaf of bitter, black peasants' bread, a hunk of cheese with a moldering rind, and red wine so rough it burned their tongues.

"We have food shortages," she said sulkily, seeing Eugénie's expression. "It was all I could get. Everything is taken to Paris, or to the army."

But the following day she brought fresh milk and eggs from the farm; the next day she trapped two rabbits and made a stew with young carrots and potatoes. From time to time she would eye the stocking purse, but made no attempt to take it from them at gunpoint, as she might have done. She said little during the following days, leaving at dawn and returning during the afternoon, her only companions the half-feral dogs that guarded her closely when they were not hunting for food.

That first day the three of them slept, exhausted after the perils of the previous night and dazed by the heat of the French summer. The two girls shared Bernard's horsehair mattress; it turned out to be well padded and surprisingly comfortable.

But Eugénie woke shortly after dawn the following morning. Sunlight was already shining through the holes in the thatch and patterning the mattress. She could feel it burn where it fell on her bare arm; it was going to be another hot day. Though she was refreshed, she felt weighed down by worry.

What are we to do? she thought. *We have no passports, no official papers, and no way of obtaining them. We are in danger if we stay here and greater danger if we leave.* Hetta's idea of journeying to Paris to save Armand was impossible—laughable. And in the room beneath them was the problem of Fabrice, who needed to rest his ankle.

As she thought of Fabrice, it was Julien's face that came into her mind as it so often did. Julien, looking up at her from the hall at Goosefield so coldly, so scornfully, the last time she had seen him; his dark eyes, once so soft as they gazed into hers, like two hard black coals.

Her heart contracted painfully. Where had he gone? Why so secretly, without a word to anyone? He was surely involved in some dangerous enterprise. Would she ever see him again? Was he even *alive?* At this dreadful thought, she gave a half sob and turned quickly to stifle it in the mattress.

Hetta was awake, her head turned, watching her. She was still flushed with sleep, but her eyes were very bright. "You are thinking of him, aren't you?" she said quietly.

Eugénie nodded. She knew Hetta meant Julien. It seemed pointless to deny it.

"I think of him, too," Hetta whispered.

Feelings of outrage and jealousy bubbled up inside Eugénie, but she bit her tongue. Julien was not a possession to be fought over. They could not quarrel, now of all times.

Hetta looked away. "You know, Cousin, he does not feel for me as he does for you. Yes, he has some regard for me, I grant you, but it is not the same."

"No!" Eugénie burst out in a fierce whisper, unable to control herself. "Indeed, it is not the same! I saw him holding your hand!"

Hetta shifted on the mattress. "It was not what you thought. Sometimes we see what we expect to see. It was me, holding his hand."

"What does it matter, when we are in such a pretty pickle?" Eugénie said wearily. "I must thank you at least for saving me from Guy Deschamps. You were right not to trust him, and so was Julien."

She damped down the feelings of hurt and betrayal that threatened to overwhelm her whenever she dwelled on Guy's treachery. She had been flattered by his attentions—so easily deceived! She was bitterly ashamed of her own behavior.

"I didn't believe Julien when he told me that it was Guy who had tried to kill him in Calais. I was bird-witted to be taken in by such a blackguard. He has poisoned half my youth and poor Armand's also."

"His smile was most beguiling," reflected Hetta. "You had no feelings for him, then?"

"None of any consequence." Even to think back on how she had flirted with him on so many occasions made Eugénie cringe. "If you had not come to my rescue, he would have delivered me up to Raoul Goullet without a qualm. Indeed that was his intention. He was behind the vile scheme to trap me."

Hetta sat up and clasped her hands around her knees. "When

I urged you to accept the bargain I thought it the only way to save your brother."

"It was."

"But it is not! You cannot give up so easily. We are in France now. There must be something we can do."

"Oh, Hetta, you know nothing!" snapped Eugénie, her patience at an end. "I would risk anything to save Armand, but I shan't have the chance! Do you not realize yet how dangerous France is? We are miles both from England and from Paris, with no hope of transport. We have almost no money, no passports, no certificates of residence. It will be a miracle if we survive ourselves!"

She turned away on the mattress, but not before she had seen, with a pang of compunction, how shocked Hetta looked at her words.

Fabrice, bored, as he lay resting his fast-improving ankle, determined that it was his mission to make Frenelle smile. He complimented her on her rabbit stew, but that did not achieve it. He thanked her profusely for permitting them to stay; neither did that. He apologized for his foolishness in falling from the tree so inconveniently; nor did that either.

Then he looked at her with his liquid, long-lashed brown eyes and praised her for her well-trained dogs. Such obedient, fine animals, so devoted to their mistress! Though he had not known her long, how well he understood their feelings.

Frenelle's smile and blush made her look suddenly pretty.

Eugénie, coming in from the well with a bucket of water, looked sourly at them both. She thought of Belle. *How fickle are men!*

They lived those days in a strange limbo, while they waited for Fabrice's ankle to mend.

"Poor Father," Hetta sighed. "He must be dreadfully anxious. If only there were a way of letting him know where we are!"

"And have him more worried still?" said Eugénie.

Hetta would talk wistfully of Thomas and Goosefield, of Jem and the Deal boatmen, of Sir Harry, Aunt Frederica, and Sandicote. She was, she confessed to Eugénie, most abominably homesick for Deal—she, the great adventurer! Sometimes in the night, Eugénie, tossing restlessly herself, would hear her muffled weeping. But she could give Hetta no comfort. She did not know if either of them would ever see Deal again.

They had been with Frenelle a week when the soldiers came.

TWENTY-ONE

They came in the dark hour before dawn. Every night Frenelle had bolted the door, but the knocking was thunderous, as if to break it down. The dogs barked: a frantic, nervous clamor.

Eugénie and Hetta clutched each other, dazed with sleep. Frenelle darted past the screen, pulling on her clothes. "Get into the roof!" she hissed, gesturing at the ladder in the corner, her eyes wide with fear.

"Fabrice . . ." Eugénie began.

"I will take care of him."

They struggled into their clothes, their mouths dry with sleep and shock, their fingers shaking. Already they could hear the soldiers below, shouting at Frenelle to control the dogs.

"You are Frenelle Duprés?"

"*Oui, citoyens.*"

"Your papers!"

"*Un moment, s'il vous plaît.*"

After silencing the dogs, she climbed the ladder again. "What are you doing?" she hissed. "*Vite!* Hurry! And draw the ladder up after you!"

Below them the soldiers were ransacking the room. The trestle table was upturned, the settle, the wooden stools. They even bundled up the mat, as if someone might have lain flat beneath it. The dogs rumbled deep in their throats; each crash made them growl louder.

Eugénie and Hetta heard the furniture being thrown over, the noise of the dogs; below, Frenelle had backed into a corner, the dogs in a protecting semicircle. Under her command, they made no move forward but sat, ears pricked, teeth bared.

"What are you looking for, *citoyens?*"

"A *gaz* balloon has been found nearby." They tossed her papers back at her. A dog lunged forward, eyes rolling, but she called him back sharply. "It carried passengers. Two girls. We have received word that they are spies from England."

The space between the thatch and the roof rafters was narrow, dark, and dusty. After a struggle they managed to pull the ladder up and stow it across the rafters behind them, praying they weren't making too much noise.

They lay flat, pressed to the rafters, hardly daring to breathe. The rafters were spaced so widely apart they each had to lie on a single plank, their arms tight to their sides in case they fell through the thatch. Each time they breathed, they drew in a suffocating mixture of hay, dust, and mites.

The soldiers had climbed up into the room below. Lamplight flickered through the gaps in the thatch; Eugénie and Hetta could see the outline of each other's body, the shine of each other's eyes.

The chest lids banged against the wall. The girls gazed at each other, their eyes wide with fear.

"What are these, *citoyenne?*"

A pause, then Frenelle's ashamed whisper. "I found them, monsieur, in the wood. I wanted to keep them. They are so beautiful."

"Stupid girl! They are evidence that the spies landed nearby. You should have reported it."

"I am sorry, I did not know."

There was a muttered conference between the soldiers, then a louder voice. "We'll take the dresses. Two young women, just as we've been informed. We'll search the countryside. They won't get far."

A chest lid was slammed down. "And if we don't find them, we'll be back!"

The girls lay where they were for an age before they dared move. They found Frenelle washing Fabrice's face. He was covered in soot, the rich blues and golds of his flying costume blotted out by a layer of black dust.

"I stood him in the chimney on his good leg and heaped logs in front of him," said Frenelle. She gave a small smile of triumph; the hand wiping Fabrice's face was tender.

"I thought I would choke to death," said Fabrice pathetically, and sneezed.

"You risked your life for us, Frenelle," said Eugénie. "Why did you do it?"

The smile faded from Frenelle's face and it grew bitter. "I hate the soldiers! They took my brother. Now they have taken his musket. It was all I had left of him."

When Frenelle had disappeared to her farmwork as usual, shadowed by her dogs, they talked urgently, sitting around the trestle table, the door shut and bolted.

"We cannot stay," said Eugénie. "The soldiers will return when they don't find us. Besides, we threaten Frenelle's safety."

"What about Fabrice?" asked Hetta.

They looked at him. He appeared in the full bloom of health, his plump cheeks no longer drawn with pain. Frenelle had rinsed out his costume for him and it hung above the stove, drying rapidly in the heat of the day. She had presented him with Bernard's best suit to wear instead, and he filled it more than admirably.

"I will stay here until I am recovered," he said. "I have my passport. Who would dare arrest Fabrice le Brun? Why, I have made an ascent from Rouen several times. The people will speak for me. They know I am no spy!"

"But you cannot stay here alone with Frenelle!" said Eugénie. "It is most improper!"

His eyes flashed. "You think I would insult her honor? I shall be like a father and protect her."

"With a sprained ankle?"

"At least he is hardly likely to be able to climb the ladder," Hetta pointed out. "Frenelle's honor will be quite safe."

"When you recover," said Eugénie, privately thinking Fabrice was already much recovered, "where will you go?"

"To Paris, *j'espère, ma petite*," said Fabrice carelessly. "I wish to find *ma chère* Belle."

Once, Eugénie would have believed him. Now she was not so sure. She thought of Frenelle's youthful bloom, her need.

"Hetta and I will leave tonight while Frenelle is sleeping," she said. "Do not tell her."

"Listen, *ma petite*. You must return to England. No aristocrat should remain in France now." Fabrice drew his hand across his throat meaningfully. "Go to the coast."

"You mean *walk*?"

He shrugged. "It is not so far. Sixty miles. Do you have money left?"

"A gold guinea."

"For that there will be someone with a little boat willing to chance taking you across the Channel."

"We have no map," said Eugénie. She felt sick with despair at the thought of leaving Armand in France, but she knew Fabrice was right.

He jabbed in the dust of the table with a finger.

"*Alors*, I draw you a map! *Voici* Frenelle and we three. *Voici* the village. *Voici* Rouen and her cathedral sitting on the river." He drew a wriggling line. "La Seine is not far from here, say five miles. This way along the river there is a big bend and Elbeuf; the other way, the estuary out to the sea between the ports of Le Havre and Honfleur. That is the route you must take." He looked at Eugénie. "It is possible you can find a barge to take you down river. *Mais prenez garde*, be careful! Soldiers patrol the locks and gangs rule each stretch of water."

Eugénie nodded, her mouth dry. "We shall walk at night and hide during the day."

Fabrice sighed. "I should be looking after you, but I cannot, injured as I am! I can only wish you *bonne chance*. It is a dangerous enterprise, *mes petites*."

"But we face it together," said Hetta.

Unexpectedly, Eugénie felt Hetta's hand reach out for hers under the table.

Frenelle was fast asleep when they left, curled in a tight self-protective ball on her pallet. Downstairs the whites of the dogs' eyes gleamed in the darkness as they woke, but they did not stir from their corner as Fabrice bade the girls an emotional farewell, tears choking his voice. "*À bientôt, mes petites belles*."

"Thank Frenelle for all she has done for us," whispered Eugénie.

They collected bread, cheese, and well water in a skin bag. Eugénie lit the wick of one of the lanterns by the door and took it up, while Hetta carried the food.

Then they were out in the night.

TWENTY-TWO

The heat of the day had scarcely lessened and the moon, full when they first arrived, was lopsided now.

It was a light, cloudless night, the stars scattered thick above them so dazzlingly bright they had little need of the lantern. The air was still and heavy against their faces and a smell of crushed summer grass rose underfoot as they edged along a meadow. Against the stars they could see the jumbled roofs of the village, sleeping fearfully under curfew. Somewhere a dog barked; an owl floated by on silent white wings, making them both jump.

Eugénie extinguished the lantern; it was safer, and their eyes were adapting to the darkness. They skirted the village in case soldiers were about on night duty. Then they followed a thoroughfare of sorts—a wide dusty track, white with chalk in the moonlight, running straight across flat countryside. On either side hedges and fields stretched away, interrupted by the occasional church spire.

Eugénie's heart was beating disconcertingly hard. What a lunatic scheme this was! They had nothing with them, no identity papers, only the clothes they were wearing and her stocking purse with its one gold guinea. She thought of the long walk to Le Havre. She had never walked such a distance in her life, especially in such uncomfortable boots! She had blisters already. How many days would it take them to walk sixty miles? They did not have enough food and water to last the journey.

"Perhaps a barge would take us to the coast in return for work." She looked doubtfully at Hetta in her boys' clothes. "How strong are you?"

Hetta flexed her arm in the moonlight; even to her it looked puny. "Strong enough."

"You must let me do any talking. Your French is not good enough."

"What?" Hetta began indignantly. She had been secretly pleased with how much of Frenelle's harsh accent she had grown to understand.

"You'll never be taken for a native of France. You must be my witless brother, who speaks little, but is able to work. I shall be"— Eugénie thought desperately, then remembered the women dipping clothes over the sides of the boats between the bridges of the Seine—"a washerwoman."

"You, a washerwoman!" chortled Hetta.

"I am glad you have the spirits to laugh, Cousin!"

They trudged on in sour silence.

Eugénie's feet hurt abominably and her clothes stuck to her. Two hours, at least, seemed to have passed. The dark hedgerows were silent, apart from the scurryings and scratchings of small nocturnal animals.

"How far is it to the river?" asked Hetta, in a small voice.

"Five miles, Fabrice said."

"I believe he was mistaken." They were tired and thirsty from the oppressive heat. They dared not drink more than a few sips of water: It had to last. But only minutes later they saw a great spire far to their left, rising unmistakably against the lightening sky. *Rouen.*

They had reached the river.

*　　*　　*

It was dawn when they left a wooded area and glimpsed in the distance the dull pewter sheen of water. Eugénie signaled silently to Hetta. *Follow me.* It seemed quiet around them, but she dared not take any risks. They crept across the towpath to the bank and crawled beneath the overhanging fronds of a willow.

They were on a vast hairpin bend. The river beneath them was without a ripple, and filling gradually with gray-green light. Further along the bank a line of moored barges waited for the lock to open. From where the girls were hiding, they could see the smoking remains of fires: the burned-out heaps of branches and twigs, the orange sparks before the flame died, and the men sprawled by them on the open ground, snoring and muttering in their sleep. In the shadows beneath the trees the great barge horses champed the dry grass.

"Should we stow away?" whispered Hetta.

Eugénie shook her head. "We'd be discovered. Walking will be safer." She remembered the bargemen she had watched from the bridges of Paris as rough and violent men, and wished she had brought the knife that Frenelle used to skin rabbits. But it had been Frenelle's only knife.

They tried to sleep.

They were woken by raucous voices, speaking in strong accents. They had been discovered.

Men stood in a circle around them. They wore red caps, the *bonnets rouges*, and it was light enough to see the threatening, bearded faces beneath, the glitter of their eyes, the way they stared lasciviously at Eugénie in the clothes that were too tight on her because they had been Frenelle's. A heavy, unwashed, animal smell came from them.

"*Bonjour, citoyens*," said Eugénie, trying to disguise the sound of her aristocrat's voice. During the days they had been with Frenelle, her sharp ear had picked up the local accent and she mimicked it now.

"Who are you?" one of them said suspiciously. "This is barge-men country."

"We want work, my brother and I. He is somewhat lacking here," she tapped her forehead, "and speaks little. But he is strong. As for me, I am a washerwoman by trade."

"Your papers?"

Eugénie drew in a breath. "We have none, *citoyens*. But we are willing to work our passages without pay to Le Havre if you will take us."

The men looked at one another. Someone sniggered. One of them came forward and seized Hetta, dragging her up. He pretended to punch her in the stomach, much to the amusement of the others. "Feeble in limb as well as mind!"

Hetta looked humiliated and furious, but afraid.

"We can't take you without papers," one of them grunted, shaking his greasy head. "We'd be in trouble."

A mutter of agreement went around.

"This side is for Paris anyway, girl," said one of them, more helpful than the others. "You need to cross over by the lock. Watch out for the guards."

Eugénie's heart sank. They could not risk it.

"You won't find anyone to take you on the other side neither, not without papers."

"Wait a minute," said one of them, inspecting Eugénie closely and evidently liking what he saw. "You, girl. I'll take you. You can hide in my sleeping quarters!" The others guffawed, leering at her.

"Thank you, *citoyen*," said Eugénie, with dignity. "But I stay with my brother."

She thought the bargemen would not leave them alone, but they did, after a terrifying time in which she wondered whether the one who had made the offer might not seize her bodily and carry her on board his barge to do with her what he would.

But eventually he, too, lost interest. She had been a moment's amusement and he had paid work to do in difficult times.

"What shall we do?" whispered Hetta, as the horses were harnessed up and the first barges began to leave. The sun was already hot, striking the brown grass between the hanging fronds of the willow.

"We'll start walking at dusk," said Eugénie, with more certainty than she felt.

They had had no sleep the previous night and were both exhausted. They curled up against the trunk in the green shade of the willow. It seemed that they had closed their eyes only a moment before something woke Eugénie: a stealthy footfall on the grass, a flicker of warm air across her face, a shadow falling over her.

She opened her eyes and started back.

TWENTY-THREE

Hetta woke instantly. The girls huddled together as the figure approached against the sunlight.

"I heard you earlier," said the man gruffly. "You'll not find work with that lot without papers. They're too wary of the National Guard. Barge owners have been arrested for employing illegal workers. But I've only two lads to lead the horses and can't afford to take on more for the better part of the journey. I could use you—hide you, too."

As the sunlight fell on him they could see he was a poor creature, wizened and humpbacked, though the eyes above the reddish beard were sharp enough. He examined Hetta in her boys' clothes, his expression fixed in a disconcerting sneer.

"*Merci, citoyen,*" said Eugénie, her voice trembling. "My brother is strong despite appearances. But which way do you go? It is Le Havre we want."

"To Paris. But if you and the boy remain with me, we return to Le Havre after delivering our cargo."

Eugénie thought rapidly. It would be a delay, but at least they would be sure of shelter and the return journey. She took a deep breath; she prayed she could trust him. "It will be a risk for you."

She held out the guinea quickly, watching his face. "But we can pay for our food."

The coin glinted gold in the sunlight. The man's long nose seemed to twitch as if he scented it. He took it in his filthy hand and bit it. "English, eh?" He looked at her thoughtfully, then stuck it in his striped trousers and closed one eye. There was something ghastly in his wink.

"If the soldiers board us, we'll hide you among the grain."

They followed him across a gangplank to a small, dilapidated-looking barge. A brown and white terrier shot out, something dangling either side of its mouth that dropped with a thud to the deck as the little dog barked a warning at the girls.

"Hush, Fidèle!" said the man, adding with pride, "She kills the lot of 'em! We've the cleanest barge this side of Paris."

They stared at what the dog had dropped. Two dead rats, their throats torn out.

His name was Reynard Graunier and his barge, *la Solange*, was as old and dirty as her owner, and as slippery, too, creeping up on heavier barges and taking their place in the lock queue.

Reynard the Fox. The name suited him. After the first meeting he largely ignored them, barking orders at his bargemen or muttering at the lockkeepers beneath his breath while his little bitch scampered about snarling, in echo of her master. But he was as good as his word, and before they went through the first lock at Elbeuf he showed them how to slip down into the hot, musty darkness of the hold, among the sacks of grain.

The hold was packed almost to the deck with cargo, but they managed to wriggle along to the far corner, away from the hatches, and still had enough air to breathe through the cracks in the deck above them. The sacks were even reasonably comfortable to lie on, though the material was coarse and scratched their skin. They lay, wondering if there were any rats trapped down below with them, their hearts thudding, feeling the movement of the barge through the lock. But they were lucky: The soldiers did not board.

The first night the girls decided to brave the stuffy, stinking living quarter, rather than sleep out in the open with the bargemen.

It was a tiny, broiling cabin in the forepeak. Planks fixed to the walls held sleeping pallets; shelves in the corner were stacked with bottles, greasy tin cups and bowls, and rolled charts. An oil lamp was suspended from the ceiling over a table in the center, attracting a dark cloud of moths and mosquitoes. Apart from a few stools and some dirty cloth bags in the corner—presumably holding the bargemen's possessions—that was all it contained.

Hetta was so exhausted from leading the horses all day and struggling to maneuver the tides, she fell asleep at once. Eugénie lay awake, sweating on the other straw pallet, while she listened for rats and cockroaches. *Soon we shall smell as foul as the others.*

It was not an uplifting thought.

Graunier's bargemen, young and strapping, were as silent as their employer. Hetta said nothing either, to stay in her role as the witless brother.

The young men showed her how to fasten the towing harnesses on the horses, how to lead them, how to use the currents to their best advantage, what to do with the horses before they reached a lock. For Hetta, who was used to the horses at Sandicote and had ridden all her life—though sidesaddle, in a ladylike way—it came easily.

But it was curious how gentle the young bargemen were with her. Did they pity her? They even averted their gaze when she went with Eugénie into the undergrowth to use it as a makeshift privy. Perhaps they assumed that she and Eugénie were lovers, not brother and sister at all.

After the first day Eugénie noticed that there were women leading the horses along with the men, so after Amfreville she helped as well, for she had ridden as a child on the family estate at Chauvais. She tucked her gleaming fair hair well under the kerchief and, shuddering, dirtied her face with river mud. She was scarcely paid a second glance. She was thankful, though, that Reynard Graunier did not send her off to market, where she might have encountered soldiers; it seemed he liked to handle money matters himself.

At night he sat on deck guarding his cargo with a musket, a shadowy sinister figure, humpbacked against the stars, his little dog, Fidèle, tucked under his free arm. Sometimes he would turn and stare back at the living quarters where they had sought refuge, and they saw the glitter of his eyes. He never appeared to sleep.

"The gangs—they come at night sometimes," said one of the bargemen, a sturdy, pleasant-faced young man called Michel. "They demand a toll—part of the cargo—before they let you move on."

That night the girls pushed the table in front of the door.

They discovered that it was mostly the major locks that were patrolled by soldiers of the National Guard, so they did not have to hide at each one. There was less river traffic nowadays because of the war, and soldiers were needed elsewhere: They heard stories of turmoil and rebellion in the countryside.

Soon they lost count of the locks *la Solange* had negotiated: each one almost identical, with its crumbling brickwork and slimy walls, and keepers taciturn with the drop in business since the Revolution; while the river narrowed darkly beneath towering cliffs, then broadened again, flowing around the long fingers of islands and past banks hung with willows, yellowing with the coming of autumn. There had been a drought all summer, and the countryside was parched.

If soldiers were policing the lock queues, demanding to see the bargemen's papers, the two girls lifted a hatch and slipped down into the hold, squirming along their tunnel through the sacks to the farthest corner.

They grew braver; and careless.

In the long evenings after *la Solange* was moored, they would sit on the bank with the two bargemen, Michel and Pierre, to eat the meal Reynard cooked on an open fire. Shortly after they joined the barge, Hetta was intrigued to see the two young men get out a pack of dog-eared cards.

"May I play?" she asked eagerly, completely forgetting her role.

They looked astonished, but nodded.

She won that game of Vingt-et-un, and the next, while Eugénie watched apprehensively and the bargemen looked more startled still.

"You are meant to be my bird-witted brother!" hissed Eugénie, when the two bargemen wandered off later to relieve themselves. "They will suspect!"

But they did not appear to do so. The next night they invited Hetta to join them, and grinned when she nodded. It became an evening ritual—the three shadowy figures playing cards in the dying firelight—and Eugénie stopped worrying.

It was growing dark when they reached Andrésy one evening, and the lock was closed. They had taken a couple of mooring posts and Hetta was unbridling the horses on the bank, when she caught sight of two soldiers with muskets boarding a barge farther along, their lantern bobbing in the dusk.

She tossed the towing rope at one of the bargemen and hastened across the plank to the boat, signaling Eugénie to follow her. There was no sign of Reynard Graunier and Fidèle.

They lifted the nearest hatch and scrambled down, their hearts jolting with shock. They wriggled through the passage they made for themselves between the sacks and lay mute in the darkness, waiting.

They did not have to wait long.

Boots sounded above them on the deck.

TWENTY-FOUR

Loud voices rapped questions at the bargemen.

"Your destination?"

"Your cargo?"

"The total number of sacks on board?"

Would the soldiers want to count them? They waited for a hatch to crash back.

"No more than two of you? Where's the bargemaster?"

"Monsieur Graunier will be back shortly, *citoyen*, but I have the boat's papers here," said Michel's voice, submissive. "They are all correct."

"You are both residents of France?"

"See, our passports and certificates, and our master's, and the orders for the grain we are to supply to the warehouses in Paris."

There was a brief silence while the papers were examined.

"We are looking for two girls," snapped one of the soldiers. "One is an English spy, the other an aristocrat, who will lose her head when she is found. One dark, one fair. Good-looking. You could not miss them."

Eugénie and Hetta clutched each other. Eugénie, breathing in wheat dust, thought she might choke.

There was another silence. Were the bargemen shaking their

heads, or were they pointing down at the hold? Had they suspected them all along?

The mutter of voices, impatient, unfriendly. Then the boots clumping away. A moment later they heard the bargemen whistling on the bank, as they continued unbridling the horses.

It was a long time before they dared extricate themselves from their dark hole, and in the end it was the overpowering heat that forced them out. Eugénie, wriggling along the passage, longing to breathe fresh, dust-free air at last, caught her foot in the neck of a sack. She tried to twist free and found she could not; she had to reach back with her hand.

Something rustled beneath her fingers. She felt not grain, but paper.

The bargemen blushed as Eugénie thanked them profusely for not revealing their two stowaways. Reynard returned, but only grunted when they recounted the brush with the soldiers.

Eugénie said nothing about her discovery until later, when she and Hetta were making a last trip behind the trees. "I believe some of those sacks are half filled with paper, Hetta! Graunier is out to cheat the bakers of Paris!"

"It only signifies if he finds we have learned his secret. If he does, I fear he will throw us off."

The thought that they needed to fear Graunier's brooding figure now, as well as discovery by soldiers, was daunting in the extreme.

And when they returned to the barge moments later, Graunier prevented them from boarding.

He raised a lantern as he stood on the plank, a grotesque, misshapen shadow. "A word with you," he said, his sharp fox eyes on their lit faces.

He took Hetta's arm and pinched it. "Where are your muscles, *garçon?*"

Hetta felt herself flush. "This way," he said, leading her by the arm and jerking his head at Eugénie. "We do not want to be overheard."

Hetta, frightened by the strong grip on her arm, glanced back at Eugénie, who put her finger to her lips in warning.

He stopped behind an overgrown thicket and released Hetta. It was dark beyond the lantern light and the dry leaves rustled. The girls gazed at him, struggling not to show their fear.

His voice was a harsh whisper. "Tomorrow we reach Conflans-Sainte-Honorine, the last staging post before Paris. I must take on more hands, for the current is fierce. As soon as we are in sight of it, climb into the hold and remain there. We shall be inspected by soldiers."

It was the most he had ever said to them.

"Thank you, monsieur," Eugénie stammered, taken aback. "We are truly grateful for the warning."

He shook his head, scowling, and said nothing more.

The once busy barge center, Conflans-Sainte-Honorine, sat where the Oise joined the Seine from the north. All the same there was more activity than at the various locks they had passed through, with a queue of barges already waiting and men hanging about, hoping for work pulling boats upstream to Paris.

The girls slipped into the hold. It was late afternoon and the sunlight had turned low and golden. Down below it was stifling, dusty, dark, and hotter than ever.

They crouched on top of the sacks just below the hatch, where a crack of fresh air filtered down. Hours seemed to pass while they waited for the sound of water lapping beneath them to tell them the barge was on the move. They dared not speak to each other, but strained their ears for any ominous sound.

At last it came. The familiar, dread thud of boots overhead.

They dived into their passageway and wriggled along it. Soldiers were evidently inspecting each barge in turn. They heard voices: demanding, brusque. Then, suddenly and shockingly, the hatch farthest from them was flung back and crashed down onto the deck, letting in a shaft of light that reached them in the far corner.

They cowered back against the sacks in their hole, unable to see what was happening. They heard a voice: A soldier was peering down.

"Not a place for an aristo, eh?"

Reynard Graunier's voice, full of contempt. "You think I'd have an aristo on board my barge? Guillotine the lot of 'em, I say!"

The soldier laughed. "She might have climbed on board when you were looking the other way, *citoyen*! Perhaps I should take a look."

"I guard my cargo day and night with grain so scarce," growled Graunier. "The people of France are all thieves these days, desperate to stop the hunger in their bellies. The drought has only made things worse. There are robbers up and down the Seine, out for what they can find."

"Too true," said the soldier. He seemed to lose interest in the hold, for they heard his voice getting fainter. Perhaps he had not cared to climb down into its hot, murky depths on such a humid evening, or perhaps he sensed a kindred spirit in Graunier.

"Is it safe to climb out yet?" Hetta whispered to Eugénie.

"Wait until we've passed the lock."

The hatch was put back in place, plunging them into semi-darkness again. The barge did not move for another age, while they waited; they were perspiring freely and yearned for a drink of water. Then at last they felt it rock and heard the slap of water against the sides. From the movement and the noises they could guess when they were passing through the lock. Then they were on their way again.

Hetta reached the hatch first. She put her hands against it.

"I can't shift it," she said, puzzled.

Eugénie tried, pushing both palms up against the wood.

"*Mon Dieu!* The bolts have been pushed across!"

"Bang on it!" cried Hetta. "It must be a mistake. The soldier did it, perhaps...."

"Or Graunier," said Eugénie. "Deliberately." Her voice trembled. "Perhaps he has realized who we are."

For all the noise they made, no one came.

They heard Fidèle's claws skittering across the deck; she snuffled at the hatch as they yelled up. They heard the tramp of Graunier's feet. Was he deliberately ignoring them?

"If we have to spend the night down here we shall die," said Eugénie. "There's not enough air!"

Panic was rising in her chest. Her hair was wet beneath the kerchief, but now she felt cold. They lay curled beneath the hatch, drawing in any air that came down.

They became aware that the barge had stopped moving. They must have moored somewhere for the night. Somewhere Fidèle was barking, a high-pitched yap.

Feet crossed the deck swiftly and purposefully, stopping overhead.

"Let us out!" Eugénie cried weakly. "*S'il vous plaît*, Monsieur Graunier, let us out!"

Bolts were drawn back. The hatch was raised. A lantern shone in their eyes, dazzling them.

A voice that was not Graunier's at all said, "Eugénie de Boncoeur, if I am not mistaken!"

TWENTY-FIVE

The next moment an arm came down and seized her, lifting her up through the hatch; Hetta followed. They were dizzy on their feet with heat exhaustion, hardly caring now that they had been discovered. They swayed together in the dusk, blinking at the lantern. They could see nothing beyond it except a tall, dark figure.

"Inside the cabin," ordered the voice.

A hand pushed Eugénie in the small of her back. She stumbled through the open door. More lantern light inside, and Graunier and the two bargemen lounging on the bunks, their dirty faces shining in the heat. Fidèle crouched on the floor between her master's legs, ears pricked, eyes bright.

Michel the bargeman, his expression unreadable, helped Eugénie to a stool and Hetta next to her. There was a pitcher of watered wine on the table, and in the silence he poured them each a cupful.

Avoiding Graunier's eyes, they drained the cups. Eugénie found it difficult to focus after so long in the dark. She buried her face in her hands, despairing. She heard the door of the cabin shut, turning it into an airless prison. Sweat trickled down her back.

"Mademoiselle de Boncoeur! I never thought to see you like this!"

She lifted her head. The man who had discovered them was standing before her. "Do you not recognize me, mademoiselle? Indeed, I find it hard to recognize you!"

There was laughter in his voice. She stared at him, puzzled: wildly curling dark hair beneath a battered hat, a sunburned face, the flash of white teeth as he grinned and executed a perfect courtly bow in the narrow space. His voice was strangely cultured when he spoke. Was he not a soldier, then?

"Xavier Saint-Etienne, mademoiselle."

She stared at him, unable to take it in. "Saint-Etienne?"

"I have forfeited my title and estate, of course, but we met once or twice in the old days before the king was guillotined, at the salons of Germaine de Staël and Rosalie de Condorcet."

She gasped. Hetta, understanding that they were not to be arrested after all, gazed at him in bewilderment and relief as he sat down opposite.

Eugénie had a faint memory of Xavier Saint-Etienne's face: She had been so young and nervous at those salons, she had scarcely dared speak to anyone. Saint-Etienne would have seemed very much older, for he was older than Armand. He had not been in Armand's immediate circle, but she knew that his political beliefs had been the same: He was a constitutional monarchist. He had wanted the monarchy to survive in France, but bound by a constitution that would make life fairer for ordinary people.

She saw the gleam of amusement in Saint-Etienne's eyes as he looked at her, and was suddenly very conscious of how altered she was from the immaculate, fashionably dressed child she had been: her hair, limp with sweat, hanging around her shoulders; her mud-stained bodice and skirt. But it was not merely her appearance. She had changed in other ways, too, though a part of her still longed to be pretty and perfumed again.

"Whatever are you doing here, monsieur?"

"I might ask the same of you, mademoiselle!"

She hesitated. Could she trust him? And he had revealed her true identity to Graunier and the bargemen! She looked apprehensively at them across the table. Graunier nodded at her: a curious, but reassuring, gesture. Fidèle jumped up to the bunk and curled herself into a neat ball on his lap. His gnarled hand stroked her smooth coat absently and she closed her eyes in bliss.

"Do not fear, mademoiselle," said Saint-Etienne. "You are among friends. We work closely with the Chouan rebels in this area. Since we first heard word from them about a French aristocrat and an English spy—two young women—who had landed near Rouen by balloon, we set our own spies on the trail. We watch the river." He shrugged, took a draft of his wine. "Unfortunately it is also being watched by government agents at the major locks."

He glanced across at Graunier. "Reynard here is one of us. He has done his best to protect you on the journey since picking you up at Elbeuf."

Eugénie was amazed. "*Merci*, monsieur," she faltered. Astonishingly, Graunier smiled at her, a gap-toothed, hideous smile.

"But how did the government agents know who we were?" she asked Saint-Etienne. "They sent soldiers searching for us, even when we were in hiding near Rouen."

"Does the name Guy Deschamps mean anything to you?" said Saint-Etienne. "The alert was sent from him."

Eugénie glanced at Hetta. "It does indeed, monsieur." So Guy was willing to deliver them up to government agents! But she was beyond feeling the pain of betrayal now.

"You must return to England, mademoiselle," said Saint-Etienne gravely. "You will most certainly be arrested if they find you. Did you truly believe you could travel to France with no identity papers and not be caught? It was foolhardy in the extreme. You have put the lives of Reynard here and his two colleagues—yes, they are not what they appear either—in the greatest danger."

"It was unplanned, monsieur, I do assure you," said Eugénie, with dignity. "We landed in France by accident, with no way of returning to England. We would never have expected such a sacrifice from Monsieur Graunier!"

"It was my fault," interrupted Hetta, speaking for the first time. She had been following the conversation without too much difficulty. How dare he patronize them, this stranger? "I cut the balloon's tethers."

Xavier Saint-Etienne leaped up from his seat and bowed. "Monsieur! I was told there were two girls."

"I am no monsieur," declared Hetta, standing up herself. "My name is Henrietta Coveney. I am a girl despite my clothes."

"Is that so?" Saint-Etienne's eyes ran over her. The corners of his mouth lifted. He was laughing at her! "Indeed, I would never have guessed."

"We knew," said Michel. Pierre, the other bargeman, nudged him.

Hetta sat down again, frowning. "I am no spy either, I do assure you," she said haughtily, "though I am English."

"You will still be arrested if you are caught, Mademoiselle Coveney. You have no passport, no certificate of citizenship in France. And for you, mademoiselle"—Saint-Etienne turned to Eugénie somberly, the laughter gone from his eyes, his face shadowed in the lamplight—"it will be the guillotine."

Eugénie poured herself some more wine; her hand shook.

Hetta noticed that Saint-Etienne's glance lingered on her. Perhaps he had never seen a woman dressed as a man before. She was not to know that he was admiring her eyes, which looked very large and dark in her pale, tense face. He seemed to withdraw his gaze from her with an effort.

"And besides endangering Reynard and the boys," he went on, "you might have jeopardized our mission."

"What is your mission, monsieur?" Eugénie asked tentatively.

The men around the table looked at one another. Saint-Etienne hesitated. "I thought you might have guessed since you have lain on it these past few hours! In those sacks of grain are forged *assignats* bound for Paris. They come from Britain. We circulate them through the gaming houses of the Palais Royal. It is our small effort to destabilize the economy and thus, the Republican government."

"But that sounds most important!" Eugénie lifted her head. "We shall endanger your mission no longer, monsieur. We'll leave at daybreak tomorrow, my cousin and I."

"Certainly not!" said Saint-Etienne curtly. "Why, Julien de Fortin would never forgive me if I allowed it!"

Eugénie's heart lurched. "*Julien?* You know Julien de Fortin?"

"How do you think we found you? It was Julien who recognized your descriptions and set us on your trail after you landed at Rouen. We thought it most likely that you would head for the river eventually, either to return to the coast or to journey to Paris."

"So Julien is in France?" breathed Eugénie. "Where? Please tell me, monsieur!"

"He is in Paris, in hiding. Unfortunately, Deschamps traced his movements from Deal to France. Julien has been working on this mission, along with an English gentleman named Jem Cuttle, who is an agent of William Pitt, I do believe."

"Jem!" exclaimed Hetta. "Is he in Paris also?"

Saint-Etienne shook his head. "He takes delivery of the *assignats* on the French coast." He looked at them through bright, narrowed eyes. "For your own safety, it is best you know as little as possible about what we are doing. But the reason I'm here tonight is that we have had warning that all goods coming into the city are being searched for counterfeit.

"Reynard and I have talked. Our plan is to unload at a private dock during the night before traveling on, and that is when you must leave the barge secretly. We'll arrange your return journey to Le Havre, but it must be on a different barge to avoid any risk."

He stretched out his long legs while they gazed at him anxiously. He appeared remarkably relaxed. "You will have to remain in Paris a couple of nights, no more."

Paris! thought Eugénie. At least she would be in the same city as Julien. And there might be a chance to visit Armand! Glancing at Saint-Etienne's firm chin, she thought it wisest not to mention this.

"While you are there, you should not venture out," he said, as if reading her thoughts. "Have you a friend who might hide you?"

Eugénie had Belle's address, but hesitated to endanger her. Manon, who had once been her maid, lived too far away, near Montparnasse, outside the walls of the city. Of the aristocracy she had once known, only Victoire was left; the others were in hiding themselves, or had fled. Victoire d'Abreville, who had turned Republican in order to remain in Paris. How good it would be to see a friendly face, to live in luxury for a day or two!

She nodded meekly.

"Good. I will pass the direction on to Julien and arrange for him to meet with you soon after you arrive. Then at least you will have a man to protect you."

"You think we need a man for protection, monsieur?" said Hetta levelly. Her eyes locked with Saint-Etienne's. "Together my cousin and I are as stalwart as any male."

"That I believe, mademoiselle."

"But we do need Julien, Hetta!" cried Eugénie.

Saint-Etienne cleared his throat. "Tomorrow, when we take on extra hands to haul us to Paris against the tides, this is what you must do, mesdemoiselles."

Eugénie shuddered. "Must we hide in the hold again?"

"You will remain in here, in the living quarters during the day. Outside, Reynard will guard you with his musket. If questioned, he will say that one of his bargemen has the sweating sickness and is being tended by his sister inside. It should be enough to frighten the soldiers away. Besides, they are still looking for two girls."

He bent down and pulled a bundle from beneath one of the bunks. Fidèle jumped down from Graunier's lap to investigate, her little tail wagging furiously.

"To cross Paris you will need passports with new identities, certificates of citizenship, and different clothes. I have brought what you need."

The girls unfolded their passports. The details of hair and eye color were correct, due to Julien no doubt. Only the names were different. Eugénie read her new name: "Madeleine Boileau."

"Listen carefully," said Xavier Saint-Etienne. "You must learn your stories well for the checkpoints. It is safest at present to be *bourgeois*, since most of the government come from that class. You, Mademoiselle Eugénie, will be a respectable young middle-class wife, a good Republican, recently married, with a husband away at the war; you, Mademoiselle Coveney, will be her maid, since it is best you speak as little as possible."

Clean clothes at last! thought Eugénie. For her there was a *robe économique* in striped satin, with a linen fichu and a tricolor cockade for her linen headdress; for Hetta, a jacket and skirt in printed cotton, with a matching fichu and a simple kerchief to cover her hair. But the clothes looked as if they had been worn before. It seemed wisest not to dwell on the fact that they might well have belonged to victims of the guillotine.

"I hope they'll fit," said Saint-Etienne. "Julien had to guess your measurements from the clothes at our disposal. I'm not convinced he is much of a ladies' man!"

Eugénie ignored the grin that accompanied those words. "And how do you propose we leave the barge without being seen, monsieur?" she said repressively.

In answer he ducked down again and pulled out two sacks. The girls stared at them, while Fidèle sniffed them equally dubiously.

"At dusk we shall pull up at a private quay in the industrial outskirts to unload. All the sacks will be brought up from the hold. You, meanwhile, will have hidden—each of you—in one of these empty sacks."

They looked at each other in horror. How would they breathe? In the heat it would be stifling.

"It is the only way you will escape arrest, and even that is not certain," said Saint-Etienne, in a manner that brooked no argument. "Reynard here will alert you when the time comes."

Reynard nodded, his eyes shifting from Eugénie to Hetta. It was still a crafty, foxy face, but now they knew he was on their side it was somewhat less unsettling.

Saint-Etienne continued. "Once you are in the sacks, you will be carried"—the bargemen winked at each other—"to a cart, then taken to a warehouse, where you will change into these clothes. I shall be waiting, with a cab and a hackney driver whom we've recruited. I will have to leave you then, for we must not be seen together. He'll take you where you wish to go." He drained the last dregs of his wine. "That is all we can do to help you until you meet up with Julien."

He made his farewells, kissing Hetta's dirty hand gallantly. "Until tomorrow night, mademoiselle."

Then he led Eugénie out on deck. Night had fallen, but it was no cooler; a hot breeze blew against her face. "I know your brother's situation, mademoiselle," he said quietly. "It is indeed perilous. You may not have heard that he has been transferred to La Conciergerie."

Eugénie shook her head dumbly.

"Suspects go there before they are tried. I fear most go to the guillotine thereafter. My spies tell me there's evidence against him and the trial won't go well."

He pressed her hand in sympathy, then swung himself lightly over the side. She saw him run to where his white horse was tethered, ghostlike, among the trees.

The girls were both too apprehensive about the next day to sleep.

Eugénie's thoughts darted confusedly between Armand and Julien and the dangers the next day would bring. "I wonder if Xavier Saint-Etienne's scheme will work," she whispered, as she heard Hetta turn restlessly on the other bunk.

"Since there is no other way of leaving this boat, we must trust him, I suppose." Her cousin's tone suggested she was most reluctant to do so.

"I saw him looking at you. He appeared much struck."

"He is a little too full of himself for my liking. I do not care for his bold looks."

"Julien is alive and in Paris!" Eugénie whispered to herself yet again. She became aware that Hetta was saying something.

"Eugénie, I must talk to you. I have tried to tell you this before."

"What, Cousin?"

"When Julien left that evening in Deal, he had already told my father and me that he was going on a mission in France. He did not say what it was, but begged me not to tell you."

"He told you, and not me!" New hurt and anger filled her.

"Don't be vexed. He didn't wish to upset you."

"He must think me a weak, foolish creature!"

"No, indeed he does not! But I was agitated at the thought of him going into danger. At the last moment I clutched his hand, begged him not to go. And then you came out into the hall."

It made little difference now. But Eugénie was caught by the sadness in Hetta's voice.

"I do believe you love him, too."

"It was nothing—a *tendresse*. Now forgotten."

Eugénie did not believe her.

TWENTY-SIX

Late that evening a cart jolted slowly over the cobbles toward a shadowy warehouse, its wheels muffled by sacking. There was no one about. This was not the usual time for unloading, and this particular quay, inconveniently far from the center of Paris, was little used. The two bargemen pulling the cart carried no lantern, though one gleamed in the warehouse when they eased open the huge doors.

"Hurry!" hissed the young man waiting inside.

"Turn your back, monsieur!" ordered Eugénie.

Saint-Etienne did so obediently, as the girls changed into their clothes. "How did you fare inside the sack, Mademoiselle de Boncoeur?"

"I vow I am bruised in every limb from the jolting of that cart!" declared Eugénie. She felt humiliated, but at least she was safe. For the time being. "And I can still taste the sacking!"

"And you, Mademoiselle Coveney?"

"Well enough," said Hetta airily, suspecting his solicitous tone. Not for anything would she let Xavier Saint-Etienne know that she had been terrified of discovery—of violent hands wrenching apart the sacks to discover them, of shouts of triumph in a dialect she could not understand. Her fingers quivered as she did up the buttons on her jacket. She glanced across at Eugénie's white face and saw how she, too, fumbled as she arranged her fichu.

"You will need money, mesdemoiselles," said Saint-Etienne. He gave them a sheaf of *assignats* each, which they tucked into their bodices.

"Counterfeit, I presume, monsieur?" said Eugénie, and tried to smile as he nodded. "Then we, too, are playing our small part in their distribution!"

Saint-Etienne looked them over and beckoned. "Come." He picked up the lantern and pushed open one of the doors a crack. "Keep silent."

"Does he expect us to chatter like housewives on such an occasion?" Hetta whispered to Eugénie as they followed him into the twilight. Her indignation made her feel a good deal better.

A hackney cab was waiting in the dusty lane behind the warehouse, its hanging lanterns unlit. Once the carriage had belonged to an aristocrat; now its crest was painted out. The driver, a stooped, elderly man, his face hidden, stood by the horses' heads.

"Give him your direction, Mademoiselle de Boncoeur," said Saint-Etienne in a low voice. "He goes under the name of Marcel."

She whispered the address to the shadowed face.

Saint-Etienne took both their hands. His fingers felt warm and confident around Hetta's clammy palm. "Our paths will cross again in Paris, mesdemoiselles, *bien sûr*. Our secret world is small." His eyes glinted in the twilight, his gaze lingering on Hetta. "*Au revoir*, until we meet again."

They passed through one checkpoint, then another. They were asked why they had left Paris.

Eugénie thought quickly. "Visiting my poor mother-in-law at

Fontainebleau. She longs for her son to return from the war—as I do."

"We will check our departures lists," said the soldier on duty. "It will be the worse for you if you are lying."

"Why should I lie, *citoyen?*" asked Eugénie, in outraged tones. "Am I now not the only one left in my family to look after my mother-in-law? Everyone has been taken off to fight—all my brothers, all my husband's brothers, those of my friends...." She sighed tragically and put a handkerchief to her eyes. "It is hard for a young girl to comfort an old woman, when she suffers herself."

"All right, Citoyenne Boileau, you may pass," said the soldier wearily. "*Vive la République.*"

He thrust the certificates of citizenship back through the window and the carriage clattered on over the *pavé*. Eugénie's heart was thumping. "Sit back," she warned Hetta, pulling her against the leather seat.

Noisy groups of *sans-culottes* in their striped trousers were still thronging the narrow streets beneath the overhanging houses. The street lanterns had been lit, and shone on greasy faces flushed with triumph and intoxication beneath the *bonnets rouges*. The girls dared not open the windows, and the heat was overpowering.

Shouts and curses echoed after them; thuds, as clods of hard mud were thrown at the carriage; a bottle missed the back window and smashed behind them. They clung together as the carriage swerved down a side street and into a quieter square.

Hetta peered out, curiosity overcoming her fear. So this was Paris, the great city she had longed to visit!

After the low houses of Deal, she had a sense of claustrophobia. On either side they were hemmed in by many-storied buildings, with rows of tiny windows rising up, even in the gray slate roofs, which were tall and pointed like witches' hats. There was dust and filth everywhere, and the smell of something rank constantly in her nostrils, without a fresh sea wind to blow it away.

The citizens of the square were behaving as if there were no revolution at all, Hetta thought, walking about on the parched grass and stopping to greet each other. But they all wore tricolor cockades and their faces were gaunt, their eyes watchful, as if an evening chat with a neighbor might have a more sinister purpose.

Liberty, equality, fraternity! Where were those high ideals now, the principles of brotherhood and freedom she had thrilled to through her reading?

In the nine months she had been away, Eugénie sensed Paris had changed. The ancient city now looked under siege, embattled; its old houses more decrepit than ever, its people sullen and suspicious. Hope had gone—the excitement of the new Republic—and had been replaced by a bitter undercurrent of anger. The Revolution had not brought what the people wanted: food in their bellies, fair wages.

She could see where the anger had manifested itself: in the dark corpses hanging from the lantern supports, putrifying in the heat. *"Les aristos à la lanterne!"* The old phrase rang in her memory.

But these were not aristocrats. These bloated bodies had once been ordinary working Parisians; she could tell by the ragged clothes they wore. The people of Paris were turning on themselves. "Don't look, Cousin!" she said.

Hetta turned her eyes away in shock. In the lamplight, flies were buzzing around the swollen faces.

As the carriage passed La Place de la Révolution, deserted now after the day's executions, she saw the outline of the scaffold against the night sky, and above it a shape she knew to be the guillotine. The stench of spilled blood seemed to fill the carriage and, looking down, Hetta saw the cobbles were clotted black.

* * *

It took them almost two hours to cross Paris. They saw few other carriages: Most had been requisitioned for the war. Those they passed had their blinds drawn down.

Night fell. The moon and stars were not visible from the narrow streets, but the air seemed to take on a thicker, hotter darkness. The driver stopped in La Place des Vosges, a dimly lit square of once fine houses of brick and stone near the Marais.

Eugénie leaned forward and tapped on the partition. "Can you take us no nearer, Monsieur Marcel?"

"The streets around here are blocked with rubbish, mademoiselle." He pulled the carriage step out and helped them down. Eugénie's legs were weak; for a moment she thought she might faint from heat, hunger, and fear.

Hetta gave her an apprehensive look. "Is it safe to walk alone here at night?" She felt out of her depth, a stranger in a strange city.

Eugénie pulled herself together. "Keep close to me, as if you were my maid. If we are stopped, I shall say our cab threw a wheel. Whatever you do, keep walking."

"Take my lantern," said Marcel, lighting the wick. "I would escort you, mesdemoiselles, but I fear I will lose my carriage to robbers if I leave it here unguarded in the dark."

Eugénie hesitated. "Would it be possible, monsieur, for you to take me to La Conciergerie tomorrow?" The walk on foot could be dangerous and she dared not risk it.

She heard Hetta's surprised intake of breath.

He sounded doubtful. "Should you not remain in hiding, mademoiselle? I am certain that Monsieur Saint-Etienne would not approve."

"I daresay not, monsieur, but my poor brother is a prisoner there." She looked at him imploringly in the lantern light. "You must understand that I cannot be in Paris without at least seeing where he is held!"

Few men could resist Eugénie de Boncoeur's pleading eyes. He bowed his head. "Very well, mademoiselle. I shall return at noon, unless I am prevented from doing so." The words hid a multitude of meaning. Eugénie knew he had risked much to bring them here.

The carriage rattled away. "You'll not go alone, Eugénie!" Hetta whispered into the silence. "I shall go with you!"

"If anything should happen..."

"Then it is my responsibility, not yours. I will not have Saint-Etienne dictate what I can and cannot do. A carriage ride will not be dangerous, surely?"

But Hetta's voice trailed away as if subdued by the surrounding presence of the night. They were alone, dark gaps yawning where the streets of the Marais opened before them.

Which one to choose? Eugénie had been here—how long ago it seemed!—for Victoire's last party in the period before the execution of the king. But now it was as if she had never known it.

As the old coachman had said, the streets were filled with rubble. The beautiful houses were for the most part boarded up, and there were gaps where boards had been stolen for firewood. There were no people about, no torches burning either side of the gates, no footmen waiting on the steps of the entrances. As they hurried along, they glimpsed great front doors hanging open on dark interiors. Mice scuttled from the lantern light. Something larger moved under a pile of broken masonry and there was the gleam of tiny red eyes.

"Pick up your skirts," hissed Eugénie, as they clung to each other in fright. "We're almost there!"

She had remembered the way.

TWENTY-SEVEN

The grand facade of Victoire's house was as it had always been: imposing, elegant, the pale stone shining. But the wrought-iron gates had been ripped from their hinges to be melted down for bullets, and the courtyard was in darkness.

"I am certain that Victoire is still here," whispered Eugénie, as they hesitated in the shadow beneath the entrance arch. "She would never leave her home to emigrate. She left it too late and would have been too frightened. Besides, she gave up her title and insisted to all that she was a Republican."

But she looked again at the shuttered windows where no candlelight flickered. A huge pile of rubbish—mattresses, broken furniture, smashed china, mud, and horse dung—was heaped darkly against the walls. "Her servants must have left, though. She would never countenance such filth against her windows."

"Will she still be prepared to shelter us?" Hetta said doubtfully.

And as soon as they crept up the steps to the front doors, they realized that Victoire was no longer living there, with or without servants. The great doors were still hanging on their hinges, but the locks had been torn away.

"Do you have the courage to go in?" Eugénie whispered.

But she felt her own seep away. She had hoped for so much: a decent supper after the frugal food they had eaten on the journey; a hip bath of hot water, brought by a maid; a soft featherbed; a beautiful dress to wear for a while.

"Do you think anyone's left inside?" Hetta whispered back.

They listened, but it was eerily silent. They might have been the only inhabitants left in a ruined city.

Eugénie pushed against the broken wood of one of the doors. It was a mistake: With a tremendous clatter that shattered the silence of the night, it fell inward. Trembling, they listened again, expecting shouts, running feet, *sans-culottes* to surround them, but no one came.

At their feet the lantern glimmered in the wood dust. Eugénie picked it up. "Come, Cousin."

They stepped sideways around the splintered door. There was a dark stain inside the threshold, where something had spilled on the marble floor and dried. As Eugénie held up the lantern, the vast hall filled with soft yellow light; but there was darkness at the top of the wide curving staircase. The air felt chill after the heat of the night.

She went across to the great fireplace. It was filled with unburned logs, lying on thick ash and dust. Dust lay, too, on the chairs that had been drawn up to the hearth. They had not been worth stealing, but whatever else had been there had gone. They stood in an empty, echoing space.

"Poor Victoire! She had so much furniture, so many valuable paintings," Eugénie said, staring around in dismay. "All looted by the mob. She must have emigrated after all. Let's hope she is safe." She felt cold suddenly and rubbed her arms where gooseflesh had sprung.

"What should we do?" whispered Hetta. "Stay here?" The prospect was not inviting.

"Why whisper? There's no one here." Eugénie sank down in one of the chairs; dust puffed up around her. "We daren't venture out again at this hour with nowhere to go, and we have given this direction to Saint-Etienne for Julien."

Hetta looked at the leaping shadows they made in the lantern light, thin ghostly figures expanding and contracting up the walls as they moved. Eugénie rose to her feet and pressed Hetta's hand. "If the mob has been here already, they'll not return. Let's see what they've left us."

They started with Victoire's boudoir, the lantern Eugénie carried casting a fragile circle of yellow light that made the shadows darker.

The four-poster bed had been left—presumably because it was too large and heavy to carry—though not much else. In a ruined bedchamber, its thread-work pillowcases, lace-edged sheets, and vast satin quilt were untouched beneath the dark red and gold tester, the pillows still plumped up, as if by the maid that very morning.

The powder room contained rows of wigs on stands. The blank papier-mâché faces stared at them as they entered, disconcertingly lifelike. They hurried out and Eugénie went to investigate a heavy wardrobe, left intact. There were still dresses hanging within it: light silk dresses, heavier winter costumes. As she opened the door, they rustled gently in the draft, as if moved by a ghostly hand.

They avoided the salon and the drawing room, and ventured up farther, to more bedchambers, the decorations ripped from the walls, the furniture taken or destroyed. At last they came to the servants' floors up in the roof: a maze of small, hot rooms with bare wooden floors.

Here nothing had been touched: trundle beds; pottery jugs and bowls for washing, some still containing scummy water; cupboards with uniforms for the male servants—livery jackets, white breeches; others full of maids' outfits. Personal possessions had been left: a prayer book, a flagon of wine half drunk, an embroidered cushion, a shawl cast carelessly down, a hairbrush tangled with long brown hair, rumpled bed linen. A smell of sweating, overworked bodies still lingered.

"They must have all run away," said Eugénie. "Unless they were arrested for working for an aristocrat." They stared at each other in the yellow light, troubled.

"Shall we sleep up here?" said Hetta. "It's hot, but it feels safer than Victoire's boudoir."

They chose the smallest room. Being so cramped, it felt more secure than the others, though they would have to share the bed, rumpled and unsavory as it was. The only piece of furniture was a wooden chest.

Curious, Hetta lifted the lid and peered in. A powdery white smoke rose up, making her sneeze. Three wool wigs sat in a row on the bottom, waiting for a footman who would never return. Her sharp eyes saw something sticking out from under one of them and she pulled it out. It was a battered leather case, heavy in her hand.

Eugénie stared. "A gun case." Their eyes met.

Hetta laid the case on the bed and flicked back the brass clasps. Lying in a hollow on the padded silk inside was an old screw-barreled pistol. Eugénie picked it up gingerly and weighed it in her hand.

"My groom at Chauvais taught me to shoot," she said reflectively.

"Careful, Cousin," said Hetta.

"It's not loaded. See? The barrel is empty and there's no powder and shot."

"No one is to know that," said Hetta.

They took the pistol with them and sought out the kitchen in the basement, desperate to find something to eat. Earlier their fear had driven away their appetites, but now hunger returned to gnaw at them.

All the cooking utensils and saucepans had been taken to be melted down for ammunition. There were a couple of half-burned candles in old wine bottles, and more in a drawer, passed over by the looters. They lit them all, until the kitchen was ablaze with light.

The scrubbed wooden table was still there, and a few chairs too worthless to steal. The range hung open, the wood gone. A mouse disappeared behind it at their approach. A large black cockroach moved rapidly up the wall away from the light.

"Let's try the larder," said Eugénie, with an optimism she did not feel.

As she opened the baize door, an overpowering stench of decay met them. They both choked and hung back as the air turned black and began to buzz; the light from the lantern had woken swarms of flies.

Little had been left, but enough for the flies. A half-eaten lamb joint turned green, a rotting pigeon that had never been plucked, its eye sunk into its head; pheasants, too, hanging limp and shriveled from the ceiling, still with their long brown and black tail feathers.

"Wait," said Eugénie. She darted in, covering her eyes and mouth with her hands, and fetched out a glass jar, then a large earthenware container. They slammed the door shut. A few escaped flies buzzed angrily past them into the kitchen.

Eugénie set down her finds on the table. The glass jar was almost full of a dark red confiture, perhaps strawberry jam; they could scrape the flaky white mold from the surface with a spoon. She took the lid off the earthenware container and saw thin dry biscuits.

They dipped the biscuits into the jam, eating hungrily with

their fingers, for there were no knives, no plates, but when Eugénie tried the pump at the sink, cold water gushed out, splashing her. "We can drink—and wash!"

They said little to each other: too exhausted, too intent on cramming in as much as possible, sating themselves with sweetness. Then Hetta raised her head.

"What's that noise?" she whispered, her eyes huge in her wan face.

Eugénie stopped chewing and listened. In the otherwise complete silence, she heard boots clip the marble above them.

They were not alone anymore. Someone was up there, in the hall.

TWENTY-EIGHT

They froze, seized with fear, unsure what to do. Silently, Eugénie reached for the pistol. There was nowhere to hide except under the table, where they would most certainly be seen. And now it was too late anyway, for the footsteps were coming along the basement passage. The line of light under the kitchen door would give them away; it was too late to do anything about it.

With painfully beating hearts, they sat and waited, clutching the edge of the table, as if its solidity might save them.

The light had been seen. The steps halted for a moment, then continued, faster. The door was pushed open violently, swinging back against the wall. They saw the giant shadow of a raised stick.

A young man entered in a rush. He wore a black coat; a hat hid most of his face. He stopped at the sight of the pistol, then started forward. He was haggard and pale and his eyes burned beneath the brim of his hat.

"*Julien!*" whispered Eugénie. Her heart seemed to somersault; she stood up shakily, and so did Hetta. The pistol crashed to the table.

For a long moment he gazed at them, and in the wonder of

reunion they gazed back, as if under a spell. Then he came over, dropping his stick, and seized their hands as if they were about to start dancing.

"Eugénie! Hetta!" Then more formally, "Mesdemoiselles!" A huge smile lit his face. Then he let their hands go, as if taken aback by his display of emotion. "You are safe! Thank God!"

The girls sank down on their chairs. Julien pulled another up and sat down. Two white faces gazed at him, lips smeared with jam.

Eugénie's smile was stiff and unused. She looked at his face and could not judge what he felt for her, only that he seemed happy to see them both.

His expression grew serious. "What possessed you to come to France? Did you not realize it was sheer madness?"

Eugénie opened her mouth.

"It was my fault we came in the first place," Hetta interrupted hastily. "I cut the tethering strings on Fabrice le Brun's balloon. I'd not foreseen that we should cross the Channel!"

"Fabrice le Brun," said Julien dryly. "I seem to remember he is often present at moments of drama. We traced him through villagers' reports to a farm cottage. But you had already left. It was your good fortune that Reynard Graunier happened to be in that part of the Seine and picked you up quickly. Two girls without money or identity papers, one a French aristocrat! The whole enterprise could not have been more dangerous. And Graunier had to spend time while on a mission, risking his own safety and his colleagues' to shelter you!"

"We had no notion of the trouble we'd cause," said Eugénie contritely. She could not bear him to think ill of her.

"At least you are safe."

Hetta wrung her hands. "You must understand that in the first place it was because we had to escape Guy Deschamps!"

He did not look at Eugénie. "You must tell me more of that scoundrel Deschamps in due course." His face cleared. "But how very well your French has improved, Mademoiselle Hetta!"

She blushed with pleasure. They were talking in French and she had found no difficulty understanding it. "All those months of your lessons in Deal must have stood me in good stead, monsieur!"

Julien returned her smile. Then he looked down at his hands.

"But meanwhile, you could not have arrived at a worse time. Paris is more dangerous than it has ever been. Robespierre is paranoid about the enemy within, scouring the country for traitors, encouraging people to report on one another. The Terror has been officially declared by the Convention. Soon there will be a time of terrible mass execution."

He took off his hat and ran his fingers through his tousled dark hair.

"We are trying to arrange your journey back to the coast and thence to England. You cannot remain in Paris." He stared around, frowning. "The Marais is a derelict area these days. It could not be more unsuitable."

"I'd hoped Victoire would still be here," said Eugénie, in a small voice. "But we have a pistol."

He looked at it. "Loaded?"

She shook her head reluctantly.

"Much use will it be." He sighed and pulled a package from his pocket. "I have brought you bread and cheese. It will not make a feast, I fear."

"We shall keep it for tomorrow," said Eugénie gratefully. She looked down at the table, hardly daring to ask the question for fear of the answer. "Have you heard how Armand is faring?"

"I know you will desire to see him, mademoiselle, but you must not. We have devised your new identities carefully. You will give yourself away if you visit him."

Tired tears rose in Eugénie's eyes. Julien looked away, biting his lip. "Have you seen Armand yourself since you've been in Paris?" she asked in a faltering voice.

Taken aback, he said patiently, "I don't believe you understand, mademoiselle. I cannot visit him: I am forced to hide during the day. Robespierre's spies know I am in Paris."

Deschamps had tracked him to Paris. Julien had had to change his nightly refuge twice already. A couple of times he had been careless, had been inches away from a knife in his back, wielded by those long white fingers.

He misread Eugénie's look of apprehension. "Don't fear for yourself and Mademoiselle Coveney. There are few left in the city who will recognize you, dressed as you are. But take no risks. Stay inside."

Eugénie's voice trembled. "I care nothing for myself—but Armand? Can you not devise a scheme to rescue him?"

He sighed. "Escape is impossible from that prison, Eugénie."

She stared at him with a stricken look, unable to speak. A tear spilled down her cheek. An awkward silence fell while he gazed around the kitchen with its dusty shelves and empty stove, looking anywhere but at her. His eyes met Hetta's for a moment. Then, as if he could bear the silence no longer, he leaped to his feet, picking up a candle in one hand, his stick in the other.

"I shall discover what wine Victoire kept in her cellar! You look as if you need a little restorative, mesdemoiselles. Perhaps the mob have left us a bottle to celebrate our reunion!"

He should not stay long, Julien thought, much as he longed to do so. He had a secret meeting with Saint-Etienne and the others that he could not miss.

He would make certain first that the girls were as safe as they could be for the night, and return tomorrow. It was unlikely that the *sans-culottes* would come back a second time: they had stripped the Marais down to its very stone.

She is here, and safe!

But doubt still lingered in his mind. *Does she feel as I do? She has never told me.*

But perhaps he'd never had the courage to ask. He knew his shyness and reserve had made him an emotional coward, and he cursed himself for it. Before she left for the coast, he would let her know how his heart felt.

The bolts on the cellar door had been shot back, top and bottom. Someone had been here before him. He went cautiously down the stone steps, gripping his knobbly Hercules stick, but the little rooms before him were all empty in the darkness. Most of the wine had been looted, but he found a missed bottle. He turned, and a fat rat slithered away behind a pile of barrels.

Something caught his eye and he bent down, holding the candle closer. It was a second before he took in what he was seeing and then he felt a sickening horror.

The remains of Victoire d'Abreville.

But he was not to know that. He saw the bones of a hand and arm outstretched that might have belonged to anyone, since all the bracelets and rings had been wrenched off. Beyond was something that might once have been a shoulder. The remainder was mercifully hidden behind the barrel. There was no stench, for the rats had picked the carcass clean.

He could not tell the girls that their refuge was a tomb.

He bolted the door properly, thankful that the top bolt was out of the girls' reach, though it was unlikely they would descend into a dark cellar. Then he made his way back to the kitchen.

Hetta Coveney had fallen asleep where she sat, against the back of the hard chair. Eugénie, however, was gazing at him with her enormous blue eyes, while she finished chewing her last mouthful of biscuit and jam. She blurted out in a little voice, "Julien, I was very foolish..."

He set the bottle on the table and sat down. "Do not dwell on it," he said soothingly in a low voice, for she appeared in some distress. "Hetta..."

"Hetta!" she interrupted bitterly.

"Hush," he whispered, gesturing at the sleeping girl. "Let her sleep."

Eugénie subsided, but an expression crossed her face he could not read.

"It was not your fault, Eugénie," he said softly. "Indeed, it sounds as if it was an accident on Mademoiselle Coveney's part." He smiled lopsidedly. "She was not to know the habit of balloons to fly on the prevailing wind! I'm only thankful you both survived." Looking at Eugénie's distraught face, he did his utmost to sound comforting. "Anyway, I daresay things can be mended. Your unexpected arrival has not jeopardized the mission, and we shall get you safely home to Deal somehow."

She sighed. *She is worried about Armand*, he thought. He hesitated, and her eyes filled with tears again. She reached across the table to him, her hand open as if in supplication.

"Julien...Julien, before my cousin wakes...That is, she will wake soon, and there is so little time for me to talk to you..."

"About Armand?"

"Well, yes, but no, not..." She frowned and shook her head, tangling her words.

"Eugénie, I wish I could be more positive...."

"That is it!" she exclaimed, "that is what I wish, also—that you might be more positive! Oh, Julien..."

He was bewildered by the passion in her voice. Did she truly think he could work magic to break the dreadful bars of La Conciergerie? Perhaps she thought he had not done enough to try and save her brother. In truth, it was impossible for him to do anything, save find some rogue lawyer willing to defend Armand for enough money. He felt a great welling of frustration and despair.

"Armand is my greatest friend. Believe me, mademoiselle, I suffer as much as you."

"I doubt it, monsieur," she said, and, indeed, she looked quite tragic at that moment, her face anguished in the candlelight.

"Eugénie. . . ."

Their voices had roused Hetta. She rubbed her eyes. "Forgive me, I must have fallen asleep!"

"Well, now you are awake, mademoiselle, we may start on the wine!" said Julien, with false heartiness. "I think it may cheer us all."

But his smile was strained as he took a knife from his boot and dug it into the cork with unnecessary force.

"Why didn't you tell him about Raoul Goullet's bargain?" demanded Hetta, after Julien had left. "I don't understand you. You said only that Guy Deschamps's behavior frightened you when you met him secretly during the ball!"

"It was the truth," said Eugénie.

"But not all of it," said Hetta.

"I don't know, Cousin," said Eugénie tiredly.

But she did know. A mean little part of her had wanted to hurt Julien by letting him think she had had an assignation with Guy. Julien had said nothing to her of his feelings when he had the chance tonight. But that was not the whole reason she had not told him about Goullet's bargain. She knew Julien would be horrified, that it would offend his principles. He would call it blackmail, say that the contract was illegal in the first place.

Or perhaps he would not care. Indeed, why should he? He was still in love with Hetta. She had seen the way he had kissed Hetta's hand in farewell. He had kissed her hand, too, but after Hetta's, and not, she was certain, with the same fervor.

"When he returns tomorrow night, you must tell him," said Hetta firmly, startling her out of her thoughts.

They were sitting on the bed in their chemises in the room they had chosen at the top of the house. Cleaner and with food in their stomachs, they listened to the bells of a church a little distance away ring out the chimes of midnight.

"What are we to do, Hetta?" As the sound died away, Eugénie rose and walked up and down the tiny attic room restlessly, making the candle flames quiver. Hetta lay back, watching her, an odd look on her face. Momentarily distracted, Eugénie wondered what she was thinking.

Hetta was wondering what Julien had said to Eugénie while she was asleep earlier. She hoped that he had made his feelings clear to Eugénie, but suspected, given Julien's frustrated manner and that Eugénie seemed in low spirits, he had not.

How much Father had liked him! They had got on so well. She remembered him saying very gently to her once, "Do not set your heart on Julien, my darling Henrietta. His is elsewhere."

She had known that, but it had not made any difference.

But now she found that seeing Julien again was not as painful as she'd expected. To her annoyance, the memory of a tanned face rose before her, the glint of laughter in hot brown eyes, the flash of white teeth. Since they had parted from Citoyen Xavier Saint-Etienne, that face kept creeping back into her mind. It was a handsome face, granted, but its owner was altogether provoking.

How very different they were—Julien, so refined in sensibility, Xavier, so very . . .

"I know Julien advises against it, but I cannot remain shut up in this house all day while Armand is in prison here!" Eugénie was saying, flinging her hands out. "After all, the only people who will recognize me in the whole of Paris now are Raoul Goullet and Guy Deschamps—if he is here."

Hetta roused herself. "So I suppose you still wish to take the carriage to La Conciergerie?"

"Of course." Eugénie sat down on the edge of the bed and looked at her cousin earnestly. "But, Hetta, you should not risk accompanying me."

"It is no risk to sit in a carriage!" retorted Hetta. Then she looked carefully at Eugénie and saw the gleam in her eye. "If that is all we are doing."

TWENTY-NINE

Julien's senses had sharpened during the years he had been in hiding: He knew when he was being followed. As he made his way back to the secret meeting in the Cordeliers district, he saw something flicker behind him in the light from the hanging lanterns.

Sure enough, down a deserted, dimly lit alleyway, he heard a soft tread on the cobblestones. When hands grasped his throat, he had already pulled out his knife, and all it took was a strong backward thrust of his wrist. There was a grunt behind him, the sound of a body falling heavily.

In astonishment, he saw the knife sticking in his assailant's heart. He felt too sick to pull it out. Averting his gaze from the dead man's eyes, he pulled the papers from beneath the coat and scrutinized them swiftly under the single hanging lantern. The man was a government agent, a member of the Brotherhood of the Watching Eye, no doubt sent after him by Guy Deschamps.

He tucked the papers away beneath his own coat; the papers of a government agent could come in useful.

Then he ran.

A little while later, in a hot attic room in a nondescript house in the rue des Cordeliers, he was in urgent discussion with Xavier

Saint-Etienne and two comrades; the girls would have recognized them as the bargemen from *la Solange*, Michel and Pierre. They had not risked lighting a candle, but the moon shone in through the dusty window.

After they had finalized their plans regarding the distribution of the forged *assignats*, Saint-Etienne said, "There is another matter. I have bad news. According to our agent in the Ministry of Justice, de Boncoeur's name is on the list of those to be tried before the Revolutionary Tribunal during the coming week. If the verdict is guilty, as we know it must be, he will be back in La Conciergerie a mere twenty-four hours before being taken to the guillotine."

Julien felt horror seep coldly through him despite the heat of the night. He put his hand to his head. "I can't tell Eugénie! She will try to see Armand—try to attend his trial at the very least. She might be recognized."

"It will be hard to keep it from her," said Saint-Etienne.

And is it right? thought Julien. "But is there anything we can do? I've heard a prison concierge called Bault takes bribes and we've plenty of counterfeit."

Michel shook his head. "No one escapes from La Conciergerie, not even for money. Our plans to rescue the queen from there have come to nothing."

"No," said Saint-Etienne thoughtfully. "No one *escapes* from La Conciergerie."

A cloud passed over the moon, plunging the room into darkness as they stared at him.

The following morning, Eugénie and Hetta came into La Place des Vosges as the church clock struck noon. Eugénie had not been certain Marcel would come. But the cab was waiting in the shadow of the houses.

The Pont Neuf was busy with the usual stallholders as they

approached La Conciergerie. It stood on the Quai de l'Horloge on the bank of the Seine, beside the Palais de Justice, where the Revolutionary Tribunal sat. Once it had been a medieval palace, but from the late fourteenth century it had been a prison. Too close to the river, it was damp and dark, reeking of sewage, and with its four pointed towers looked like something out of a sinister fairy tale, with an ending that would not be happy.

In the hot sunshine, crowds were streaming down the Boulevard du Paris to the entrance on the east side, by the Cour du Mai: notaries, lawyers, financial agents, stock exchange brokers, auctioneers, priests, each recognizable by the clothes they wore. Eugénie, peering through the window as the carriage came to a halt on the Pont Neuf, thought with a pang of the prisoners, desperate to settle their financial affairs and make a last confession before they went to the guillotine.

There were other carriages drawn up among the stallholders on the bridge, ready to transport the most important visitors back to their businesses. She tapped on the partition. "Monsieur, would you wait here for us awhile?"

The old coachman looked dubious. "Citoyen Saint-Etienne said nothing about bringing you to this place, mademoiselle. I should not have done so."

"He need not know," said Eugénie, passing through a wad of *assignats*. Marcel hesitated before taking them, but his wife was infirm and his sons out of work. He nodded reluctantly. "Very well."

"Look how many visitors there are," whispered Hetta. "Surely we can get in, too?"

Eugénie shook her head despondently. "We'd have to pass the concierge and he doesn't know us. At least let's go and see who has been tried this morning." She needed to reassure herself that Armand's name was not among those on the list.

In the Cour du Mai, dark in the sunlight, details of the morning's trials in the Liberté and Egalité halls had been nailed to the doors. Since it was past noon, the trials were over for the day and spectators were spilling out into the small courtyard, mingling with hopeful visitors to the prison and soldiers marching in a fresh intake of prisoners to a chorus of loud jeers. Eugénie managed to push her way through the commotion and ran her eye swiftly down the list of names: Armand's was not there.

She broke free of the crush and rejoined Hetta. Beneath the *bonnets rouges* faces bobbed past them: gloating, tear-streaked, bitter, vindictive. The morning's trials had been good entertainment for those who relished the guillotine's bloody spectacle, for the accused had all been condemned.

What has taken possession of my countrymen? Eugénie thought. The Revolution had turned men into monsters. Where was true justice now? Not in these once hallowed halls, with their travesties of trials.

And then in the crowd, she saw a familiar face.

It was Belle Fleurie.

But how could she signal to her without drawing attention to herself? She hopped up and down, not daring to call out, or wave. Under the bright, harsh sun people still thronged the Boulevard du Paris, and Belle was gone.

Eugénie turned to Hetta. "Belle Fleurie is here somewhere! The milliner who gave shelter to Armand and me before I came to England? But I've lost her!" The crowds were parting, people hurrying off in different directions.

She felt a pluck at her sleeve. "Eugénie! Can it be you?"

She turned, and there was Belle, like a pebble miraculously thrown up from the crowd: a little more lined, grooves of sadness around her mouth, but her *maquillage* as brave and hectic as ever, and her eyes full of joy.

"Come," Belle said urgently, and led Eugénie, with Hetta

following, along the Quai de l'Horloge. They stood in the cold shadow of stone pillars and gazed at each other, Hetta a little apart, uncertain.

"*Ma chérie!*" whispered Belle, her eyes brimming. She stroked Eugénie's hand. "Why, I scarcely recognized you, you are so grown up! You had my letter about your brother, is that why you are here, *ma petite*? But it is *trop dangereuse!*"

"I am here by accident, Belle." Eugénie turned to Hetta. "This is my English cousin, Mademoiselle Coveney. We are disguised, as you see."

Belle regarded their clothing in turn with the expert eye of a *modiste*. "Ah, the disguise is *parfait*! A well-to-do madame of the *bourgeoisie*, and her maid? If I did not know you, I would not suspect." She wrung Hetta's hand emotionally. "Any relation of Mademoiselle Eugénie is as close to my heart as she is!

"Listen, *ma petite* Eugénie. I have seen your brother. He is in a private cell, as well as can be expected. I have been taking clean laundry in to him twice a week." Belle nodded at a covered basket on her arm.

"You are allowed to do that?"

"*Oui*, I bribe one of the concierges, Monsieur Bault." She winked. "He and I are good friends now. He and the other one, Richard, are not as rough as some of the jailers." She made a face. "Too fond of the bottle, *ces bêtes*, and vicious with it. But Bault will take money for a visitor's pass. This day as always I take in clean laundry, and bring out your brother's dirty linen—shirts and undergarments."

"Oh, Belle, I know you can't afford the bribes!"

"I make enough, even now." She smiled wryly. "When times are hard, it is surprising how much women will spend on frippery to cheer themselves." She leaned closer. "There is a way you can see your brother. But I should not mention it to you. If anything happened to you, I would never forgive myself."

"Please tell me!"

"It is always very busy in the records office—new prisoners being registered, visitors coming through. The clerk gets flustered."

"You think we can slip through?"

"Take my basket. If you are stopped, say that Belle Fleurie is unwell today. But you are her friend and have come in her place. Take money for Bault."

"Will he let me through?"

"I do not know, *mon enfant*. Make sure Mademoiselle Coveney carries the basket, as a maid should. Produce your papers and remember your story. You will know Bault, for he stands by the doors with his guard dog. But it is a risk. If Bault suspects you are related to Armand de Boncoeur—indeed, none other than his sister . . . !" Belle made an expressive *moue* and touched her neck.

Eugénie gripped her hand. "Thank you, Belle. You have given me hope."

Belle smiled sadly. "Let us pray there will always be that." She patted her reddish hair, now streaked with gray beneath the outrageous hat, with a casual hand. "Have you heard anything of that blackguard, Fabrice le Brun?"

Eugénie chose her words carefully. "It is thanks to Fabrice that we survived our trip to France. It was his balloon that brought us safely here through many dangers."

Belle's eyes opened wide in disbelief. "*Vraiment?* He is a hero, then? Where is he, my daredevil?" She looked around in sudden hope.

"He is resting awhile on a farm near Rouen, but he will soon be on his way to find you, Belle."

She shook her head. "And when will that be, I wonder. A year, two? Ah, the perfidy of men!"

THIRTY

A bulky middle-aged man in dark clothes stood inside the prison entrance, an ugly black mastiff beside him, jaws dribbling.

The man's sharp eyes scanned the incomers, as did those of the dog, as if they worked as a team. Occasionally the man stopped and questioned someone, and the dog would strain to sniff the terrified visitor as he produced his papers.

"Citoyen Bault?" Eugénie spoke with a *bourgeoise* accent; she had no difficulty in making her voice sound tremulous. She wondered if the dog could smell her fear. "I am a friend of Madame Fleurie. She has been taken sick and asked me to bring in some linen for her. It belongs to one of your prisoners—Citoyen de Boncoeur."

At Bault's feet the dog growled low.

"Quiet, Ravage!" He scrutinized Eugénie under heavy lids. "Your name?"

"Citoyenne Boileau."

"Your papers?"

Bault looked them over, frowning. "Married so young?"

"My husband is away fighting the Austrians. We'd only been married a week!" Eugénie put a hand to her eyes.

Bault grunted. "Let me see inside the basket."

Hetta's fingers shook as she drew back the covering. She could feel the man's gaze pierce her. Inside were pillowcases, a linen shirt, a shift. He felt beneath the pillowcases, blunt fingers with wiry black hairs scrabbling about. For what? A secret message? A knife?

He withdrew his hand. "Give the basket to one of the porters to take in."

Eugénie had not been expecting this; she thought quickly. "I promised Madame Fleurie to take it in myself." She pressed a small wad of *assignats* into Bault's hand. "Such a faithful dog," she said, simpering down at him. The dog glared up; she dared not pat it in case she lost her fingers. "Perhaps you might buy him a bone? And a good dinner for yourself?"

Bault was startled. This young wife was wealthy, as well as pretty.

Eugénie widened her eyes in feminine helplessness. "I don't know the prisoner. That's why I have brought my maid, *citoyen*. I would not want my poor dear husband to hear of me visiting a male inmate alone, you understand. This is the least I can do for Madame Fleurie, who has been such a good friend and comfort to me in this lonely time."

"Go on, then," said Bault impatiently. He had her money, Citoyen de Boncoeur was a good inmate—caused no trouble though his execution was certain—and there was a fellow approaching now that did not look like an official and must be questioned. Since the queen had been transferred here last month, there were endless spectators trying to get in and gawp at her, taking up the jailers' time. With more than double the number of prisoners La Conciergerie should take, they were short staffed anyway.

He put a thick hand on Hetta's arm, as she was about to follow. "But not the maid. She remains outside."

Hetta did not look at Eugénie. She knew she would be trying to hide her shock: She would have to brave the prison on her own.

"The clerk will take your name and details," Bault said to Eugénie.

The dog whined, and he cursed it, but under his breath in case it should offend pretty little Madame Boileau, who, given the way the war was going, would surely be a widow soon.

The clerk's office was a scene of great commotion, a small room divided by a glass partition, in which the records clerk, a rough, officious little man with wild eyes, entered names in the register, yelling out orders and swearing and insulting those around him while he did it.

After he had examined her papers again, sucking his teeth suspiciously—though Eugénie protested that the concierge himself had allowed her through—she was sent to wait on a crowded bench set against the wall. The men and women huddled on it had been bullied into silence. With a shock she realized they had their hands tied behind their backs: They were prisoners waiting to be taken to their cells. Many of them were weeping openly; some looked cowed, others defiant. When a lover tried to murmur comfort to his terrified sweetheart, the clerk shouted at him to keep quiet.

Eugénie balanced the linen basket on her lap and clenched her fingers on the handle. At her feet two condemned men lay on a worn mattress on the litter-strewn floor, staring at nothing, their faces empty of hope as they awaited the cart that would take them to the guillotine. In the small courtyard outside the window, a soldier guarded another condemned prisoner—a wretched woman—who lay on a sickbed, waiting for her own execution.

At last a jailer arrived, and Eugénie was taken along a dank, filthy passage. She passed a row of crowded cells with barred windows in the doors: She could just make out through the gloom inside, the shapes of men lying on straw pallets. There was an over-powering reek of sweat, urine, and sewage.

She followed the silent jailer into a small hall formed by two vaulted arches. Behind iron grilles she saw a courtyard: women, walking up and down. To her astonishment, they were elegantly clothed, their hair dressed immaculately. Some of them washed linen in a fountain.

The jailer led her up a staircase and along another dirty, straw-covered corridor of closed doors, though the air was fresher here. He stopped, took a key from a bunch at his belt, and unlocked a door. He jerked his head at Eugénie, his eyes on her breasts; his breath stank of alcohol and garlic. "Be quick about it. I haven't got all day."

The key turned behind her.

The small room was almost bare, with a brick floor. Her swift glance took in a trestle bed, a table, two prison chairs, a washing bowl and jug. A linen bag hung on the back of the door. Armand was sitting at the table, head sunk in his hands. He looked up as Eugénie came in, and turned so white she thought he was about to faint. She held her finger to her lips warningly, gazing at him, unable to move.

Her great fear had been that she might not recognize him—that prison might have changed him irrevocably, both in looks and personality—but on the outside he was still recognizably her brother, though his hair was long and his face gaunt. But he was clean shaven, and the linen shirt he wore, laundered by Belle, spotless.

He leaped to his feet, his blue eyes wide and amazed. She found she could move at last.

Then they were in each other's arms.

"My dearest Eugénie, my darling little sister, how did you man-age it?" he murmured into her ear. "I thought my eyes deceived me! I believed you in England!"

She hugged him tightly. *How thin you are, I can feel each rib!* she thought, dismayed. "I was in Deal, but now I'm here, and there's so much to tell you, but I have no time!"

"This is so dangerous for you! I never thought to see you again. . . ." Tears were running down his face, though he was smiling.

She wiped them away. *One of us must be strong.* But now she could not help weeping, too, soundlessly, for all those months he had endured behind locked doors, in filth and degradation.

"We will get you out of here, Armand!"

"It is impossible." He released her, but kept hold of her hand, examining her tear-drenched face as though he wanted to commit it to memory forever. "They have kept me alive too long. My trial must come up soon. I cannot see a good outcome, Eugénie."

She took a deep breath. "I've met Julien again, and we will think of something. Do not despair."

He shook his head. "You'd both face the guillotine." He gripped her hand tighter. "Eugénie, you must stay safe for my sake—for the name of de Boncoeur. Do not take any risks, promise me that."

"I cannot do that, but I will be careful." She looked down at their clasped hands and saw scar tissue on his fingers, fading now to pink. "What happened?" she said in horror.

"It is of no consequence. Go, before you are suspected! And, Eugénie, beware of Raoul Goullet and Guy Deschamps, should you come across them. It is because of them I am here."

A strange expression crossed her face. "There is no need to tell me that, Armand." She kissed him on both cheeks. "Don't give up hope. We shall think of a way to rescue you. There is one open to me already."

And then she was gone before he had time to ponder her words.

* * *

Hetta, waiting outside in the sunlight, tried to avoid the lecherous gaze of the men who pressed around the prison doors.

Two men came out, their voices carrying above the others. One was dressed in the same dark clothes as the concierge, Bault, the other in the height of fashion.

She recognized the second man immediately. It was Guy Deschamps.

THIRTY-ONE

Eugénie came out of Armand's cell, the empty basket on her arm, keeping her face under control. Her hat, pulled well down, hid her red eyes.

"Thank you, *citoyen*," she said to the jailer. "My business is done. The wretched aristocrat complained about a tiny stain the flat iron had made on his shirt! Ungrateful beast!"

"Soon he will have no need of a shirt," said the jailer, with a wink.

"What do you mean?" said Eugénie, trying to keep the apprehension from her voice.

"He is an aristocrat, and after his trial—*phut*!" He sliced a hand across his neck in a grotesque gesture.

It took all Eugénie's self-control to follow the jailer in an unconcerned way back to the entrance, while he dawdled down the passages, inspecting one fetid cell after another. He had an evil grin on his face, as though he would very much like her to remain as an inmate. Now and then he took her arm in a familiar manner to direct her and gave it a squeeze. She felt sick with fear and disgust at the thick stench of his closeness. He left her at last, and was shouted at impatiently by the records clerk as he went.

Bault was no longer at the entrance, but soldiers were still bringing in prisoners. Eugénie tried to walk through them nonchalantly, but the soldiers' gaze followed her. At any moment she expected to be questioned, or even arrested.

But then, somehow, she was outside in the courtyard and no one had stopped her.

Hetta was agitated. "Guy Deschamps is here and has seen me!"

"We can't run," said Eugénie, though her heart sank. "It will only draw attention to ourselves so close to the prison." They left the courtyard cautiously, but there was no sign of Guy among the passersby on the Boulevard du Paris. Was he even now informing the National Guard of their whereabouts?

"Walk as normally as possible to the Pont Neuf," whispered Eugénie. "I see the carriage waiting for us. We can get away."

The bridge, earlier so busy, had quietened as the day wore on, the stalls abandoned and empty. Few were crossing now: a ragged man pulling a cart, a solitary rider on an old nag, a half-starved girl with a crying baby. Their carriage was the only one left standing in the late afternoon sun.

They hastened toward it, looking behind them nervously, but there was no sign of any pursuit. "I can't understand why Guy didn't report us to the soldiers as soon as he saw me," said Hetta breathlessly.

"He wants to keep me alive for Le Fantôme," said Eugénie in a strained voice. "If he'd reported us, we would have been arrested and in due course gone to the guillotine."

When they reached the carriage, the horse was waiting patiently, chewing its bit and shaking its head against the flies, but Marcel was not there.

"We've been far longer than we expected," said Eugénie, as Hetta looked around in rising panic. "Perhaps he has gone for refreshment."

They waited warily in the shadow of the carriage, but still there was no sign of the old coachman.

"Let's climb inside," said Eugénie at last. "The blinds are down and we won't be seen."

She opened the door on the dim interior and tried to pull the step toward her. After a second she realized that something large was half wedged beneath it. She put out her hand and touched softness, a liquid stickiness. When she looked at her wet fingers, they were redder than the evening sunlight.

Marcel was very dead.

She slammed the door shut and leaned against it, trembling. *"Mon Dieu!"* she said over and over to herself. Those open eyes, sightless but fixed on her in the semidarkness, the mouth agape in horror.

"Eugénie? What is it?"

She shook her head. "Don't—don't open the door! Marcel has been killed!"

Hetta looked at her, aghast, while Eugénie shuddered against the closed carriage door. "Who could have done such a thing?"

Eugénie tried to shrug. "The Revolution has bred murderers. It might have been thieves after his takings, or *sans-culottes* who suspected him. Poor old man."

"We must get away from here," said Hetta.

"I am sorry, Cousin," Hetta said painfully, during the walk back to the Marais. "When we were in England, you told me of the dangers in France and I didn't believe you—I didn't understand. I do now."

Eugénie took her arm. "It does not signify. All that matters is that you are with me, Hetta, and I do not have to bear all this alone.

"We must be careful," she said, as they came at last into the deserted street where Victoire's mansion stood in shadow. "Be as quiet as possible, in case anyone has broken in while we were out."

But the courtyard was silent, and when Eugénie pushed open the broken door, the house was as quiet and shrouded in gloom as when they had left that morning.

"Hush." Hetta paused on the threshold as the door creaked back. "Let's wait a moment before going in."

"There's no one here," said Eugénie. She crossed the hall and stood at the bottom of the stairs, looking up into the shadows. They listened, but could not hear a sound.

Hetta shivered and decided to say nothing. When she had followed Eugénie inside, there was enough daylight left to see a footprint in the dust on the stained area. It had not been there that morning.

Eugénie lit the candles in the tarnished candelabra, and sank into one of the moldering chairs by the empty fireplace. It had not been the first dead body she had seen, but she felt profoundly shaken by it, and cold to the bone despite the humid evening. At last she took up one of the branched candlesticks and walked unsteadily to the staircase. "I shall look for a shawl among Victoire's things."

"Let me come with you," pleaded Hetta.

"There's no need. Why are you so anxious, Cousin?"

Victoire's boudoir remained eerily possessed by her: the hanging canopies, the lace-edged sheets, the looking glass that had once reflected her face. Cracks of remaining daylight came through the shutters and crisscrossed the walls. Eugénie could almost smell the perfume in the air as she set the candlestick among the cut-glass bottles on the dressing table and went to the wardrobe. There was a rustle of silk and taffeta as she opened the door.

She pulled a shawl from a folded pile in the corner and turned.

Something on the dressing table caught her eye, tucked between two bottles, white in the candlelight. She had an extraordinary sense that this had happened before: that she was back in time in Deal.

The letter was in the thick black handwriting she remembered all too well, and sealed with her own family crest. It could only be from Raoul Goullet. How had he known she was here?

Had *Guy* somehow discovered where they were hiding? Had he forced the information from Marcel, and then killed him casually? Could Guy have brought the letter and still be inside the house? She gazed around in sudden fright, but there was no one there and nowhere to hide in the great empty chamber.

The tone of the letter was abrupt and impatient.

> Ma chère Eugénie (for I swear you will be mine),
>
> You have returned to Paris, but I have had no word from you in answer to my previous letter. Do not provoke me. I am becoming impatient, and an impatient lover can be dangerous.
>
> I have had word that your brother is due to go before the Revolutionary Tribunal this week. He will face the death sentence unless I take steps to save him. Do you wish to see his head roll away beneath the guillotine's blade?

Eugénie felt the blood drain from her face. She forced herself to read the rest calmly. She could hear Hetta's voice, perturbed, calling her name from below.

> I shall send my coach for you at the hour of ten tonight. I invite you to take supper with me in my private apartment at the Palais Royal. I shall expect your answer

> then. You know the answer I demand of you. I do not
> wish to force it from you by other means.

"Eugénie?" Hetta's voice was on the landing outside.

Her fingers trembled as she pushed the letter deep into her bodice.

After she had eaten a little bread and cheese, she told Hetta that she was feeling much recovered.

Hetta looked at her doubtfully. Eugénie had scarcely said a word as she ate, and indeed seemed altogether distracted, almost jumping out of her chair when the church clock chimed nine.

But it was not so very surprising. How anxious she must be about her brother! Then there was the horror of finding Marcel, coming so soon after the visit to the prison. Thank goodness Julien was coming tonight. She mentioned as much to her cousin, hoping to cheer her.

To her surprise Eugénie jumped to her feet, looking distraught.

"Julien! What time was it he came last night?"

"The church clock struck midnight when we were in our bed-chamber," Hetta said, puzzled.

"And he had come some two hours before." Eugénie shook her head wildly. "Oh, what shall I do? I cannot see him, not now. It is too much to bear!"

Hetta watched bewildered as Eugénie began to pace up and down the candlelit kitchen, muttering to herself under her breath like a lunatic, "Oh, pray that he comes later! He will try to stop me, I know, and put himself in danger."

"Do you wish to see him or not?" said Hetta, at a loss to understand.

"I cannot see him, Hetta, I cannot explain! When he comes, tell him I am indisposed—unwell." She picked up a candlestick.

"Where are you going?"

"Upstairs, to Victoire's bedchamber. I shall come down when he is gone."

She hastened from the kitchen, with Hetta staring after her. Had they quarreled the previous night? She heard Eugénie's quick footsteps dying away and shivered despite the heat. She hated Victoire's chamber. There had been violence in there, *sans-culottes* slashing their way around the walls, yet leaving the bed eerily untouched.

It was dark now and she would have to go and sit in the hall, on her own in the emptiness, while she waited for Julien.

Hetta had hardly sat down in the old armchair, in a flickering pool of candlelight, when she heard a sound.

Julien? How could she know for sure?

A whimper rose in her throat. She crept to the shutters and opened one a crack. She could see nothing; night had fallen in the courtyard.

Light gleamed from a lantern. A shadow slid through the door, past the broken locks, followed by a figure she knew well—had once thought she loved.

"Julien!" In her relief she longed to fling herself into his arms.

He set down the lantern he was carrying and came toward her. "Mademoiselle Hetta!" He kissed her hand almost absently and looked around. She felt the old pain, as his face grew anxious. "Where is Mademoiselle Eugénie?"

"She is in low spirits. Monsieur—Julien—I must talk to you..." She grabbed his hand to startle him into seeing her properly. "Come, sit down."

"What is it?" he said impatiently, but he followed her and sat down in the other chair beside the empty hearth.

She leaned forward and saw his dark gaze rest on her, but not thinking of her—thinking of Eugénie. "Today we went to see Armand."

He looked appalled, as she had known he would. "That was madness!"

"I was not allowed in, but Eugénie managed to visit him alone." She spoke rapidly to stop emotion creeping into her voice. "But Guy Deschamps saw me outside La Conciergerie. He did not report me. But when we returned to our carriage we found Marcel murdered."

"Marcel?" He sounded shocked.

"Eugénie saw his body. When we returned here I found a footprint in the dust. I believe Deschamps came while we were out, after discovering our whereabouts from Marcel."

Julien looked distracted. "Are you certain he is not here still? Where is Eugénie? We should leave immediately."

"She is upstairs in Victoire's boudoir, still recovering. Comfort her, if you can, Julien."

His face grew frigid. "She will want no comfort from me."

"She loves you, Julien! Can you not see that?" Hetta slapped her skirts in impatience. "I do not know what has passed between you, but now is the time to remedy matters before it's too late."

A few months ago it would have been the greatest sacrifice she had ever made to send the object of her desire straight into the arms of her rival. Now she had the faint but undoubted satisfaction of knowing that it was the right thing to do.

Shall I ever find love myself? she wondered sadly. But now was not the time for such thoughts. She had an odd sense of urgency, of time speeding up before some terrible event.

"Quickly!" she said to Julien. "Go to her now!"

THIRTY-TWO

He looked at her a moment, then seized his lantern and climbed the wide staircase two at a time, soundless in his leather-soled boots. He remembered the positioning of the rooms, the great reception rooms dusty and ruined in the darkness, and above them Victoire's boudoir. Had Eugénie remained there, or would he have to search through this great ghost-ridden mausoleum to find her?

But in Victoire's bedchamber Eugénie was standing before the long-cracked looking glass in a circle of candlelight, studying herself, her face intent and somber. She had changed into an ornate evening dress of deep blue silk that must have been one of Victoire's, and had dressed her fair hair into long curls. The candlelight turned her skin to palest gold. A tricolor rosette was pinned to one shoulder and she touched it, then brought her hand to her face, pinching her cheeks to redden them and smoothing her lips from a tiny pot of salve.

He smiled tenderly at her vanity, with a lift of the heart. *She cannot be so troubled*, he thought, *if she is trying on Victoire's clothes for amusement!* But there was something disturbing about her grave demeanor, her intentness of purpose as she gazed at herself. He felt a stirring of unease.

"Mademoiselle Eugénie? Do I interrupt?"

She saw his face in the looking glass. Her skin was suffused with pink, from the folds of the gauzy fichu at her breast up to her cheeks.

He bowed. "My apologies for bursting in upon you. I'd heard from your cousin that you were unwell. I was concerned."

"Concerned?" she said—sarcastically, he thought.

He dropped the formalities. "Eugénie, what are you doing up here alone? What is this playacting? You look as if you were about to go out to dine at some grand mansion!"

She laughed hysterically, but said nothing.

"I heard from Mademoiselle Coveney that you visited Armand today!" He cursed himself for his accusing tone as soon as the words were out.

Her eyes flashed. "I could not be in Paris without seeing him. If others dare not do so, then I must!"

He felt a flush of anger. "What are you implying?"

A fury rose in him that he should feel the need to prove to her of all people that he was not a coward. After all they had been through together! The moment to speak of his love for her was lost: Things had suddenly developed in a way he'd not intended. Now they were both glaring at each other.

She hesitated, as if realizing she had gone too far. "I know you are in hiding and can do nothing." She cast her arms wide. "But where are his other friends when he needs them?" She bit her lip. "There is only me."

"What are you talking about?" What dangerous scrapes would she get herself into now? "Eugénie, for my sake, do not attempt anything without telling me first."

"What? You believe yourself my keeper?"

"No, but I heard what you suffered today."

She turned from him restlessly, and went over to the nearest window, opening a shutter and peering out over the night-filled courtyard. "It's so hot tonight and stifling in this place!"

"You will be seen against the candlelight!"

"By whom? There's no one out there."

"Please, Eugénie! Deschamps may know you are here. It is too dangerous to remain here. You and your cousin must leave as soon as possible. I beg you, come somewhere safe with me—for my sake."

The plea came out involuntarily, straight from his heart, and she hesitated and looked at him, her eyes wide and questioning.

He put his hand on her bare arm. He had meant it to be a soothing, persuasive gesture, but, disconcerted, found her flesh warm and soft. He fancied he could even feel her blood coursing against his palm, stirring his pulse so that he felt on fire with heat. She stared up at him, as startled as he by the contact.

His heart thudded heavily. How lovely she was! His hand was still on her arm. He cleared his throat. "Eugénie..." he whispered. "There have been misunderstandings between us in the past. They mean nothing—to me at least. Do you forgive me for them?"

"Oh, Julien, it is you who should forgive me," she said earnestly. "I said foolish things to you in Deal and have regretted them so long." She shook her head. "But it is too late."

He was caught by her note of anguish. From somewhere a church clock began to chime. She stepped back, and he had to release his grip on her arm. His hand dropped uselessly to his side.

"Take Hetta to a safe hiding place," she said. "I have to go."

"*Go?*" He was mystified, apprehensive. "Where?"

"Do you care?" she said bitterly.

His feelings overwhelmed him. "Care? Of course I care." He spoke wildly, his tongue loosened at last. "I love you, Eugénie."

There. It was so easy, after all.

She hesitated a long moment, then spoke shyly. "Do you—do you truly, Julien?"

"I have always, from the first, my darling." He gazed into her brave, defiant eyes, red lidded with exhaustion and grief. He saw them soften with emotion as she looked back at him.

"But it is too late, Julien."

"What do you mean?" He stepped closer still. "*Ma chérie,*" he murmured. "*Mon amour.*" He was so close he fancied he could smell the scent of her skin, her hair. He felt drunk with longing. He yearned to sweep her into his arms, to press his mouth against hers. But she was standing rigid before him, her face despairing, and he could not move.

"You must go from here," she whispered. "It is safe no longer, as you say." Tears began to stream down her face. "This has been our last meeting, Julien. Take Hetta and go. She has loved you from the first. Find your happiness with her."

"What are you saying?" he demanded, in pain and bewilderment. "She is your cousin, and I like and admire her exceedingly, but you must know I do not have the same feelings for Hetta as I do for you!"

She tried to smile through her tears. "I have not always realized that, Julien," she said in a small cracked voice. "I have been greatly jealous on occasions, I confess, bird-witted as I am!"

"Not you." He caught her hand, pressed it between his as if he would never let it go. "But why should we part now?"

There was an unmistakable noise in the courtyard; they heard it through the open window. The swift clip of horses' hooves on the cobbles, the rattle of wheels. The horses snorted and were still.

Eugénie gave a little gasp and wrenched her hand from his. "There! That is the reason! Do not stop me, Julien. The carriage has come for me and I must leave!"

* * *

Hetta, alone below, heard the carriage draw up, though the rumble covered the clip of another rider over the cobbles, and the sound of that person dismounting, tethering his horse. But she heard the footsteps outside, careful but confident.

She stood up, her heart thumping, her limbs turned to water. She had enough presence of mind left to blow out the candles, but now she was surrounded by darkness. Her instinct was to warn the others, but she knew they must have heard the arrival of the carriage, too. Should she hide down here? But where? Every item of furniture had been destroyed.

The glow of an oil lamp. The slit between the double doors filled with light. She thought she would faint with terror.

A man stood in the entrance, a dark silhouette. He advanced, holding the lamp before him, and it lit the handsome features and auburn hair of Guy Deschamps.

Hetta steadied herself on the back of the chair, as the lantern light found her.

"What is it you want of us, Monsieur Deschamps?" she said in French, her voice trembling, but cold and clear. "Is it revenge?"

He stared at her, seeming taken aback. Then he recovered himself, making a graceful bow. "I have come for Mademoiselle Eugénie," he said quietly, smoothly. "Not for you, mademoiselle. Return to England, if you can. I will help you. Paris is no place for your games."

"I thank you for your advice and offer, monsieur, but I have no intention of returning yet," said Hetta. She clutched the back of the chair. "Mademoiselle Eugénie is not here. See for yourself. I am alone."

"I do not wish to accuse you of lying." He smiled at her, almost pityingly. "But there is candlelight in the window above."

The next moment he had sprung toward the staircase, the lantern in one hand. The light went with him, illuminating the line of the scabbard at his belt. His shadow raced up the wall as, lithe as a beast following a blood scent, he leaped up the marble stairs two at a time.

THIRTY-THREE

Still gripping Eugénie's hand, Julien pulled her to the window. *"Whose carriage is that?"*

"Mademoiselle Eugénie has agreed to come with me," said Guy Deschamps's voice from the doorway.

Eugénie and Julien turned, each as startled as the other, though Julien was not to know that. *"You!"* he said. He turned to Eugénie in outrage and pain. "You would go with him? You have thrown away my love like some idle frippery!"

"No, I beg you, Julien, believe me! I did not know that Guy . . ." She stared at Julien, her eyes brimming with tears, but he had no compassion now.

"My apologies for interrupting," came the hated voice, gloating and complacent. "Yes, it is I, Guy Deschamps. Fully recovered from our fight in Calais, as you see, and demanding satisfaction!"

"Then you shall have it!" said Julien, through clenched teeth. "Not least for ordering an agent of the Watching Eye to kill me because you'd failed yourself!" He heard Eugénie's indrawn breath, but it would make no difference; she was besotted with Deschamps.

"This time, however, I will succeed in killing you, monsieur,"

Guy said smoothly, though he had flushed with anger. "Name your weapon!"

Julien looked at Guy's rapier, glinting in its sheath in the candlelight, Guy's hand hovering over it. He had not had the stomach to withdraw his knife from his pursuer the previous night, and he wore no sword. "I have no weapon," he said. "For a fair fight we must use our fists."

Guy shook his head sadly. "Oh, no, de Fortin," he said. "I want the lady and I mean to have her. So . . . I use my sword." He drew it as he spoke.

Eugénie gasped. "Do not kill him, I beg you!"

"He won't!" said Julien. Icy fury gripped him. Deschamps had stolen Eugénie from him. All this time she'd loved a traitor! She had betrayed him herself, while smiling so sweetly.

But his survival instinct warned him to watch and be wary, not to lose control. As Guy's blade flashed, he circled around it, dodging each stab.

But it could not last. A man armed with a sharp, cutting edge that could slash through flesh and bone on contact, against one who had nothing, save the knowledge that his love had been stolen from him by his rival.

Guy lunged. Julien jumped away just in time, darting behind the bed hangings. Guy slashed at them, his blade glittering. His temper was rising, but skilled swordsman as he was, he damped it down. "Come out and surrender, de Fortin," he called softly. "You know I must win."

"You must kill me before I surrender to you," panted Julien. "Only a coward like you would take on an unarmed man in a duel!"

"This is no duel, de Fortin. This is a fight to the death, and we both know whose that will be!"

"You've tried to kill me already and failed," Julien taunted him, dodging behind the head of the bed.

"But this time I will succeed!"

Guy took another stab at the canopy as if to illustrate his words. Lumps of crimson velvet, padding, silken tassels, fell on the pillows like gouts of blood. Julien ran the length of the bed as a whole curtain came down in front of him in a cloud of dust. He bundled it up and flung it at Guy, but Guy leaped to one side, laughing.

Guy struck out again, missed Julien, and hit one of the posts of the tester. For a second his blade lodged in the wood, and as he cursed, struggling to free it, Julien ran backward, keeping one eye on Guy while looking desperately for a makeshift weapon. He glimpsed Eugénie's white face; she had backed into a corner of the room.

And now Guy was after him again, his rapier free.

Julien thrust the edge of the dressing table at him and dodged behind it, as bottles smashed to the floor in a shower of glass, silver stoppers rolling in all directions. The bedchamber filled with a cloying perfume.

Guy leaped on top of the dressing table and jumped down, his sword in front of him, his green eyes glittering in triumph. "This time I win, de Fortin!"

Julien backed away from the blade, his heart thudding. A breeze from the window lifted his sweaty hair. He was against the wall and would have to edge along it, past the window, while watching Guy. Once he reached the far corner he would be forced to stop, and Guy would block his escape.

"I shall stick you like a pig, de Fortin," said Guy, smiling. "Now where shall I choose to plunge my sword, I wonder?" He stood still, as if pondering. "Heart, belly, groin? Which would cause the most agony, the longest death?"

"Guy! You cannot do this!" Eugénie rushed forward, her arms outstretched, as if to pull Guy back.

"Keep away, for God's sake, Eugénie!" Julien shouted.

"There is no need to watch, *ma chérie*," said Guy calmly.

But for a minute he was distracted. Julien slid sideways, as Guy's eyes flicked away from him. For a second he was out of range of the sword tip, but then Guy moved, too, his eyes focusing on him once more, ruthlessly matching him pace for pace.

But Julien could see what Guy with his back to the open doorway could not: that Hetta, advancing silently from the dark landing, had entered, was crossing the bedchamber, and that there was a pistol in her hand.

"Put down your sword, Guy Deschamps!" she called out. "Or I shoot!"

Guy turned, his sword arm dropping for a second. "You won't shoot, Mademoiselle Coveney," he said levelly. "Any bullet will go straight through me and hit your friend de Fortin, here."

Hetta hesitated, and bent down suddenly. The heavy pistol skidded across the floorboards under its own weight. Guy whirled, but Julien already had it grasped in his right hand. He pointed the long barrel at Guy, swearing inwardly at himself for not being able to hold it steady. Would Guy realize it was not loaded?

They all heard the click as he drew back the cocking piece. Guy shrugged, with admirable aplomb. "Who is talking about a fair fight now, de Fortin?" But he had gone white. He stood motionless, his sword arm at his side, waiting for death.

"Get down, girls," said Julien grimly. He glanced to his left, as if to check that they were out of range. The first rule of the swordsman was always watch your enemy's eyes, and he forgot it for that instant.

Guy leaped forward, pushed him violently sideways, swung himself over the windowsill, and disappeared.

* * *

Hetta ran to the window and peered down into the darkness. She could see nothing. The rubbish heap below would have broken Guy's fall.

Julien picked himself up and staggered blindly to the bed, laying the useless pistol beside him. He sat among the ruined curtains, his head in his shaking hands.

Deschamps believed I would shoot him in cold blood, he thought incredulously—*as he would have killed me without mercy*. There was something chilling in that.

They heard the creak of carriage wheels first, the clop of hooves, then Hetta saw the carriage lurch away through the entrance arch, a dark rectangular shape against the white stone. A horse whinnied nearby, almost beneath her, then a figure on horseback followed the carriage.

"Guy is gone after the carriage!"

Julien raised his head. *"Eugénie?* Where is Eugénie?"

He jumped up giddily, rushed to the landing, and shouted her name through the dark echoing layers of the old mansion.

There was no reply.

PART THREE

The Reckoning

CHAUVAIS AND MONTROUGE

September–December 1793

THIRTY-FOUR

Julien slumped down on the edge of the bed again. "She is gone with Deschamps."

"I know she loves you, Julien! I know it!" He caught a note of despair in Hetta's voice, as if she had reached the end of her patience. "We must think how to rescue her!"

"She does not wish to be rescued. She has made her choice."

"Oh, you poor fool!" She perched beside him, her dark eyes glaring into his; he was taken aback by her vehemence. "Forgive me, but you know nothing! I do not believe she climbed into that carriage of her own free will. She has never told you of the letter she received from Raoul Goullet!"

"Raoul Goullet—Le Fantôme?" he said, bewildered. "What letter?"

"He proposed a bargain. If Eugénie agreed to be his wife, he would arrange for Armand to be freed." Hetta spread her hands. "He made it sound as if he were offering her a favor—that he would overlook the fact that she had reneged on a contractual agreement and would not bring her before the law—but it was blackmail nonetheless. And Guy knew all about it!"

"But that contract was never legal in the first place, would never have stood up in court."

"And now she has given in—she has gone to Goullet!"

"We do not know that for certain."

"You still believe she has a secret arrangement with Guy? I tell you, Julien, she hates and fears him now!"

Julien was silent; old jealousies racked him.

"It must have been seeing Armand in prison today, so helpless, that made her give in," Hetta said.

He shook his head. "I knew nothing of this offer. I would have warned her not to accept, whatever she did...." Doubt churned inside him. "If that is what she has done."

"What? You still believe she is in love with Guy!"

His gaze fell and he stared at the sea of broken glass and splintered wood around them. He thought of Eugénie's last words to him, her tormented face. She had tried to convey the anguish of her choice to him and he had not understood.

"I see now I have been wrong all along," he said quietly at last. "There is so much I should have said to her..."

"It is too late for such thoughts, Julien. Have you any notion where she might be taken? We must go after her!"

"It is not as simple as that, Hetta." He rubbed his face wearily. "First I must think what's best to do."

She stared at him in outrage. "I thought you loved her! Yet you would let another man kidnap her for his wife while you waste time *thinking*?"

He ran his fingers through his hair. "I know how it must look to you. But in truth I am now in the most devilish dilemma."

"What do you mean?"

He hesitated. "It seems I must decide between—my love and my best friend."

She stared at him, puzzled, impatient, and he blurted out, "I learned last night that Armand is due to come up before the Revolutionary Tribunal. We—that is, Saint-Etienne and myself—are planning to rescue him tomorrow." Her face was rigid in the candlelight so he could not tell what she was thinking. "We dare not delay," he went on. "Armand's trial could be any time during the next few days. Once he has been sentenced, he will be held a further twenty-four hours before execution. It is our only chance."

"You think the trial is certain to go against him?"

Julien nodded. "He is an aristocrat, a royalist—a traitor to the Republic."

"But you love Eugénie!"

"I love Armand also, Hetta," he said quietly. "He is as dear to me as my own brother. We have been through so much together. I cannot abandon him now that he is facing death. Eugénie herself showed me that."

Hetta jumped to her feet and paced about furiously. "I tell you, Julien, I care nothing for Armand de Boncoeur, whom I have never met, but I do care about Eugénie, who is my best friend!" She stopped; it was true, she realized. "If we delay in rescuing Eugénie, you will lose her. She will be Goullet's wife!"

The decision was impossible, cruel. How could he choose between Armand and Eugénie? His heartache must mirror that felt earlier by Eugénie herself. He put his head in his hands.

After a moment he looked up, his eyes wide, fired with the sudden realization of their own immediate danger. What a fool he was! He jumped to his feet. "We cannot linger here! Come, Hetta." He held out a hand to her, which she ignored. "We must leave before Guy Deschamps dispatches the National Guard to arrest us. Then we will be unable to do anything for Eugénie or Armand!"

Her face was very white in the candlelight. "But where can we go? Is anywhere safe in Paris?"

Guy Deschamps flicked at his coat with a furious hand as he rode behind the carriage. No damage was done to the exquisite cut, but the precious silk would have been stained. He had landed on a pile of rotting mattresses and broken his fall, but they were covered in mud, mold, and horse dung. But at least he was sound in limb, if not in humor.

On his way he stopped at the nearest *violin*, the local Guards' headquarters, and curtly told them de Fortin's present whereabouts. If he had failed to murder de Fortin—so far at least—then the Republic with its killing machine would do the job for him nicely. His report took no more than a minute, and then he was trotting on to catch up with the carriage, smiling to see La Boncoeur's little white face through the back window staring out at him.

In the next twenty-four hours, while Le Fantôme made arrangements for his marriage ceremony, he would have plenty of time to dally with her.

THIRTY-FIVE

The gardens of the Palais Royal, once immaculate, with their rows of carefully tended horse chestnut trees hung with lanterns and tables and chairs set out beneath them, were sadly changed since the Revolution.

Now weeds grew up through the paths, the fountains were dry, the lighting poor, and the shops and awnings lining the sides of the garden tawdry and dilapidated. The raucous clientele who frequented the gardens on a summer's evening, however, were more intent on pleasure than ever, while the walks teemed with starving beggars, running in the shadows like rats.

The gaming houses grown up around it were temples to money, where men sweated nightly with greed and fear. The grandest and most notorious of these was found inside the old palace itself, and belonged to Raoul Goullet.

Guy Deschamps held Eugénie's arm in a vicious grip as they mounted the steps. Inside the marble hall he nodded at the concierge. The man was trained to show no surprise, but his eyes flickered at the filthy state of the usually *très elegant* Monsieur Deschamps's coat and breeches.

Still holding Eugénie tightly, Guy pushed her into the antechamber that led to the salon.

"Let go of me!" Eugénie hissed. "I have come of my own free will, or have you forgotten?" Her eyes blazed at him. "If you wish to use brute force, like the animal you are, you may, but there is no need, I assure you."

He chuckled. "It suits you to be in a temper, *ma petite mademoiselle.*" He leaned into her ear and whispered, "And it excites me, too."

"You are despicable, monsieur!"

"A lovers' tiff," said Guy, winking at the concierge, who had followed and was holding the door to the gaming salon open, his face impassive.

The candlelight in the great room disoriented Eugénie after the darkness of the streets. She almost tripped over a chair, so that Guy had to take her arm again. His touch was repellent to her now—she, who had once longed for it!

Everywhere candles shone, from the gilded brackets on the walls to the silver candelabra on the gaming tables, where tobacco smoke rose in misty wreaths. A huge crystal chandelier hanging from the ceiling shone on moldings picked out in gold. Long mirrors on the wall panels reflected light. Under her feet the deep carpet deadened the sound of the men playing at the round green-topped tables: the soft shuffle of cards, like the sea, the click of yellow counters pushed out over the baize. Dealers hovered around the tables, footmen waited attentively for orders or rushed about with glasses on silver trays. There was an expensive smell to the air: of cigars, the best wines, gourmet food, and something indefinable that might have been money—vast, undreamed-of quantities of money.

Few looked up from the serious business of gambling away fortunes to watch Eugénie led blindly through the room.

Guy opened the door that led to Raoul Goullet's private suite and shut it behind them. In a small but richly furnished room, a table had been laid for two, with gleaming cutlery and wine glasses. "We are alone at last, *ma chérie!*"

Eugénie thrust his arm away and glared at him. "I know your true nature, Guy. You are a traitor, a murderer!"

He laughed, as if pleased by the description.

"You refer to the death of the old cabdriver, I imagine. Self-defense, my dear Eugénie. He tried to kill me with his bare hands. Besides he was a counterrevolutionary! We must rid Paris of such vermin." He smiled disarmingly at her expression of horror. "How very beautiful you look tonight."

"I will never listen to your flattery again, monsieur!"

"I wonder." He put out a hand and touched her mouth. "Sometime soon I shall have a chance to warm those frigid lips." He watched her face, amused. "I do assure you that I will be altogether a more satisfactory lover than your poor Monsieur de Fortin, who will turn up here at some point, I am certain—unless the guards have already caught him. When he does so, he will find himself caught in a nice little trap!"

He pulled out a fob watch. "But now I must go and report to Monsieur Goullet, who should be arriving any moment." He looked her up and down, the smile still on his face. "Perhaps I should tie you up first, in case you change your mind and escape?"

"There is no need," Eugénie said coldly. "I am here to give Monsieur Goullet his answer."

Silly little fool! Guy thought, as he left the room. Did she really believe Goullet would keep his side of the bargain once he had her?

The Pale Assassin entered the supper room quietly, dismissing the footman who held open the door for him.

Eugénie drew in her breath and stood up trembling, struggling to take control of her fear. The sight of him so close sent a chill through her. She had not seen him for months, but that pale, waxen face, so curiously ageless beneath the old-fashioned powdered wig, had haunted her dreams. How long would it be before he died? She might have to suffer years of being his wife.

"Monsieur Goullet." She curtsied.

"Mademoiselle Eugénie." He took her reluctant hand, but instead of kissing it, examined it minutely. "You have not been caring for yourself." His thin lips pursed in disapproval. "Your skin is rough. There is dirt beneath your fingernails."

Eugénie felt a wave of indignation, but said nothing as he waved her to a chair at the table. He touched her neck with his black-gloved fingers and she flinched. "That dress has not been made for you. It does not fit properly." He reached for a cut-glass decanter and poured wine into a glass, which he offered her.

"*Non merci, monsieur.*"

He drank from it himself, running his tongue over his lips. "A pity. It is the very best vintage."

"I wish to conduct our business without further ado, monsieur."

"I fear I never mix business with pleasure," said the Pale Assassin. He tinkled a little bell and the footman entered again, this time with a silver tray laden with food.

Eugénie had not eaten properly since leaving *la Solange.* She was ravenous, and the food—thinly carved slices of white meat in a rich wine sauce, surrounded by a host of little dishes containing all manner of delicacies—smelled delicious. At last she began to eat.

The Pale Assassin observed the glow of her skin in the candlelight with the desire and pleasure of the obsessed collector who sees his greatest prize within his grasp. Her coloring beneath the dirt was more beautiful than any of the precious possessions already in his collection; a bath, a fresh *toilette*, and new clothes would restore her perfection.

But first the formalities must be dealt with properly. The ceremony must be seen to be legal, with a priest to conduct it, a lawyer, and witnesses.

Eugénie pushed her plate away; a pulse beat in her throat. "How do I know I can trust you to carry out your side of the bargain, monsieur?"

Goullet's expression did not alter; she could not tell what he thought. He began to cut himself a piece of cheese very precisely, the mother-of-pearl handle shining between his black-gloved fingers. Then he reached into a pocket and pulled out a piece of crumpled paper, its edges charred, and showed it to her. She looked at it blankly. It was a floor plan, the drawing smudged, but the writing beneath it, still legible, was Armand's.

"He was planning to rescue the queen from the Temple prison," said Goullet, smiling coldly. "Through the chimneys. Ingenious, but lunatic, and now fatal evidence against him. However, I will make sure the Tribunal never sees it."

He held the plan out to the candle flame, where it flared briefly before the blackened shreds scattered on the cloth. He dusted his gloved fingers together and regarded her, waiting.

She bowed her head in acknowledgment. "But—I still have one condition before I accept."

He stared at her unnervingly with his strange, light eyes. "And what is that?"

THIRTY-SIX

It took Julien and Hetta more than an hour to reach the house in the rue des Cordeliers, dodging through a maze of alleyways and muddy lanes in order to confuse their trail, until they reached the slick, black water of the Seine and the Pont Notre Dame to the Left Bank.

Now Hetta lay on a pallet in a dusty, windowless cupboard of a room at the top of the house, a bundle of clothes brought from Victoire's mansion at her feet. The room was even smaller than the cabin on *la Solange* and almost unbearably hot; her light linen chemise clung to her as she tossed and turned, worrying over Eugénie. She had opened the door a crack for air, and lay listening to the murmur of urgent voices in the adjoining room.

Julien—and Xavier Saint-Etienne. He had shown her the cupboard where she was to sleep with a mocking flourish, as if it were a comfortable bedchamber in some country chateau, and his black eyes dared her to complain.

Julien was arguing, his voice raised. "Can we not rescue Eugénie first? Anything may happen if we leave her in Goullet's grasp."

"Her life is not in immediate danger," said Saint-Etienne, "but Armand will die. We dare not delay."

Silence, then Saint-Etienne said, gently for him, "I am sorry, de Fortin."

"And what will happen to Eugénie if we are both arrested?"

"It is a risk we have to take."

No! Hetta wanted to shout, longing to confront the overbearing Saint-Etienne. But the wretched truth was that he was right: Armand should be rescued first. It was life or death for him, while Le Fantôme was unlikely to harm the prize he had sought so long.

It seemed Julien had given in. At length Hetta heard him say, as if he were forcing the words out, "Tomorrow, then."

Shortly after dawn the following morning, the clerk's office in La Conciergerie was quiet. Farther down the passage the barber was cutting the hair of the guillotine's new victims, but the day's intake of prisoners had not yet arrived. The night clerk was yawning over his register and looking forward to being relieved shortly by the day clerk.

He was startled by the sound of boots coming along the stone passage, followed by a rap on the door and the entry of two young men.

The clerk groaned inwardly. More work, just at the end of his watch! Then he frowned, suspicion flooding him. These two looked unimportant, poorly dressed. How had they got past the prison concierge?

"Your papers, *citoyens*," he snapped, suddenly alert.

The taller of the two stepped forward. With a quick gesture he flipped aside his coat, showing a red sash beneath. *Mon Dieu*, he was a government agent! He should have noticed that this one had a commanding presence about him.

The young man produced his papers and the clerk gazed down. The name was known to him: He was one of the formidable Le Fantôme's agents. His companion's papers were in order, of course, signed with Fouquier-Tinville's flowing signature. He began to feel apprehensive: He did not want Le Fantôme to complain to Robespierre about the administration of the night office.

"May I inquire your business here, *citoyens?*" he said timidly.

"We have government orders to fetch the prisoner Armand de Boncoeur for further questioning," the agent rapped out. "We believe he is still withholding information relevant to his forthcoming trial."

The clerk stared at him in confusion, then pretended to check his register, though he knew all too well what it told him. There must have been some almighty mess-up somewhere, and he prayed the clerk's office would not take the blame. Already in his mind's eye he saw the dark blade of the guillotine slicing down toward his own neck.

"My apologies, *citoyens*, but Armand de Boncoeur has already been removed."

"Removed?"

"For a short time only, you understand—before he stands trial tomorrow. But for the very same reason. He was taken out for further questioning not an hour ago."

Goullet had returned to his own mansion after their discussion at supper, leaving Eugénie in his rooms at the Palais Royal, where she spent the night in one of the luxurious bedchambers, waited on by a maidservant. She knew there were footmen stationed outside her door, but she made no attempt to escape: She had made her decision, and the Pale Assassin had accepted her condition. Besides, she knew if she tried to return to the mansion in the Marais she might be followed, which would put both Julien and Hetta in danger.

As he left, Raoul Goullet said to her, "I have arrangements to make for the ceremony tomorrow evening. I shall not return before then."

"We are to be married so soon?"

"Indeed. I have waited too long already."

"But what of Armand?"

"You will see Armand shortly," said the Pale Assassin, and he smiled.

Eugénie had bowed her head silently. She wondered what she would do with herself all day, shut away in Goullet's jewel box of an apartment while she waited in trepidation and fear for her future to begin.

She did not sleep well, listening all the while for Goullet's footsteps, but he kept to his word and did not return; neither did she see Guy Deschamps again that night.

She fell heavily asleep as dawn was breaking, and slept late into the morning. When she awoke a thin-faced woman was waiting anxiously by her bedside.

"Apologies, *citoyenne*," said the woman. "I have come to take your measurements for the wedding dress. We have little time if the ceremony is to be this evening. Citoyen Goullet wants a dinner dress, a morning dress—a veritable trousseau of clothes! We have not had such an order since the Revolution, nor such exquisite fabrics with which to work. Madame *la modiste* will come in herself shortly to show you her designs."

Blinking in astonishment, Eugénie looked around. An army of girls surrounded her bed, laden with silks, satins, and sewing materials. A maid placed coffee on her bedside table and withdrew discreetly.

After she had been measured from head to foot and the dressmakers had hurried away to work in an adjoining room, she was allowed breakfast. Then she suffered herself to be bathed and scented by unfamiliar and inscrutable maids. Not since she had lived in her guardian's house before the Revolution had so much care been taken over her *toilette*, but she could not enjoy it—she who had once spent hours primping and preening.

Alone at last, a muslin wrapper over her chemise, she curled up in an armchair. To comfort herself she thought of Armand. Goullet must have arranged for his release by now. That had been her condition: She would not marry Goullet until she saw with her own eyes that Armand was free.

A light knock came at the door. "The *modiste, citoyenne*," announced the footman, and ushered in a woman carrying a sheaf of designs tied with ribbon. No doubt the dressmakers would still continue sewing to Goullet's instructions whatever her opinion, Eugénie thought wearily, glancing up.

A second passed in which she could not believe her eyes. She waited for the footman to withdraw.

"*Belle!*"

They hugged each other fiercely, heedless of the designs sliding to the polished floor.

"Le Fantôme wanted the best and found me." Belle was never given to false modesty. But her eyes were frightened. "He tracked me down last night, as he does everyone in the end. I sat up drawing all night and took these to him early this morning for his approval. He said if I could carry out his wishes in a day, he would make sure I'd not be arrested for sheltering aristocrats."

"You braved so much when you took in Armand and me," said Eugénie in distress.

"Pah! You think I would have turned you away?" Belle stood back and surveyed her, hands on hips. "Now, did he force you to this marriage?"

Eugénie shook her head. "He has agreed to secure Armand's release from La Conciergerie if I marry him. I had no choice, Belle."

"But you may have years of being Goullet's wife!"

Eugénie nodded numbly.

Belle drew in her breath. "This cannot happen. When I can do so without suspicion, I shall slip away to Monsieur de Fortin's secret lodgings. We have been in communication since his return to Paris, and I know where he is hiding. He will gather his friends and rescue you."

Eugénie clutched her. "No, Belle, no! I forbid it! You could jeopardize Armand's life!"

Belle stared at her, troubled, irresolute.

"Please, Belle. Do nothing. For Armand's sake and mine."

THIRTY-SEVEN

That evening Eugénie waited in the supper room for Goullet's arrival. She had been served a meal she was too nervous to eat, and it was still early: He would not be arriving yet. She was sitting on the chaise longue beneath the thickly curtained window, glad of some time to herself, when without warning Guy Deschamps entered.

"Permit me to say that in that dress you look more ravishing than ever, *ma chère* Eugénie," he said thickly as she looked up in shock. He had known she would be alone; he had planned to arrive early so he would have plenty of time before Goullet arrived, and had instructed the footman not to enter while he was there.

"You have said it, now go!"

Her chemise *à la Républicaine* was in the new simple style, fastened down the front with tiny silk-covered buttons; the pale pink silk of the dress reflected a glow onto the skin of her neck and shoulders. Guy stepped closer to touch her, but as he approached, she seized a carving knife from the table and waved it fiercely. Its serrated edge caught the candlelight.

"Don't come near me!"

"Eugénie, *chérie*. Why such anger toward an old friend?" He pulled a wry face. "I have spent all day carrying out Goullet's commands, and it has been a wearisome business to find a priest and lawyer for him." He sighed, watching her. "It is not easy to find those who will leave Paris in such troubled times, even for a short journey."

She looked startled. "Leave Paris?"

What pleasure to tell her: a little revenge of his own.

"Surely he has informed you of his plans? The ceremony tonight—private, of course—will take place not in Paris, but in the chapel at Chauvais, witnessed by your brother. Then he will learn that he has lost both his beloved sister and his estate. Goullet has devised the most exquisite revenge, has he not?"

Eugénie turned pale. He stepped closer, but she waved the knife so threateningly he was forced to draw back.

"Eugénie, *chérie*! You would prefer Goullet to me?" He tried to catch hold of her, laughing, but she sidestepped him, her eyes flashing in her white face.

"If you come any closer, I will not hesitate to plunge this straight into your treacherous heart! If you do not believe me, you will find yourself most tragically mistaken, monsieur!"

He did believe her at that moment, and he did not want her to report his behavior to Le Fantôme. All he had desired this evening were a few stolen kisses: There would be plenty of opportunities to seduce her once she was married, when, frightened and repulsed by her husband's cruelty, she would come to him for comfort. Meanwhile, he was not going to risk jeopardizing his future.

He shrugged easily, hiding his ruffled pride. "You may reject me now, mademoiselle. But I tell you, in a month's time—nay, less—days perhaps, you will welcome my advances. It will be all you have to rescue you from the most stultifying boredom. People can die of boredom, you know."

He shook his head in mock pity.

"Once you are married, Le Fantôme will lock you in while he

goes out. You will play the hostess at his dinner parties so that men as warped as he can envy and lust after his most perfect possession, but he will never let you leave the house. You will be his plaything, and some of his games will be very sinister, my dear Eugénie. He does not regard you as a human being, but as an object."

She was silent, pale as candle wax, but the knife did not waver. He delivered a parting shot for good measure as he reached the door.

"Sometime tonight the reckless Julien de Fortin will no doubt attempt to rescue you, informed by Belle Fleurie of your where-abouts. We have set the trap and when he falls straight into it, the National Guard will be waiting!"

He retreated to the gaming salon, and sat down at a small empty table near the door to Goullet's apartment. He had time to fill now before Goullet arrived, so he ordered a large brandy from a white-wigged footman. It would ease both his humiliation at the hands of the de Boncoeur chit and the tedium of two coach jour-neys, out of Paris and back.

He had taken Armand de Boncoeur from La Conciergerie early, and with the help of armed Guards, bundled him off to Chauvais and left him there, a prisoner. Poor fool! He had thought he would be tortured again: It had been most amusing.

Guy ran an experienced eye over the gamblers in the salon as he lounged at the table, waiting for his brandy. It was early: all the tables not yet full. The gamblers were always of a certain type and he could see examples of each: the usual ugly old *bourgeois*, who would make or break his fortune tonight; the desperate poor man in a lumpy, ill-fitting coat at another table, perhaps a farmer, face sunburned, here for a night on the town; two loutish youths, full of bravado, egging each other on to higher stakes.

His lip curled contemptuously. It should be a good night for the salon.

The footman reappeared with his brandy on a salver. The bulbous glass was placed before him.

"And now, monsieur, let us get matters straight between us."

Guy looked up in amazement, and beneath the footman's white wig the dark eyes of Henrietta Coveney looked coolly back at him.

She sat down opposite, took off the wig, and laid it carefully on the table; her own long hair was pinned up and she was wearing breeches and a footman's coat from Victoire's mansion.

He hid his shock. "Your attire is most fetching, Mademoiselle Coveney," he said, as he threw back the brandy in one, and with its fire blazing inside him, looked her over. "You have left the pistol behind, I see, for which I am heartily grateful, though"—he sounded hurt—"I was wounded, in spirit, at least, to think that you might have used it on me!"

"It wasn't loaded," said Hetta shortly.

The charm went from his voice. "You have come to save your cousin, I imagine—a futile endeavor. I cannot believe you have come for the gambling!"

"You are wrong, monsieur," said Hetta. *Her French had improved enormously since he had last heard it in Deal*, he thought. "And I suggest we play together, not for money, but for rather different stakes." She leaned forward over the green baize and looked him straight in the eye.

Guy felt the curious pull toward her that he had always felt; that direct gaze of hers was distinctly unsettling. He could not help but admire her audacity and courage in coming here tonight. What did she think she could achieve by throwing herself into such danger? But he would humor her for the time being.

"Which game do you wish to play, mademoiselle?"

"Quinze."

"A game of chance?" he said, incredulous.

"It is a fair and honorable game, monsieur. We shall both sport upon an equal hazard."

"And what stakes do you propose?" he said sardonically, but tantalized in spite of himself.

"It is very simple," she said. "If I win, I take Eugénie away." She watched as his eyes went involuntarily to the closed door of the apartment nearby.

"And if I win?" he said.

She hesitated before speaking, but her voice was firm.

"Then you have both of us. Or rather, Monsieur Goullet has Eugénie and you have—*me*."

He raised his eyebrows and smiled slowly.

She did not smile back; it dawned on him she was serious. Her eyes were still on his face, waiting for his answer. He did not want to gloat, but it was almost irresistible: Did she truly believe she would be able to walk freely out of here with Eugénie de Boncoeur, when Le Fantôme would be turning up shortly, accompanied by the National Guard? A ferocious excitement rose inside him that he could not quell. La Boncoeur might have rejected him tonight, but here was another offer and Henrietta Coveney was a challenge he had long desired.

He clicked his fingers and ordered a footman to bring him another brandy and wine for his young companion. "I accept your proposal, mademoiselle," he said once the footman had gone, his smile growing hard. "How could I refuse a challenge with such a prize?" He summoned a dealer without further ado. "Bring a pack of cards. We wish to play a private game of Quinze, for private stakes. No onlookers, no interference of any kind."

But Hetta held up her hand. "Monsieur," she said to the dealer, "all stakes are held to account honorably here, I take it?"

"*Bien sûr, mon petit monsieur*," said the dealer, with a patronizing smile for the boy's youth.

"Then we should have our agreement in writing and sign it,"

said Hetta to Guy. "Bring us paper and pen also, *s'il vous plaît, monsieur.*"

The dealer gave Guy a questioning look. Guy nodded, the fug of his second brandy warming him delightfully. "It is a little unusual, but let us humor the boy."

Hetta wrote out the terms they had agreed. Amused, Guy signed his name and she did the same, folding the paper carefully as the dealer watched impassively. Then he took the paper away with him and left them alone.

Guy turned back to Hetta, meeting her gaze.

"It will be a dangerous game." He lifted the brandy to his lips. "A very dangerous game for you, I fear, Mademoiselle Coveney."

THIRTY-EIGHT

"The best of five," said Hetta.

They shuffled the cards and cut them. Guy had the lower card and so was dealer. He shuffled them again and, following the rules of the game, Hetta cut the pack. Guy as dealer had the right to choose which card he kept from the cut pack and which he gave to her. The winner would have cards that totaled fifteen, or came closest to that number.

He gave Hetta an Eight, keeping a Three for himself. She was able now to ask for further cards, one after the other, in the hope of totaling no more than fifteen, but she had to judge when to stop. She took too great a risk, and her last card gave her a total of more than fifteen. Guy totalled twelve and won the game.

He won the next game, too. He thought he detected a trace of anxiety in her dark gray eyes, and felt a leap of triumph and pleasure.

Zut! He was too impetuous and lost the next game.

The salon felt insufferably hot. The fumes of alcohol and cigars caught in the back of his throat. He ordered another brandy and downed it. She had not touched the wine in her glass and said nothing, her eyes intent on her cards.

Two games to her, two to him. Now the deciding game.

They shuffled and cut the cards. He cut the lower—a Two—and so was dealer.

As Guy shuffled the cards again and Hetta cut, the implications of what he had agreed came home to him. He had signed his own name to the terms and the dealer had witnessed it. If he lost, it would be impossible to back out without losing face. Le Fantôme would never let the de Boncoeur girl go whatever happened, but he, Guy Deschamps, was risking his standing with his mentor and his future career in the new Republic, all because he felt a *frisson* for this girl.

I cannot lose, he thought. He kept the Ten for himself, and they shuffled and cut the cards once more. His total so far was thirteen: hers, eight. He dared not take another card.

For years Guy had cheated in gaming halls when in difficulty and had perfected his sleight of hand. But tonight he knew he was clumsy, befuddled with brandy and the allure of the young woman with whom he played. He wondered if he dared risk cheating.

But luck came his way. One of the oafish young men he had noticed earlier knocked his wine glass over himself and jumped to his feet, bellowing for a footman. The sunburned farmer shouted something. Distracted by the noise, Hetta looked up from her cards and turned.

In that second Guy slid a high-numbered card from the middle of the pack to the top. It was the card she would have to take from him and it would take her well over fifteen.

He was going to win.

On the other side of the salon the rich, ugly old man had lost a great deal of money. He paid his losses to the dealer, wad after wad of *assignats*. It had not been a good night for the two young men on the neighboring table either. They were paying out what looked like all their savings. No wonder one of them had been so alarmed that he had upset his wine.

The old man gulped down his own drink, as if to drown his sorrows, and idly glanced about him. There seemed to be some sort of commotion in the far corner where a young man and a boy had been playing cards quietly together. The boy had jumped to his feet.

"You are a cheat, monsieur!" he shouted, in a voice that had not even broken yet. "You are a cheat! I saw what you did!"

The young man playing with him saw the watching faces. He also leaped up, his hand on his sword. "No one calls me a cheat! I demand satisfaction."

The old man left his chair with astonishing alacrity for someone so elderly, particularly one with such a painfully hunched back, and strode across the room, his hand on his own sword hilt.

"I object, monsieur!" he said, in an educated voice, and pointed at Hetta. "You cannot fight a duel with someone who is still a child! This boy can be no more than thirteen. It would be cowardly in the extreme."

"Are you calling me a coward?" said Guy, gritting his teeth.

"I am indeed, and on his behalf I will give you the satisfaction you desire here and now!"

Merde! Damn this interfering stranger! Yet to refuse would look suspicious. Guy's disparaging glance swept over the old man, considering his chances. Elderly, and with a deformity! He could get this out of the way before Goullet arrived.

Hetta had already recognized Reynard Graunier, of course, from the moment she entered the salon, though he had shaved off his red beard. Julien had told her he would be there tonight; and the bargemen, Michel and Pierre.

"From time to time they like to make certain that the *assignats* are given a helping hand into circulation." Julien had grinned crookedly. "To amuse themselves they visit the gaming houses of Paris in turn, losing fortunes in counterfeit."

"Is that not very dangerous?"

"Oh, indeed! They are daredevils, all of them, led by the worst of the lot—Xavier Saint-Etienne!" He had nudged Xavier, and they had both laughed.

"I accept your challenge," Guy said to Graunier. "Call your seconds!"

The old man picked the two oafs at the nearby table, and they came over, large and burly now they were on their feet. And the hunchback had straightened and did not look so very old after all, but wiry and fit, though his ugliness did not disappear so magically.

The dealer shook his head. "Monsieur Goullet will not approve of this. Dueling in his salon!"

"But he is not here yet, and if you report this, I will make sure you lose your job tomorrow and very possibly your head," said Guy quietly. "Now find me two seconds!"

The footmen lifted the tables away hastily to make space for the duelists. And then from nowhere, a slight, dark stranger entered the salon, so quiet and unassuming that no one noticed him until he came up to Graunier and said in a low voice, "I have an outstanding matter to settle with this man. Permit me to take him on for you."

Their eyes met. Without a word, Graunier passed his sword to Julien de Fortin.

Guy knew at that moment he had been set up. He turned on Hetta. "You! You planned this!"

She looked back at him levelly. "But it was you who cheated, monsieur."

He pulled himself together, recovering quickly. "It is unwise to take me on, de Fortin. You know I am the better swordsman."

He stared into the young fool's dark eyes, but they did not waver.

"Tonight we are equally matched, Deschamps! It will be a fair fight at last."

Guy shrugged; he felt supremely confident as the alcohol surged through his blood. The salon reeled and steadied. He focused on his opponent, so slight and tense with determination it was laughable.

"So you wish to be beaten again, then, weakling? *En garde!*"

Outside, a carriage pulled up beneath the steps of the Palais Royal.

The Pale Assassin reached out a black-gloved hand and drew down the window. He looked out at the soldiers of the National Guard waiting in the torchlight. Rowdy noise reached them from the gardens, where the patrons were enjoying their evening to the full. There was also noise from the open windows of his gaming salon above: the clash of swords, the crash of chairs and tables overturning, shouts and curses. Dark figures dashed across the candelit windows.

This did not disturb Raoul Goullet unduly. Gambling salons always had their share of unruly behavior. As the night wore on and quantities of liquor were consumed, fights broke out, duels were fought. No doubt the *fracas* inside would quiet down immediately with the presence of the National Guard.

The officer in charge came up to Goullet's carriage and saluted respectfully, for Citoyen Goullet was one of the richest and most powerful men in the new Republic, in with the government and with Robespierre himself.

"I am certain that Julien de Fortin is in there somewhere," Raoul Goullet said, out of the window. "My colleague is watching for him inside. Station your men out here for the time being. You will remember de Fortin's face, no doubt."

The officer had been on duty during the attempted rescue of the king, so it was a statement, not a question, and it was true that Julien de Fortin's face at the time of that failed rescue was not one the officer was likely to forget. Undoubtedly, a villain's face beneath the dark hair: aristocratic, sneering, putting all the Republic's dreams at risk. To arrest such a criminal would bring great credit to him personally.

"*Oui, citoyen.* I will find and arrest him."

"Make sure you do. I have a private matter to undertake, meanwhile."

The Pale Assassin tapped on the partition, and the carriage moved on past the corner of the building. It stopped in the shadows at the back entrance to his apartment.

"Wait for me here, Gaston," said the Pale Assassin to his driver. "I shall return with the young lady in a moment."

He did not wish to be distracted by the arrest of Julien de Fortin: He would leave Le Scalpel to oversee that. He was about to claim Eugénie de Boncoeur for himself at last. The years of planning and plotting his revenge on the Boncoeur family were about to come to fruition.

THIRTY-NINE

Weaponless, Guy sank slowly down the wall among shards of mirror glass. He was shocked and stunned and sweating profusely; his heart hammered from exertion and fear. He cowered, waiting for the fatal blow, de Fortin's face swimming above him. "Get it over with, can't you?" he said, through clenched teeth.

Julien held the rapier poised above him, but brought it no closer. "It is over already. I have received full satisfaction. I would not sully this blade with your traitor's blood—unless, of course, you do something foolish."

At the onset of the duel the majority of the gamblers had made a swift departure. Those who were left had stayed at their tables, shrinking into their seats as the duelists darted around the salon, blades glinting as chairs toppled to the floor. The farmer appeared too nervous to move. The footmen stood in a huddle by the main doors, where Graunier and the bargemen also lingered, watching the duelists closely.

"Time for us to go, I think, *mes enfants*," Graunier muttered to Pierre and Michel. "Take the seconds as cover."

Before Guy's startled seconds knew what was happening, they were each grabbed by a muscular bargeman and felt a knife pierce their coats. Then they were marched without ceremony to the doors.

The soldiers outside saw a small group of men descending the steps, close together. Three of them chatted affably, while their companions, who must have had a bad night of it, looked pinched and apprehensive. The soldiers glanced expectantly at their officer, but he shook his head. None of the gamblers was Julien de Fortin.

The old one, hunchbacked and ugly, raised his hat. *"Bon soir, citoyens,"* he croaked.

The officer nodded impatiently. As the sound of the gamblers' feet died away on the cobbles, he looked at his men. "Time to go in. Search the palace. If de Fortin's in there, he won't get away."

Needing no encouragement, the soldiers surged up the steps.

Julien heard the boots crossing the hall outside. With his free hand he swiftly lifted the wig from the table where Hetta had left it and fitted it over his dark hair.

The footmen were confused and alarmed. When the soldiers burst into the salon, now a deserted, desolate scene of broken furniture and shattered mirrors, they pointed at Guy Deschamps, still slumped in the far corner.

"That man! He is the one who caused the commotion. He is the one you should arrest!"

The soldiers saw a dissolute figure crouched in the far corner. A young gentleman in a white wig, exuding an air of authority, held a rapier over him. "I leave this rogue to you, *citoyens!*" he called out as they approached.

Guy, spluttering with rage, slurring his words, was hauled to his feet.

The officer stared at him. Perhaps his memory was not so good after all. He could not remember de Fortin's features as clearly as he'd thought. But this young drunkard looked pale, and his unpowdered hair was dark with sweat. He most certainly had the look of a traitor about him.

"Julien de Fortin, you are under arrest!" he said.

The farmer came forward without a word to join Julien and Hetta; the bright brown eyes of Xavier Saint-Etienne glinted at them. The soldiers, intent on arresting Guy, who was putting up a furious struggle, did not notice as they went swiftly to the door of Goullet's apartment.

Inside, Saint-Etienne's strong brown hands went around the throat of the terrified footman. "Where is the mademoiselle?"

"Gone with the master but five minutes ago!"

"Gone where?"

The footman tried to prize the ruffian's fingers from his windpipe to no avail, and gasped out, "When I carried out a portmanteau for the young lady I heard him tell the coachman—Chauvais."

Chauvais! The three of them looked at one another in dismay. "How the deuce are we going to get there?" said Julien. He ran through the candlelit antechamber to the outside door and opened it onto the empty night, as if hoping that by some miracle the carriage was still there.

There was a crash behind Hetta as the footman fell to the floor. "Knocked the poor fellow clean out, I do believe," said Saint-Etienne with satisfaction, and dusted his hands together. "Best to keep him quiet for a while."

He looked at her. "You play a thoughtful game—for a woman," he said softly. "I watched you in the salon, mademoiselle. Perhaps we should play together sometime. We might find ourselves well matched."

She raised her dark eyebrows. "I doubt it, monsieur. Besides, the game is over, is it not?"

"Only just beginning, I fancy," said Saint-Etienne, with a grin. "Come, we must acquire ourselves some transport!"

A driver, lounging against the side of the carriage as he waited for his master to return from an evening's dalliance with a doxy in the gardens of the Palais Royal, was not aware that a figure had slipped out of the shadows behind him until he felt a pistol pressed against his throat.

"Don't make a sound!" hissed Julien, clapping his hand over the man's open mouth, though it was doubtful any cries would have been heard above the din in the gardens.

The driver made strangled noises behind the restraining hand and tried to shake his head. He was not to know the pistol was unloaded. In his shock, he was dimly aware that someone was climbing up into his driving seat and that someone else—a boy?— had opened the carriage door and jumped inside.

"Your papers, *s'il vous plaît*!"

Trembling, he fumbled inside his coat.

"*Merci, monsieur!* Now, a little walk!"

The pistol still against his throat, he was pushed none too gently toward a dark arbor nearby, recently abandoned by a pair of revelers. His hands were bound tightly to one of the ornate chairs with some material that happened to be Julien's pocket kerchief.

Then his assailant disappeared. He opened his mouth to yell for help, and saw out of the corner of his eye the carriage he had so recently driven himself career off down the narrow street, its lights extinguished and the horses clipping the cobbles at a fast trot.

FORTY

When Raoul Goullet had taken Eugénie out of his apartment, gripping her arm in case she should have a last-minute change of heart, she had felt the distorted bones of his fingers beneath the black leather glove. The tender flesh of her arm was still bruised. Now she pressed against the corner of the carriage, as far away as possible from Goullet, as it swayed through the dark streets of the city.

In the confined space, the man's presence so close was chilling. She saw the shine of his pale eyes watching her; his white face loomed ghostlike in the darkness of the unlit carriage.

From time to time they were stopped at a checkpoint. The soldiers examined Goullet's papers, saw he was a government agent, and saluted. They peered in at Eugénie.

"My fiancée," said the Pale Assassin. "I have her papers with me." Le Scalpel had produced a fine set of forgeries.

"No need, Citoyen Goullet," they said, winking at one another. Even government agents were allowed time off.

Then they were out of Paris, and in open country.

It was a warm, clear September night, but the wind was rising, rattling the windows of the carriage. Under the huge yellow globe of the moon, fields stretched away on either side, untended and overgrown since the war. Beyond them, the darkly tossing trees had already shed many of their leaves after the long summer drought. The drought had cracked the surface of the roads, which had been neglected during the Revolution, and the carriage groaned and creaked as the driver swerved to avoid potholes.

It was about a two-hour journey to Chauvais from Paris: Eugénie remembered as much from the time she had traveled with Armand to Paris to live with their guardian, the Comte Lefaurie, after their father's death. She could bear the silence no longer. She spoke, above the whining of the wind through the window fittings.

"Why should we travel to my family estate for the wedding ceremony?"

"Chauvais no longer belongs to your family," Goullet said, barely civil now he was sure he had her. "The estate has been forfeited. It is owned by the government and promised to me by Robespierre himself."

She heard the malevolence in his voice.

"Why do you hate my brother and me so much? I must know, if we are soon to be—husband and wife." The words stuck in her throat.

"Very well." He leaned forward and lit one of the carriage candles with a lucifer. "I want to see your face." His smile was ghastly in the flickering light. "It is not a pretty story."

Eugénie affected indifference. "We have time enough to fill."

"It will afford me some satisfaction to tell it at last to the daughter of Sébastien de Boncoeur."

He raised his voice above the rattle of the carriage; it was a soft, sibilant voice, without emotion.

"Your father died a gambler and spendthrift, and left Chauvais bankrupt." He raised a gloved hand. "No, do not protest. Do not speak until I have finished.

"One ill-fated evening, when your father was still a novice at cards, I accepted an invitation to join his table for a game of Bouillotte.

The stakes were high, but I thought I'd win easily enough. In the event, I lost all I had to him—my entire fortune. What was worse in society's eyes was that I had cheated. I was kicked out of the club—disgraced—another beggar crawling in the filth of the streets.

"I planned to murder your father in revenge and retrieve my money bags, but he outwitted me." Goullet clenched his teeth. "So, after months of groveling in the gutters, I returned to Chauvais one dark night and forced the steward at dagger point to show me where the gold had been stored.

"He led me to an empty stable before I killed him. In the light of my oil lamp I saw the bags on a beam at the back. I put the lamp on the beam and examined them. One bag alone would restore me to wealth.

"Your father must have seen the light in the stable. Suddenly he was in the doorway. He was weaponless, but threw himself upon me. We struggled; I believe I knocked him out. I reached up for a bag and in my haste tipped over the oil lamp. The straw went up in a sheet of fire, the boiling oil spilled out over my hands.

"Somehow in my agony I escaped alive. I left your father to burn. But he did not die, as I'd hoped. I learned later that a young groom had dragged him out, unharmed apart from smoke inhalation. It was I who was now marked irrevocably, the flesh of my hands almost burned away."

Goullet stretched his gloved hands toward Eugénie and she shrank back.

"The scars are livid still. Over time my left hand withered to a claw; the middle and ring finger of my right hand mended crookedly."

She heard the bones crack as he flexed his fingers, smiling. "I find, though, that this hand seems to possess extra strength.

"I began to rebuild my fortune under a new name. But while investing himself, your father discovered that my business matters were not all they should be. Unaware of my identity, he exposed my company and once more I was ruined."

There was a sheen of sweat on the parchment skin of Goullet's face; he wiped his lips with a silk handkerchief.

"I had to find a way to ruin your father as he had ruined me. My chance for revenge came when your mother died. Your father was devastated. But he was also now single and rich. By that time I had collected a group of like-minded young followers—*protégés*, you might call them. I sent them out to—*divert*—your father. He spent many a night in the gambling halls of Paris, plied with wine, forgetting his sorrows while he lost his money; and I waited for my chance, careful never to show my face.

"I followed him one night. It was late, the city streets deserted. He was lurching from side to side—in his cups, I thought. I took out my dagger. But before I could plunge it between his shoulder blades, he turned, saw me, and staggered, clutching his heart.

"He died at my feet. There was a smile on his face as if he knew he had outwitted me again. But it is I who will have the last laugh. His ancient retainers are eager to save their own skins in these days of the Terror. One has squealed. I know where the gold is now."

"You are a monster, monsieur," Eugénie whispered. Tears of anguish had sprung to her eyes. "I cannot marry you."

"It is too late for regrets, mademoiselle. Besides, what of your brother?"

She felt the blood rush to her face; her heart was hammering. "When Armand knows the truth about you he will stop this travesty of a marriage! He would not want me to marry our father's murderer. He would rather die himself! It was your evil scheme to ruin my father that killed him, even if your dagger did not!"

The Pale Assassin examined her curiously, and with some disapproval. "It is unbecoming for such a porcelain beauty to show spirit. I want you composed for the ceremony. Calm yourself."

Eugénie leaned forward, her hand shooting out to strike him. But just as swiftly the Pale Assassin's right hand caught her wrist, gripping it so cruelly she screamed out in pain. "I warn you, mademoiselle, never try that again."

Nursing her wrist, Eugénie withdrew to her corner of the carriage and stared out speechlessly. Then, in the depths of her despair, it came to her that the landscape was familiar: In the moonlight she saw they were traveling through the forest of Chauvais. The road that once had been tended and smooth was now no more than a rutted track, white with dust, beneath the oak trees.

On the road behind them, a dark shape materialized into another carriage traveling at some speed, the horses cantering. Goullet glanced through the back window and checked his fob watch. It would be carrying the priest and the lawyer: Le Scalpel had hired a carriage to bring them out here at much this hour. The driver must be an imbecile to push the horses on such a road, but soon they would catch up and fall in behind his carriage.

But Gaston was driving the horses faster, as if in response. The carriage jerked and swayed over the uneven surface of the road. In her corner Eugénie clung to the strap, sickened at the thought of being thrown against Raoul Goullet.

"What are you doing, Gaston?" he roared.

"There are robbers after us, monsieur!"

"Nonsense, fool! Those men are traveling to Chauvais at my request!"

But now the carriage was so close behind he saw the passengers as moonlight flashed between the trees and illuminated them: a boy and a dark-haired young man. Could that be—*Julien de Fortin*? How in hell's name had he escaped Le Scalpel and the soldiers? The driver, face hidden beneath a broad-brimmed hat, was recklessly trying to overtake; in a moment they would be pushed off the road into the leaf-strewn ditch.

Goullet reached for the pistol hidden beneath his coat and drew down the window.

In the driver's seat above, the coachman whipped the horses ever faster in his terror. He saw, too late, a pothole in the road that had been hidden in the shadow of the trees and tried to swerve around it. Traveling at speed, the carriage tilted.

Below him there was a cry of protest from the young mademoiselle, then a shot exploded in a cloud of sharp-smelling gunpowder, echoing through the trees. Startled birds flapped from their roosts. The horses reared in fright. The carriage, already unbalanced, tilted further and crashed into the ditch.

Eugénie, half stunned, saw a flame lick along the silk lining of the carriage from the candle, now hanging at a right angle in its shattered holder. Nothing was in its proper place: She had slid down the seat from her corner and was wedged at the far end. She felt around feverishly and her hand went into empty space. The door closest to her had burst open.

The carriage was on its side in the ditch. Coughing, she managed to jump out, landing in deep, soft leaves. She clambered up the ditch, staggered as far as she could, and sank down blindly on the grass between two trees, drawing in lungfuls of air.

Behind her the carriage began to burn, the horses screaming as flames, blown by the wind, licked at their harnesses. Wrenching free, they careered down the road, manes and tails flying.

A pale figure emerged from the shadows. She felt a hand claw her arm and Goullet hauled her to her feet. He began to struggle through the trees, clutching her to him. Branches and brambles caught at their clothes.

She fought his grip, but the twisted fingers were ruthless. Then she let herself go deliberately heavy, her feet dragging through twigs and leaves, and heard him grunt with the effort of pulling her along. Behind them the carriage illuminated the night with a hellish glow.

FORTY-ONE

The gunshot had blown a hole through the roof, rocking the pursuing carriage violently. Hetta and Julien ducked down in shock and lay flat on the floor, on the voluminous fur rugs that had so recently concealed them on the journey through Paris. They felt the carriage slow and come to a halt. The horses shifted uneasily, still unnerved by the shot and the acrid smell of burning behind them.

"He has Eugénie!" Saint-Etienne had opened the door, an oil lamp in his hand.

"We must pursue," said Julien, "take one of the horses each!"

"The trees are too dense. Best go on foot."

"Come on!" cried Hetta. She jumped out, past Saint-Etienne's arm, and made for the side of the road.

"He's armed, mademoiselle!" Saint-Etienne shouted after her. The two young men looked at each other.

"I'll go with her," said Julien quickly, taking the lantern from Saint-Etienne. "You stay here and hold the horses. We'll need the carriage later."

He and Hetta found Eugénie wandering dazedly in the darkness beneath the trees, searching for the road. There was no sign of the Pale Assassin.

Hetta flung her arms around her. "Cousin!"

Eugénie hid her face against the footman's coat. "In the end I was too much trouble to drag along," she said, her voice trembling. "He cast me down, cursing the de Boncoeurs most despicably. He is gone, Hetta, I do believe forever."

"I doubt it," said Julien grimly. He reached out a hand to Eugénie and then, as if recollecting their last meeting, withdrew it.

She seemed to come to her senses, stepping back from Hetta and gazing at them both, her eyes wide in her white, smoke-streaked face. "Armand! He is at Chauvais. He was to be a witness at the wedding. We must find him!"

They were no distance from the chateau, though once Saint-Etienne had driven their carriage through the gates, the avenue meandered through fields of rotting wheat, the once-lush pastures of the estate dry and yellow in the dim dawn light.

Weak with the delayed shock of her escape, Eugénie's eyes filled with tears as they approached the great chateau of Chauvais at last. Austere and untouchable in its pale cool stone, pointed turrets reaching to the sky, from a distance her family home looked as it had done before the Revolution. But behind a tapestry of ivy and moss, its doors were barred, every window shuttered, the terrace thick with the unswept leaves of many autumns.

Inside the carriage Hetta pressed her hand. "It is very beautiful, Cousin."

"It was—once."

"And will be again."

Eugénie shook her head. "I see now that things will never be the way they were between the aristocracy and the peasants. We cannot go back to the days of the Ancien Régime, Hetta. The Revolution has changed everything. Armand and I will have to think of a new future for Chauvais—if we can ever reclaim it from the government."

Saint-Etienne brought the horses to a stop and they climbed out of the carriage into the utter quiet of the dawn. For a moment they all gazed up at the sleeping house without speaking, caught in its spell of silence. Then the wood pigeons began to coo in the trees that lined the avenue behind them, and close by a blackbird began to poke about in a drift of leaves.

"Where is Armand?" cried Eugénie. "Armand!" Her voice floated up into the lightening sky, tiny, insignificant.

"Hush, mademoiselle," said Saint-Etienne. "We should not draw too much attention to ourselves. Armand may well be being guarded."

They looked up at the magnificent flight of stone steps that led to the entrance, where bolts had been nailed across the doors. "I suspect he hasn't been taken into the house at all," said Saint-Etienne. "If we can't get in, neither can anyone else. He must be somewhere on the estate itself."

"And how do you propose we search such a vast expanse, monsieur?" said Hetta. She was torn between irritation and admiration of the way Xavier Saint-Etienne had taken charge; it seemed to sum up her feelings toward him very well. "It could take days."

"Then let us keep together and search close to the house first," said Julien. He looked at Eugénie's weary, desperate face and longed to comfort her. If they were to discover Armand here at all, would they find him alive? But she had not met his eyes, and he dared not take her hand.

Then he saw her expression clear. "I believe I know where he might be!"

A man, face and clothes blackened by the carriage fire, had watched since their arrival. As the four figures hastened across the forecourt, he crept from his hiding place behind a large stone urn and began to trail them.

* * *

Armand knew where he was now. The day before he had not, sweating beneath his blindfold, his hands bound. From the jolting movement and the close air, he knew he had been thrown into a carriage, but not where the journey would end.

But he knew who his persecutor was: the traitor, Guy Deschamps. There were two others with Deschamps: soldiers of the National Guard—no doubt to protect Deschamps from the dangerous aristocrat they were conveying.

When the carriage stopped at last and Armand was hauled out, he smelled clean air, heard birdsong; there was a breeze on his face and sunlight warm on his blindfold.

He had been brought out of Paris.

Stumbling, he was led for miles, it seemed, then shoved down onto a hard surface—bricks?—and the blindfold ripped from his eyes.

At first he could see nothing, dazzled by the daylight. He waited for his head to be thrust back, the sword prick at his throat that would pierce his windpipe, then the choking, drowning blood.

But it did not happen.

The soldiers spat and kicked him as they rebound his legs. Deschamps laughed contemptuously as he thrust his face into his. "You know where you are, *mon brave*? Chauvais!" His handsome features were distorted by his smile. "*Au revoir* for now. You won't be alone long. After all, we have to get you back to Paris in time for your trial!"

They left him without further word.

Armand realized he was in a stable—or what remained of it—his back against a stone manger. The timbers above him were badly charred, and he remembered his father telling him about a fire when he was a child. When the estate became bankrupt the stable had never been rebuilt.

He chafed his bonds uselessly against the stone behind him.

Why had he been brought to Chauvais? There was some devilish purpose in it. And at the end he would surely face death.

The day began to fade, the wind rose and died away; the night was very long and dark. Just before dawn, he dreamed he heard breathing.

He believed he was dreaming still, when the pale light at the stable entrance darkened and the face of his own dear sister looked down into his, crying out his name over and over again.

When at last Eugénie had finished hugging him, Julien cut through Armand's bonds and helped him up. Saint-Etienne clapped him on the back so that he staggered, protesting, against a broken beam. But he was grinning in amazement as he rubbed his chafed wrists and ankles: It felt as if he had not smiled for a very long time.

"*Mes amis, mes chers amis*, how did you know I was here?"

"It is a long story," said Eugénie, and she held him close as if she would never let him go, "and now you have all the time in the world to hear it."

He would not face the guillotine after all. *He was not going to die.* He could not believe it yet.

Blinking in the light, looking from one face to another as if each were a miracle, he saw a beautiful stranger, dressed in boys' clothes but most assuredly female. "Let me introduce Miss Henrietta Coveney, Armand," said Eugénie. "Our cousin and my dearest friend!" The girls' glances met, as if in confirmation.

"I am so very pleased to meet you at last, monsieur," said Hetta. She put out her hand shyly and Armand, gazing at her, clasped it in his filthy one. Julien saw Saint-Etienne stiffen, and smiled to himself. Xavier had never liked competition.

In a corner something moved behind a pile of partly burned wood. A rat? Saint-Etienne moved toward it, his finger to his lips. He kicked out and the wood toppled in all directions, revealing a crouching figure, his hands protecting his head.

"I advise you to state your business at once, monsieur," Saint-Etienne rapped out. "You are outnumbered, as you see, and one of us has a sword."

The man who staggered out was short but powerfully built, his clothes blackened and scorched, his grizzled hair singed. He looked around at them, scowling.

"It's Goullet's coachman!" whispered Eugénie fearfully.

Julien glanced at her and stepped forward, his hand on his rapier. "What do you want with us?"

"I mean no harm to you, *citoyens*," said Gaston the coachman sulkily. "I'm here to impart information."

"What information?"

"Information about the money." Seeing their baffled faces, the man added, "The gold I once brought here, the gold that was later put in this very place and then removed."

Eugénie put her hand to her mouth. "He means the fortune that our father won from Raoul Goullet, Armand!"

A strange, closed look came over Armand's face. He turned to her. "I never wished you to learn of our father's gambling habit. It led to the ruin of Chauvais."

"You don't want the money, then?" said Gaston slyly. "All that gold could set this place right."

"It's lost," said Armand. "I searched for it myself at the start of the Revolution."

"One of your servants gabbed to my master to save his neck. He'd had orders from your father to hide it in a safe place."

"Why are you telling us this?" said Julien. "You know who we are—what we are."

The man shook his head. "I've no quarrel with the aristocrats. My master weren't one and he were worse than the lot of you together. He were a cruel man, a devil. He'd have killed me if I'd left him. I knew too much about his evil ways." He came closer, bringing the reek of smoke with him. "I tried to save his carriage for him tonight, beating the flames out with branches. Fear he'd blame the ruination on me made me do it, risking my own life."

"You speak of him in the past," said Eugénie breathlessly.

The coachman nodded. "He's dead. Found him on my way here, facedown in a ditch. The shock, and him not a young man. Now are you coming with me to find the money, *citoyens*?"

"Careful. It may be a trap," said Xavier to Julien in a low voice. Ahead, Eugénie and Hetta, with Armand between them, were following the coachman over the cobbled stable yard.

"I'll go with the girls while you watch the forecourt," said Julien to Xavier. He could not bear to let Eugénie out of his sight.

Pigeons flew with a clatter of wings from crevasses in the walls as the coachman led the way through a succession of desolate courtyards. Julien wondered how many secret visits Gaston had made with his master to Chauvais in search of the gold. Eugénie gazed about her, exclaiming softly in recognition, clutching Armand's arm. She did not look back at Julien.

The coachman stopped. "This is the place."

The sun had risen and it was now fully daylight, though the courtyard, small and weed strewn, was half in shadow. In the center was a well with a rusty pump.

"Dry," said the coachman. "Hasn't been used for years, the servant said, what with all the droughts. That's where the gold is, down there." He looked back at them, his blackened face mocking. "Who's first down, *citoyens*? I want my share."

"Climb down, if you must," said Armand wearily. "Take a bag. I've a mind to leave the rest to rot. '*Cheat's gold*,' my father called it."

"But out of bad, good things can come, Armand," said Eugénie. "One day we may rebuild Chauvais with it. Even our father would have desired that."

Gaston approached the well and leaned over its circular wall. Julien saw him peer down, a dark figure in the dappled light. The next moment there was a deafening noise, ricocheting around the courtyard. Blood sprayed in all directions. Gaston fell back, hitting the cobbles.

Something had happened to his head.

Julien thought he would be sick. Somehow he made himself move his lumpen legs forward. He tugged off his coat blindly and threw it over the coachman. But they all had seen the horror. The girls huddled together, gasping soundlessly, too shocked to scream. He called out, his voice shaking, "Who are you? Declare yourself! You have just murdered a man!"

A voice reached them, booming eerily up the well walls.

"I am Raoul Goullet! I am Le Fantôme! And I am coming up to kill you!"

FORTY-TWO

The Pale Assassin had scrabbled about in the dirt and darkness after the long climb down. The bags were lumpy and hard beneath his gloved fingers. He could feel the outline of each precious gold coin.

It was rightly his, his long lost fortune! He might have lost Eugénie de Boncoeur, but this at least was left to him.

It was a shock when he heard voices breaking the silence above him, but easy enough to shoot the face that looked down, a shadowed disk against the circle of light sky. He had always been an excellent shot. Fury bubbled inside him. They were distracting him from what he wanted to do.

He did not know he had gone mad.

He pointed his pistol upward in his strong right hand, and began to climb the ladder. Grasping the rungs above him was difficult with his crippled left hand, but he could manage to climb by keeping most of his weight on his feet. He would kill whoever was at the top, the thieves who wanted to steal his gold!

He was almost there when his left hand clutched a faulty rung. It came away from its fixture on one side and hung down, throwing him off balance. One of his feet in its thin-soled shoe, muddy from tramping through the forest, slipped beneath him.

A terrible wail escaped his lips. He hung, dangling in space, his legs flailing, the pistol dropping far below. His glove began to slide on the broken rung, and inside the glove his distorted bones had no strength left.

His backbone broke as he hit the bottom, and he died instantly.

The sound of the fall, booming up through the well, reached them all.

Julien peered down cautiously, but from the way the body was lying twisted far below, he knew without a doubt that Raoul Goullet was dead.

"You are safe at last, Cousin," Hetta whispered to Eugénie.

Eugénie took a quick look down the hollow of the well at the broken body and turned away; she was trembling. Without a word, Armand put his arm around her. Sister and brother stood motionless together in the sunlight. Their age-old enemy was dead, but would they ever feel safe again?

There were swift footsteps across the courtyard, and Xavier Saint-Etienne stared down at Gaston's blood-spattered body. *"Mon Dieu!* I thought I heard a shot." Julien opened his mouth, but Saint-Etienne shook his head. "Tell me later." He spoke urgently. "A carriage has arrived at the entrance. Two men, a cleric and a lawyer from the look of their clothes."

Eugénie put her hand to her mouth. "The men who were to see me married!"

"They disappeared in the direction of the chapel. I think we might disappear ourselves—in our carriage, and speedily."

"It is too dangerous, Xavier," said Julien. "We cannot pass the checkpoints in daylight. We should hide somewhere here until nightfall."

They were starting to argue when a man approached noiselessly across the courtyard, startling them all. He was unarmed, dressed like a peasant, and appeared about to challenge them, alone as he was, when he caught sight of the dead body lying on the ground.

"*Georges!*" cried Eugénie. She broke away from Armand, gathered her skirts, and ran toward the stranger.

"Who the devil is Georges?" said Saint-Etienne.

"Eugénie's old groom," said Julien resignedly. On the journey to England he had heard much—too much—about Georges the groom, who had taught Eugénie to ride, shoot, and climb during her childhood at Chauvais. He had teased her, but half seriously. He found himself ridiculously relieved to see that Georges was not a young man; indeed, that his pleasant but nondescript countenance looked somewhat lined and careworn, as well it might after four years of revolution.

The man gazed at Eugénie in amazement and dawning joy, then abruptly fell on his knees. "*Ma petite mademoiselle!*"

"Please get up, Georges," cried Eugénie. "We'll have no more of that at Chauvais, will we, Armand?"

"And the master here, too!" said Georges. He rose to his feet and spoke with dignity. "I have done my best, Monsieur le Marquis, but there are few of us left willing to work for no wages save what the land yields. The estate has suffered."

"I thank you for your great loyalty," said Armand gently. "There is more than enough now to pay you and the others."

"You have found the gold?"

"Please take what you are owed. I leave you in charge, Georges."

The groom looked somber. "I saved your father from the stable fire and he trusted me thereafter. It was I who carried the bags to the well on your father's orders, but I needed help. I couldn't keep the hiding place secret and always feared thieves." He looked again at Gaston's body, but it was not his place to ask questions. "I will remove that for you, Monsieur le Marquis."

"I fear there is another also—in the well," said Armand. He tried to smile. "It has been an eventful morning."

"And will be more so if we do not leave now!" muttered Saint-Etienne. When Armand de Boncoeur did not appear for his trial, it would not take long before the National Guard was on their trail.

Armand looked at Saint-Etienne's impatient face. "There is one more thing you can do for us, Georges."

FORTY-THREE

Late in the evening, they slipped away from Georges's cottage, where they had hidden all day, to a track on the estate that ran between meadows. In the dusk a large farm horse stood between the shafts of a cart, identical to all the others drawn into Paris daily from the surrounding countryside. At the front, a sacking awning covered curved wooden slats, giving a little headroom above the planks of the floor; the back was filled with hen coops.

The hens clucked sleepily as Saint-Etienne pulled aside the sacking and Julien helped the girls up. Eugénie sat close to Armand in the darkness; he was shuddering uncontrollably, the fear of being discovered again and returned to La Conciergerie too great to bear.

The roof pressed down on them; there was scarcely room to crouch, or air to breathe. They felt the cart shift as Saint-Etienne climbed into the driver's seat and gathered up the reins. He tugged a battered hat down over his face like any farm yokel and clicked his teeth. The horse pulled strongly away.

Their destination was Montrouge, near the catacombs outside the southern walls of Paris. They were going to seek shelter on the farm that belonged to Manon, who once had been Eugénie's maid.

*   *   *

The farm stood on the red-earth slope, away from the village, among windmills and heathland. The living quarters were built over the animals' stalls, and all night long, inside the tightly drawn green serge curtains of Manon's bed, Eugénie and Hetta heard them move about below, the horses champing softly, the cows mooing deep in their throats.

But they also heard the rumble of the death carts, bringing fresh corpses from the guillotine nightly to be stacked in the tunnels of the old quarries. Eugénie lay sleepless, picturing the bodies jolting and sliding in a pool of blood. One of them might have been Armand's. Or her own.

Manon's family had given them a warm and somewhat awestruck welcome, heedless of their own danger in sheltering aristocrats wanted by the government. They saw only Eugénie's delight in her reunion with their daughter; and the young marquis, who had always been kind to her, looking so pale and ill. How could they turn them and their friends away when they, too, hated the government? And the young men helped on the farm, which was a blessing in these difficult days when there was no money to pay wages for extra hands.

The sultry days of autumn passed. Belle paid a secret visit and brought news of the city: of Queen Marie Antoinette's execution, of the leaders of the liberal-minded Girondin Party going *en masse* to the guillotine, suspects imprisoned without trial. Christianity had been banished and replaced by the worship of Reason: the Virgin Mary was now the Goddess of Liberty and her statue wore the *bonnet rouge*. In the new Revolutionary government, Robespierre, prim faced above his stiff cravat, ruled over a dictatorship, and the streets stank with the blood of those he called traitors.

After Belle's visit the young men grew restless.

Hetta longed to send word to her father that she was alive and well. France's war with Europe and England still continued, and while it lasted it would not be safe to return home.

As she went about her work on the farm, she was preoccupied, and not only with worry over her father. It pained her to admit it to herself, but she was falling in love with Xavier Saint-Etienne. She kept her growing feelings for him secret, unaware that he was watching her as she watched him.

After Belle's visit she saw the glint in his eye, the frustration of having to rely on gossip heard in the cafés of nearby Montparnasse to tell him what was happening in Paris. She knew that he would not remain on the farm much longer, and wondered how she would bear it.

Early one morning, she contrived to leave the farmhouse at the same time as he did. They each had been allocated a duty: Hers was to help with the milking of the cows. This morning there was ice between the cobbles as she followed him across the yard, and frost rimmed the thatch on the barn roof. Winter had come.

"Saint-Etienne!" She had not intended to sound so imperious. He turned and his eyebrows shot up.

"You are leaving the farm, are you not, monsieur?" she said, struggling to keep the emotion from her voice.

"I must," he said, and he came back toward her. "For a while, at least. I have to return to the heart of Paris to fight this tyrannical government." There was no mockery in his face, but something else entirely as he looked at her. "Do you understand that, Miss Henrietta?"

"I do," she said softly, "for of all things, I hate oppression most."

They had stopped sparring at last, and there was only the truth left.

She looked back at him as she stood shivering in the cobbled yard wearing ill-fitting clothes borrowed from Manon, and her eyes glowed.

His heart leaped strangely; he found he was nervous—he, Xavier Saint-Etienne, and she a mere slip of a girl! But what a girl!

He took her hand with its dirty, broken nails and pressed it to his lips. "Then we are together in that, mademoiselle."

"We are," she said, and smiled slowly. "Together, aren't we."

It was not a question. And if it had been, by that time he had pulled her fiercely into his arms, and his kiss was answer enough.

Armand told Eugénie his own decision that same evening, when they found themselves alone for once in the dark farmhouse, crouched before the smoking fire, the tallow guttering in a dish. He was not his old self yet, and she wondered if he ever would be. There was a haunted look in his eyes and he spoke little, and in confined spaces he still shook from head to foot.

"I must leave," he said. "With winter here, there'll not be enough food to go around. My duty is to return to Paris and bring down the Republic as best I can."

Fear filled her at once. "You're not recovered yet."

"This is the only thing that will make me well." His eyes blazed a moment in the old way. "I need to feel I am fighting back."

"But you cannot fight the government alone!"

"I won't be alone. Xavier and Julien will be with me."

"Julien?" she whispered. "Julien is going, too?"

Julien had gone out to look at the stars high in the winter's night. He wanted time alone to prepare his farewell to Eugénie—to choose the appropriate words so that he would not look a fool if she appeared not to care. His heart ached with uncertainty: She had given him no sign that she still had any feelings for him.

He went as far as the meadow and stopped by the fence. The moon bleached the grass with a cold, inhuman light, and the stars glittered like icicles.

There was a soft tread by his side. He lifted his lantern and, astonished, saw Eugénie, a borrowed shawl around her shoulders.

She would have scorned such an unbecoming garment in the old days. She had lost weight, and looked vulnerable beneath the heavy wool. For a moment in the moonlight he saw her as she might look when old, and his heart filled with love and trepidation. "Mademoiselle Eugénie!"

"Armand tells me you are leaving."

"Someone has to keep an eye on your brother." He gave a tense, lopsided smile. "I can't allow Saint-Etienne to lead him into scrapes!"

She did not smile back. "Will the Terror ever end?"

He did his best to sound comforting. "The people are sick of blood. They may rise against the government in protest soon, who knows? And in the government itself, there are mutterings against Robespierre led by Danton's followers."

"So it might not be too long before you return?"

Her eyes fell, but he had heard the yearning in her voice. He looked at her in amazement. Was it possible she did still care about him? He put out a hand and tentatively touched the hideous shawl; he could feel her breast beneath it, rising and falling quickly.

"Eugénie?"

She gave a little despairing gasp. "Oh, Julien, there is so much I want to say before you leave! And yet I find myself—quite tongue-tied."

He shook his head. "No, no, it is I who am tongue-tied. I have tried on so many occasions recently to say . . ."

"Say what?"

He gripped her shoulders and she seemed to melt against him, her beloved face looking up into his searchingly, so that his words came out without difficulty. "How much I love you, *ma chérie*."

"Do you truly, Julien? Still? In spite of everything? Our foolish quarrel back in Deal, when I thought you loved Hetta?"

"But then I doubted you when you left Victoire's mansion with

Deschamps. I am as much to blame, if not more." To Julien's joy even this confession did not make her withdraw; she rested her head against his chest, as if thinking.

He laid his head against hers and still she did not pull away. Her hair was like silk on his cheek and she smelled, not unpleasantly, of hay; he found he preferred it to the expensive colognes she had once worn. "We must learn to trust each other," he said softly. "We've not done so in the past, but we shall do so now."

"We will," she murmured, and nestled closer. "I have been so foolishly jealous, Julien! I could not believe you loved me for what I am."

"I cannot always say what I want to say," he whispered back. "Sometime you must teach me how to charm you as Guy Deschamps did, but for the moment can you accept me for what I am, too?"

"I do, I do," she said earnestly. It was remarkable how few words could put everything right. "Guy Deschamps meant nothing to me, believe me. I was very young and silly to be taken in by his flummery. I would not want you to have such false charm for all the world!" She sensed him smile above her. "You will not die when you go back, will you, Julien?" she asked in sudden fear.

He kissed the top of her head. "I have no intention of doing so! And especially not now, my darling."

Then she shivered and stepped away a little. "I do not know what has happened to Guy without Goullet to protect him, and I do not want to know. Perhaps it is right that he pays for the evil he has committed, as Goullet has done. Yet once Guy, like Armand, was full of fire for what the Revolution might bring— liberty, equality, fraternity."

"But he used the Revolution for his own ends," Julien said gently. "His motives became twisted, like those of so many in the Revolution. His ambition turned him into a traitor and murderer."

He searched for her hand beneath the bulky wool. It was so little and cold. He held it tightly, and they were silent awhile, pressed close together. Below them they heard the iron wheels of the death cart rattle into a tunnel opening.

Eugénie shuddered, her face full of anguish in the moonlight. "I believe I shall never laugh again, Julien."

He looked down at her tenderly. "You will, I promise you that. This time will end."

She shook her head. "The Revolution has brought nothing save fear, bloodshed, and death."

"Men in the future may think differently."

"How, when it has wrought so much destruction? I cannot think of anything good that has survived."

He wanted to banish the sadness from her face forever, and he would start now. Her eyes widened as he bent his head to hers. "I can," he murmured.

Their lips were very close. "What?" she asked breathlessly.

"Love," he said. "Love survives everything, Eugénie."

And then to prove his point, he began to kiss her.

WHAT HAPPENED AFTERWARD?

The Traitor's Smile ends here, but I find myself wondering—as writers often do—what might have happened afterward to Eugénie, Armand, Julien, Hetta, and Xavier, whom the story leaves at the height of the Terror.

The Terror was, in fact, only to last another seven months, brought to an end in July 1794 by the execution of Robespierre himself—who let out a terrible scream of pain and despair as he went under the guillotine. The Revolutionary Tribunal was abolished and all suspects released from prison. Though France remained unsettled for some while, Julien would have been able to return to studying law, becoming a successful barrister in the "Directory," the first period of stable government. As his wife, Eugénie would have been a celebrated and charming *salonnière*, especially after peace with England was declared in 1802 and the English flooded back to Paris. Her aunt Frederica would be among them, no doubt, eager to resume her shopping trips and keep an eye on her nieces.

Armand would have been able to recover Chauvais for the de Boncoeurs after 1796, when land belonging to the aristocracy that remained unsold could be reclaimed. I imagine him joining the army like his late father, fighting bravely in Napoléon Bonaparte's amazing Italian Campaign of 1796, and in Egypt in 1798 against the English (Armand would always consider himself wholly French, despite having had an English mother). His greatest battle would always be against his fear of confined spaces.

Xavier, too, would have reclaimed his family estate, but his daring adventures would have continued until France was stable again. Perhaps he would have thrown his lot in with Napoléon, who crowned himself emperor in 1804; perhaps he would have been a spy abroad during the Napoleonic wars. I'm sure he would have found a way to smuggle Hetta back to Deal soon, though, so that she could tell her father she was to marry the most impossible Frenchman. Hetta would not have approved of Napoléon's suppression of women's rights; I see her writing fiery political pamphlets, published anonymously in England, and trying to join Xavier on his various escapades.

If you visit Deal, you'll find the old part hardly changed from Hetta's time—exquisite little Georgian houses, narrow alleyways. I stayed for a night at the Three Kings, still there on the beach, though it has been renamed the Royal.

Though Paris is much changed from the still-medieval city that Eugénie and Hetta knew, you can find reminders of the Revolution everywhere: in the Musée Carnavalet; in the Place de la Concorde (once the Place de la Révolution), where the site of the guillotine is marked; in the haunted front courtyard of the Covent des Calmes, where a terrible massacre of priests took place. Their bones are on display in the crypt, and when I was down there alone, the lights went out! In the curiously peaceful Catacombs, the skeletons of many of the guillotine's victims are piled neatly on top of one another: You can find Robespierre and other famous names from the Revolution. And in La Conciergerie it is all too easy—despite its antiseptic, cleaned-up appearance and the little you are allowed to see of it—to imagine what it must have been like—and how impossible to escape from.

Was Eugénie right in saying that the Revolution had brought nothing "save fear, bloodshed, and death"?

When the monarchy was reestablished in 1814, it was bound by a constitution, just as Armand and his friends had desired. Both the constitution and the Revolutionary laws, drawn up in an astonishingly short time, were the foundation of modern France. The tragedy of the Revolution was that in order to control the people by imposing the Terror, it was forced to sacrifice the very ideal that it had struggled for: the freedom of the individual. *Liberté.*

Patricia Elliott

HISTORICAL NOTE

On January 21, 1793, the guillotine fell on King Louis XVI, sending the French Revolution into a deeper and more violent spiral that would forever alter the history of the country and its people. Though the Revolution had been well under way before this date, the execution of King Louis XVI marked the eve of anarchy and terror.

In 1789, in the midst of a financial crisis and widespread hunger, members of the peasant and bourgeois classes banded together in mobs to wrench power from France's most privileged classes: the nobility and the clergy of the Catholic Church. Chaos, murder, and violence were rampant. Mobs rioted in the streets of Paris, women charged the court of Versailles, and militias burned the Bastille to the ground. Nobles, fearing for their lives and their titles, tried to flee to neighboring monarchies. The Catholic Church, once omnipotent, found its power dwindling against new, secular institutions. As the Revolution gained support, the nobility and clergy lost more and more power. In 1792, Louis XVI lost his reign, and the people elected a National Convention to draw up a new constitution. Initially dominated by the moderate Republican Girondists, the National Convention abolished the monarchy, set up a republic, and tried and executed King Louis XVI for treason.

The people were taking back France from the privileged few, and France entered a period known as the Reign of Terror.

From September 1793 to June 1794, Parisians lived under the shadow of the guillotine. The *Comité de salut public*, lead by Maximilien Robespierre, was established to protect France from "enemies of the Revolution" but ultimately played the role of executioner, sending tens of thousands of people to the guillotine. The *Comité*'s violent presence exacerbated tensions between the rival political factions, the Girondists and the radical Jacobins, which lead to the Jacobins—and Robespierre—seizing control of both the *Comité* and the National Convention, and uniting under the Reign of Terror.

During Robespierre's year in power, he further cleaved the old France of the *Ancien Régime* from the new France of the Revolution by banning the Catholic religion and enforcing the state-run Cult of the Supreme Being, as well as replacing the Catholic calendar with the secular Republican Calendar. Thousands of political and nonpolitical figures were executed by guillotine as the Revolutionary Tribunal and the *Comité* rose to unprecedented and violent dominance.

These radical changes and mass executions were feared not only by the French people, but also by some members of the *Comité* itself. On June 27, 1794, the National Convention denounced Robespierre and his followers, and in a coup known as the Thermidorian Reaction (so-called for the month in the Republican Calendar in which it occurred), arrested Robespierre and proclaimed him an outlaw, swiftly executing him by guillotine without a trial.

Robespierre's execution marked the end of the violent bloody year of the Reign of Terror. In the years that followed, France still remained unstable as the fires of the Revolution began to wane. Rivalries between royalists and Republicans set off a series of insurrections against new iterations of Republican governments, as the royalists fought an unsuccessful battle to restore the power of the Catholic Church and traditional monarchical rule. It was not until late 1795, when Napoléon Bonaparte led the charge of Republican militia to suppress a royalist insurrection with heavy cannon fire, that the Republicans seized lasting control. However, the new government of the Directory slowly began increasing conservative control, ultimately terminating elections.

After a failed military campaign in Egypt in 1799, Napoléon returned to France—a hero to the French nation. The following month, Napoléon's brother Lucien led a coup d'état against the Directory, breaking down the last government of the Revolution. With the signing of the Constitution of the Year VIII on Christmas Eve 1799, Napoléon rose to power as leader of the new Consulate, ending the many years of hardship of the Revolution and ushering in the age of the French Empire.

Time Line of the French Revolution
From the Years 1793–1799

1793

January 21	Execution of Louis XVI in *Place de la Révolution*
February 1	War declared on Great Britain
February 25	Food riots throughout Paris
March 7–10	Rioting in Paris against the Revolution
March 10	*Tribunal révolutionnaire* (Revolutionary Tribunal)—a court for trials of political offenders—established by Revolutionary leader Georges Danton
April 6	*Comité de salut public* (Committee for Public Safety), created by the National Convention and headed by Georges Danton
May 10	National Convention moves to the *Palais des Tuileries*
May 12	National Convention forced to establish an army—the *sans-culottes*—to protect Paris
June 2	The Jacobin Club, now one of the most powerful political groups in France, arrests 31 Girondist deputies, their political rivals. Jacobins secure control of the National Convention. They push for public education, controls on food prices, and a large army of conscripted men.
June 10	Under the leadership of lawyer and prominent political figure Maximilien Robespierre, Jacobins take over *Comité de salut public*

June 24	New constitution ratified by the National Convention
July 13	Politician, physician, and journalist Jean-Paul Marat, influential for extreme radical and democratic opinions, stabbed to death in bathtub by Charlotte Corday, a young Girondin conservative. Marat considered a martyr for his cause.
July 27	Maximilien Robespierre elected deputy of *Comité de salut public*
August 10	Festival of Unity held to celebrate new constitution
September 5	Reign of Terror begins
September 6	Revolutionary army established to support *Comité de salut public*
September 17	Law of Suspects passed, permitting arrest of anyone suspected of supporting "tyranny or federalism"
September 22	French Republican Calendar established, Year I
October 14	Marie Antoinette tried by Revolutionary Tribunal
October 16	Marie Antoinette executed by guillotine
November 10	Celebration of Reason at Cathédrale Notre Dame de Paris; rededicated as Temple of Reason. Churches close and religious holidays, references, and religion itself are banned.
December 4	Law of Revolutionary government; power centralized under *Comité de salut public*

1794

April 5	Danton, president of *Comité de salut public*, guillotined with supporters
May 7	Robespierre invents new faith, the Cult of the Supreme Being, to replace both Catholicism and the Cult of Reason. Cult of the Supreme Being, which recognizes a god but emphasizes fidelity to liberty and democracy, is officially announced by the National Convention.
June 8	Robespierre leads procession through Paris and holds Festival of the Supreme Being on Champ de Mars to inaugurate new national religion
June 10	Law of 22 Prairial passed, allowing *Tribunal révolutionnaire* to condemn suspects without witnesses. Law also greatly broadens charges that could be brought against a suspect; nearly any criticism of government becomes criminal.
June 27	Robespierre and his followers denounced by the National Convention and arrested in what is known as the Thermidorian Reaction, or end of the Reign of Terror
June 28	Robespierre executed by guillotine without trial with 115 others from *Comité de la salut public*
November 11	Jacobin Club closed by order of the National Convention

1795

May 31	End of *Tribunal révolutionnaire*
June 8	Louis XVII, son of Louis XVI, dies in prison

July 14	"La Marseillaise" adopted as French national anthem
August 22	Constitution of 1795 (Year III) ratified, bringing in a two-party system comprised of a legislative branch and a five-member executive Directory. Directory of Five represents the first period of stable government, though lack of funds soon creates administrative chaos and corruption.
October 3	Royalists organize an armed protest against the National Convention; Napoléon Bonaparte given command of improvised Republican forces
October 5	Napoléon suppresses royalist insurrection with heavy cannon fire; hundreds killed
October 26	National Convention is closed and officially replaced by the Directory
November 2	The Directory takes power

1796

March 9	Wedding of Napoléon Bonaparte and Joséphine de Beauharnais
May 10	Napoléon's Battle of Lodi, Italian campaign. Napoléon made commander of French army in Italy, overcoming Austria and its allies. Success earns him respect and a hero's status in France.

1797

September 4	Three members of Directory stage Coup d'état of 18 Fructidor (eighteenth day of the twelfth month of the Republican Calendar) with support of Napoléon Bonaparte and the military.

Two conservative directors removed, as well as conservatives from *Corps Législatif* (legislative assembly) and other positions, bringing Republican power back to the Directory.

1798

May 11
Law of 22 Floréal Year VI passed, expelling 106 leftwing deputies from Council of Five Hundred—the lower house of the legislative assembly—and terminating Council elections.

May 19
Napoléon leaves for campaign in Egypt and Syria, intending to threaten Britain's trade with India. After capturing Malta, defeating the Ottoman army at the Battle of the Pyramids, and winning other battles, Napoléon is stranded when French fleet is destroyed by British at Battle of the Nile. Napoléon abandons campaign and army, leaves for Paris in August 1799.

1799

June 18
Coup d'état of 30 Prairial Year VII (also known as the Revenge of the Councils) removes two directors

October 9
Napoléon returns to France a hero, despite failure of Egypt campaign

November 9
Coup d'état of 18 Brumaire, lead by legislative leaders including Napoléon's brother Lucien, forcibly ends the Directory

December 24
Constitution of the Year VIII ends the French Revolution; establishes Napoléon as leader of the Consulate, France's new government